Taming the Mafia Boss
An Opposites Attract Age Gap Romance

Broxy Hart

Contents

CHAPTER ONE

ANDRIANA

*I*N THE THEATER OF *life, unexpected guests often steal the show, revealing the hidden truths behind the curtains of our comfort.*

"Mia!" I called. I looked around frantically for any sign of Jose, my boss, as I tidied up my stuff, preparing to leave for the day. Mia peeped out of the restroom, a half-smile on her face.

"Take a chill pill, Andriana. We're closed," she said as she glanced at her wristwatch. "Only a loser would walk in here right now." She slammed the door shut again, and I contemplated leaving her behind and heading home.

I had the most stressful day today. Our usually small restaurant welcomed a good number of people, and I wanted nothing more than to be in bed right now.

Shifting uncomfortably, I headed toward the door, looking out of the transparent glass into the silent neighborhood before walking back to a nearby seat. Only a true loser would walk in right now. It was almost 11 p.m., several hours past our closing time.

I heard muffled voices a few minutes later, before the door leading into the restaurant was thrown open. I lifted my head slowly, praying it wasn't what I thought it was, when I saw a group of men walking into the restaurant. Jose suddenly appeared from nowhere, rushing toward the entrance with a large smile on his face. He was smiling so hard that I feared his lips would tear.

I watched in horror as he welcomed them in. I couldn't do this tonight. I muttered a curse when the last man made his way in. But my throat went dry when I saw who it was. Alex Rocco! CEO of Rocco's Construction. I didn't give a shit about the construction company, but Alex was particularly popular among the ladies because of his extremely handsome features.

He caught my gaze as he stepped in and paused, looking indecisive. My heart stopped beating as I watched him. He was the most handsome man I'd ever seen. I'd never been caught off guard by a man before. It seemed surreal.

"Excuse me?"

I blinked twice, focusing my attention back on him. It was time to cut back on all the romantic novels in my collection.

"Uh?"

The other men seemed almost invisible as I watched him, and I wondered how that was even possible. How could the presence of one man have such an enormous impact on me?

"It looks like you're closed. I'm so sorry. We'll leave now." His gaze was still fixed on me, which I found unsettling. Usually, no one looked at me for more than two seconds, the first being a mistake. I almost smiled at my own joke.

"What in God's name is wrong with you tonight, Andriana?" Jose asked with a hint of irritation.

I collected myself and shrugged off the silly little attraction I was feeling when I noticed the hard glare Alex was wearing. *Oops.*

"I'm so sorry. Did you ask me anything?" I said.

Jose placed his hand on his forehead and shook his head dramatically before facing Alex. "I'm so sorry, sir. She's usually a lot more clear-headed than this."

Alex sighed impatiently, shifting his feet uncomfortably. "So are you still open?"

"We're closed," I said, making eye contact with him.

"Of course we're open! Why not?" Jose forced an ugly laugh, throwing an angry glare at me.

Alex shrugged casually before moving toward a different seat from the one Jose directed him to. He sat among the other men instead.

"Get yourself together, woman! And come serve our meal!" someone yelled.

I sighed angrily, trying to keep my emotions in check as I walked over to their table. I felt like a zombie as I approached them.

"What would you like to order?" I asked, looking at anyone but Alex.

"What do you have available?" Alex said gruffly, watching me.

"There's nothing available right now, as we've closed for the day."

"Don't be silly!" Jose yelled from behind the counter, rushing toward us. He picked up the menu from a nearby table and handed it over to Alex.

"See me before you leave tonight," Jose said, throwing me a glare.

I watched in silence as the men skimmed through the menu, my heart beating wildly in my chest.

"I think we'll go with waffles and cream," Alex said, dropping the menu on the table. I sighed in relief. That was the quickest meal to make on the menu.

"Okay, I'll just—"

"Hold on now, Alex. What do you mean waffles and cream?" someone asked as I turned in the direction of the kitchen.

"Ain't no way I'm eating that," someone else added, his voice edged with laughter.

I glanced at Alex, who was well-dressed in a beige suit. He looked like the perfect gentleman. I wondered what business he had with these rough-looking men.

"We need something strong, like pasta."

Alex shook his head slowly. "They're closed already. Look at the time. Let the little girl go home."

Little girl? I frowned.

"We don't care if they're closed or not. They let us in."

The rest of them nodded in agreement, and I threw a warning glance at Jose. Thankfully, he wasn't paying attention to our discussion. The man was right; we let them in. We shouldn't have let them in if we had no intention of feeding them. And where the heck was Mia?

It took about thirty minutes before I was able to get their order ready, and by the time I was heading toward their table, I could see the exasperation on their faces.

"You should've told us you couldn't make it instead of wasting our time here," I heard someone say.

"Just let's enjoy the meal, Blade," Alex said, nodding briefly in his direction.

Blade. I glanced at him. He had been acting like a proper douchebag since they walked in.

"I'll only keep quiet if the meal is nice."

"Let's eat!" someone else shouted excitedly, winking at me as I dropped the last dish on the table.

"Thank you," Alex muttered gruffly as I walked away from the group. Mia had tidied up the kitchen by the time I got there, and she smiled broadly when she saw me.

"It's the least I could do, Andriana. I'm sorry."

"It's okay." I sat on the bench close to her. Now we had to wait for them to finish their meal.

"Hey!" Mia squealed excitedly, shifting closer to me. I narrowed my eyes on her. "What?"

"He's so handsome, oh my God!"

"Who?" I looked around, feigning ignorance, but my sudden movement caused a bowl to fall, making a shattering noise.

"What's going on over there?" Jose cried out, running toward us.

Mia made a crying face. "I'm so sorry, oh my God."

I was about to roll my eyes when I saw she had actual tears in her eyes.

"Oh, c'mon now, Mia. It's okay," I said.

"I should've just listened to you earlier. At least all of this wouldn't be happening."

"What the hell is going on here?" Jose asked with a frown as he approached us.

The mere sight of him made me mad. I'd never seen anyone so selfish.

"We have guests outside. I'll need you both to behave yourselves." He turned to leave, then paused by the door. "Even if that's a hard thing to accomplish."

Mia started to laugh after he left. "He's such a fool."

A fool I couldn't deal with any longer. I had put up with his nonsense attitude for a good while, and I'd had enough.

Mia stood suddenly, looking alert. "I think they're done with their meal."

We both scurried through the kitchen door leading toward the restaurant. Thankfully, they were done with it.

"Who made this food?" asked the annoying man who kept making silly demands.

I ignored him, piling their plates on my tray. I didn't have the time for chitchat. We were already way past our closing time.

"Why are you so feisty?" He placed his hands on my waist, caressing it softly.

"Hey!" I slapped his hands away from my body. "Are you out of your mind?"

"Blade?" Alex called out, throwing a warning look at him.

"Come here." Blade pulled me toward himself, his lips curving into a wicked smile.

"Hey, get off me." I slapped his hands away from me, pushing and kicking with all of my strength.

"Blade, behave yourself," one of the men said, glancing over at Alex.

"Here," Alex said, dropping a pile of money on the table. "I'm sorry for any inconvenience caused."

"Thanks, man," I said.

The rest of the group stood up, casting angry glances at Blade, who looked unbothered by everything going on.

"Come here." With a movement so quick, he grabbed my shirt, rubbing his hands frantically against my breast. I don't know what startled me more: Mia's high-pitched scream or Alex Rocco's sudden movement. In a quick second, he was standing between me and Blade.

"Mind your own business, Rocco," Blade growled, his hands reaching for me once again. I burst into tears, cleaning my eyes with the backs of my hands.

"Touch her, and you won't leave this place alive," Alex said calmly, his voice almost inaudible. At this point, I wanted nothing more than to be in the quiet of my own home, safe from all this chaos.

The other men glanced at each other in disbelief. "What did you just say, Rocco?" Blade asked with a daring look at Alex.

"You heard me right, Blade. You've caused enough trouble for us already. Get your mind right, and let's get the hell out of here."

"Wow," Blade muttered, taking a cautious step toward me.

"Let's get out of here, Blade," someone else said. The entire room was filled with an unsettling silence as we all waited.

"He's your man, right?" he asked, smiling softly.

I shook my head, glancing at Alex, who was already moving toward the door.

"Blade?" he called out, pointing toward the exit.

He took another step toward me. "This is not the end, lover girl. Bye, for now."

Mia slammed the door shut immediately after they left. "Oh my goodness! Oh my God."

"Andriana, are you okay?" Jose asked, walking slowly toward me.

"Don't." I held out my hands, narrowing my eyes at him.

"You caused this, sir!" Mia said. "We shouldn't be out here working into the late hours of the night. This could've been avoided, and we're going to report this case to the police tomorrow."

She grabbed our stuff from where we left it and faced me. "Let's go. I doubt I'll be coming back here ever again."

Jose's eyes filled with horror once he heard Mia's last words. "This isn't my fault. I had no idea this was going to happen."

"C'mon, let's go," she said, leading me toward the door.

"Please, be careful," I said to Mia. On our way down the street, the men were gathered by the side of the road, talking in really loud voices. I caught Blade's hateful glare and quickly looked away.

"He's such a bully," Mia said, her grip tightening on my hand.

"Shh." I looked around. There was no one else in sight as we made our way down the street.

"Try to see if you can get a taxi." I glanced at Mia, who nodded immediately.

"Why didn't I think of that? Oh my God! He's coming! Blade!" Mia yelled.

The moment Mia's voice echoed through the quiet night, a loud, shattering sound hit the air. I turned around to see Blade walking determinedly toward us, the moonlight casting a light on his hard face.

"Run!" I screamed, running as fast as my feet could go. I didn't care about anything else as I ran down the road. I didn't care about the bag I dropped while running, or even the fact that I couldn't hear Mia's footsteps behind me. I had just one goal in mind. Home.

CHAPTER TWO

ALEX

B LADE WOULD BE THE death of me. If he wasn't getting into
trouble somewhere, he was busy causing trouble. I regretted the
day I had to join ties with him and his men. Ever since, it had been one
problem after another.

I'd never seen a mafia member as stupid as he was. He acted without
thinking, like he wanted to be discovered. I knew folks like Blade had
nothing to lose, so I tried to avoid situations that would bring us
together.

Just tonight, he had contradicted three of the gang rules and was
still showing no sign of remorse. He said that was the way things had
worked with the former gang leader, Nick, and he'd been fine. I wasn't
Nick, and I wasn't about to risk my life for some reckless reason.

"You disobeyed a direct order, Blade. I gave out an instruction and
you didn't listen," I said calmly, my gaze fixed on him. I was beyond
pissed at this point. This could've been totally avoided if he had just
behaved himself. I hated getting involved in reckless scenarios like this.

"I don't owe you any loyalty, Alex. You're not my master. I'm not obligated to do whatever you say," he answered, his eyes blazing with mischief.

"Very well." I turned to my men. "The deal is over. Let's go."

"That's not possible. We made a deal," Jay said while taking a step forward. He's a mountain of a man with a shaved beard and a scar running down his cheeks. He's a member of the rival gang, not one of my men.

"I don't get involved with things like this, Jay. Why do you think I've kept a low profile for such a long time? I can't work with Blade. He'll get me in trouble."

"You decided to get involved, Rocco. That had nothing to do with you. You could've just ignored it as usual."

The rest of the group nodded, glancing at each other. They were right, but that didn't make what they did okay.

"I will get the girl. I'll have my way with her and send you the videos," Blade said.

I closed my eyes. What did the innocent girl do to deserve such pure, undiluted hatred from him?

"You will do no such thing, Blade."

"I already told you, Alex, save your commands for your own men."

"What about loyalty, Blade? What about protecting the innocent?"

He shrugged. "You embarrassed me because of a girl tonight. I won't back down until I find her, and then, like I said, I'll send you the pictures."

"You've broken three codes tonight, Blade. You almost revealed all of our identities to those people at the restaurant, you preyed on the innocent, and then you shot in the air for no reason."

He nodded his head. "And what about the code you broke, Alex?"

I know he was just trying to sound smart, so I ignored him. "Let's forget this happened tonight, everyone." I turned toward the rest of the group. We were six in number. Blade and his men: Vito, Marko, and Don, and then I had my right-hand man with me: Enzo.

"We know the rules, and when we stick to the rules, a lot of things will be different. Let's just try to abide by the rules. It's as simple as that. We all have important responsibilities outside of this, and little things like this could destroy the real world for us."

Blade had always been the stubborn one. I knew from the way he set his foot that he had a different idea in mind, but his judgment always brought us trouble.

"You know one thing I'm going to do, Rocco?" he asked, walking toward the door. When I didn't reply, he started to laugh. "I'm having a lot of fun with this. C'mon, boys. Let's get the hell out of here."

Enzo turned to me after the last man walked out. "Blade is such a pain in the ass. It's so annoying. What has that innocent girl done to him?"

I shrugged. "Get the car ready. What was the final outcome of today's meeting?"

"Are you really going to let Blade get to that girl? He's going to brutalize her; she'll wish she never existed."

"Get the car ready, Enzo. We're going home. I've had a long day. I can't bother myself with some random girl."

"Boss, I think you should—" he stopped halfway through his speech when he noticed the glare I threw in his direction.

"Okay, boss." He pulled the door open for me to go in and made his way briskly toward the front. My mind drifted back to the girl from the restaurant, and I tried to take my mind away.

"Fuck it."

Enzo glanced at me through the mirror, his features uncertain.

This is none of your business, Alex. Whatever he chooses to do with that girl is none of your concern, I thought to myself. I caught Enzo's gaze through the mirror, and this time he met my gaze, narrowing his eyes.

"Did you just?" I asked.

"I couldn't care less about the girl, you know," he said. "But we put her in this situation. She clearly stated that they were closed, and now Blade is assaulting her and attempting to kill her. This could fall back on us."

"That's none of my business." I looked out of the window, humming a song to myself.

"Think of everything you've built, Alex. You might think this has nothing to do with you, but you were the only one they recognized, and you're going to be implicated."

"It has nothing to do with me. A few court cases would solve the problem."

He shrugged. "I've done my best. Just have some men watch over her tonight, then talk to Blade. And voila! She's safe; we're free."

The penthouse became visible as we approached. The apartment, usually a testament to opulence, felt sterile and cold. The rhythmic hum of the car coming to a halt shattered the silence.

The door leading into the house was thrown open, and Elliot, my housekeeper, hurried out. "That's enough, Enzo," I said.

"Welcome, sir," Elliot said, opening the door.

I nodded my head in his direction as I made my way out. It had been a very stressful day, and I wanted nothing more than to be in bed now. But the thought of leaving that girl alone tonight kept bugging me.

"This is none of your business, Alex. Don't get involved," I muttered, unlocking my room door.

I will get the girl. I'll have my way with her and then send you the videos.

That fool.

My mind drifted back to the number of innocent people who have been killed by reckless acts like these, and I sighed. I should put a call through to Rick.

I battled with the thought several hours into the night before finally calling Ricky. He was one of my men.

He picked up on the first ring. "Hey, boss."

"I'm sure you must've heard about what happened tonight. This kind of news travels so fast."

He sighed. "You know, just Blade being Blade."

"I want you to help me watch over the girl tonight. Obviously, she's in danger."

"Uh... give me a minute." I heard the sound of the keyboard, and I knew he was looking her up online.

"Andriana Rodriguez, twenty-three years old. She stays down Allen Lane."

"Just keep watch over her tonight. I'll find a solution to this tomorrow."

"She's a lucky one," Ricky muttered. "You usually don't care about things like this. She should thank whatever God she serves."

I sighed. "Goodnight, Ricky."

Sleep didn't come easy. The day's events replayed in my mind, a tangled mess of threats and bribes. But slowly, the tension in my shoulders eased as everything turned dark. This was easily the best part of my life.

————-

The smell of freshly cooked chicken hung heavy in the air as I stood awkwardly on the porch swing of the pastel house. This was just plain stupid. I had woken up this morning to two missed calls from Ricky, which was very unusual. The night had gone by with several attempts from Blade's men to reach the girl.

The door was pulled open, and the girl from the restaurant appeared in the doorway, a flour-dusted apron tied around her floral dress. Her eyes widened when she saw me.

"Mr. Rocco?" She looked around uncertainly before her gaze landed on me. "Can I help you?"

She looked a whole lot better than she did yesterday, more at peace.

"Hello." I wasn't one to beat around the bush, but at the same time, I didn't want to startle her.

"Come in." She shifted toward the side of the door to make way for me.

"Come in? You're very brave. Do you always let random strangers into your home?"

She looked indecisive for a moment before smiling. "You're not totally a stranger. In case you don't know, Mr. Rocco, you're very popular in this community. And also, there's CCTV outside of my house." She smiled softly, meeting my gaze.

I walked inside, my face almost covered in disgust as the pink interior came into view. It was a bizarre contrast to the iron grip I had in most situations.

She looked around uncertainly as she walked toward me. "Why are you here, Mr. Rocco?" she asked, arms folded. "Your presence here is really unsettling after what happened last night."

"I'm here to offer you a deal."

"What kind of deal?" she asked with a funny expression on her face.

"What's funny?" I asked, growing impatient. I had no interest in any of this, and I wouldn't be here in the first place if I hadn't gone and involved myself with Blade. Now I had to protect my own image by protecting her.

She shrugged. "You, of course. All of this. How'd you even find my house? And what the hell are you doing here? This is crazy."

Just remain calm, Alex. You can do this, I told myself.

"You come to work for me. You're a good cook, they say, so I'd need you as my private chef."

"Chef?" She burst into laughter, swinging her head back. "Wow, that's a really great way to classify my culinary skills: Chef Andriana. Why haven't I thought about this before?"

The smile faded away when she noticed the look on my face.

I almost used my don voice when I realized she was just a girl, oblivious to all of the chaos outside of her perfect little world.

"I'm dead serious." That was all I could say as I met her gaze.

"Huh?" She looked confused as she watched me. "That sounds a little bit suspicious." She frowned. "No, it's very suspicious, highly unusual."

I shook my head. Using my don voice would be highly essential.

"And why would I want to work for you? Your friends nearly assaulted me yesterday." She crossed her arms.

Because your life is in danger, dumbhead, I wanted to say. *And you're about to be killed if you don't do as I say.*

"Because it'll be a lot better than where you presently work," I said instead, watching her.

"Hmph. The devil you know is a whole lot better than the angel you don't know," she replied.

Oh God.

"Forget about it, Mr. Rocco. I'm not interested," she continued.

I thought about it for a while. This was all I needed her to say. I should just leave. But I knew Blade and what he was capable of doing.

I looked around the room, which was painted in a deep shade of pink. She seemed to have her life together. It would all be a huge waste if Blade got in touch with her.

"Why aren't you interested?"

She shrugged. "It just seems too good to be true. I don't like things like this. I like when things come with a little bit of struggle." She waved her hands. "This just feels like charity."

"You're working for me, girl. You'll be paid for your time. It's okay if you're not interested; I'll get someone else." Getting really impatient, I made my way toward the door. This was more than I'd ever done for anyone. I tried my absolute best.

"How much?" she asked as soon as I pressed the knob.

"Ten times whatever your current boss pays you."

"What?"

CHAPTER THREE

ANDRIANA

A LEX ROCCO'S WORDS, SPOKEN with so much confidence, sent me into shock. What was he talking about? What did he mean by ten times whatever I was paid at Jose's?

"This seems too good to be true." I watched him, unsure of what to say.

He shrugged. "It's up to you, there are a thousand other chefs I could use if you're not interested in this."

I started to laugh. "First, I'm not a chef. I'll need you to reduce your expectations of me a good deal."

"Second?" He faced me, crossing his arms over his chest. He looked genuinely interested in what I was about to say.

"Second, if there are a lot of other chefs you could use, why are you here? You could've just put a poster in front of your home or office. You know, save yourself all this stress."

He looked like he could strangle me any moment now, so I took a few steps back. "Just kidding."

He glanced at his wristwatch. "You've successfully wasted fifteen minutes of my time. I never joke with my time."

"Sorry about that."

I knew he was about to leave the moment I saw the scar on his face deepen into a frown.

"Wait!"

He paused without glancing back. There was something really odd about him. It looked like he wanted to be anywhere but here. And that was my problem with all of this: Why was he here if he didn't want to be?

"What's it going to be like?" I asked.

"Nothing much. I just need a ch—" he paused, throwing a warning glance in my direction. "I just need a good cook to make my meals. I'll need a receipt of your payments at your previous job, as that'll determine your pay."

I nodded slowly. "And when do I start?"

"Right away." This time, he turned to look at me, his face blank. Apart from the fact that he was acting a little weird right now, he was insanely attractive. Fucking attractive. I looked away from him. It was impossible for someone to be this handsome. Not only impossible. It was unfair. How could one person possess this much beauty when there were thousands of other people who lack in that aspect?

I realized he was giving me time to think about it with the way he was looking around my house. That gave me more time to drool over him. He was tall, and his shoulders strained the seams of his leather jacket. He wasn't a model out of a magazine, with a chiseled jawline or perfectly coiffed hair. But there was something absolutely captivating about him.

Suddenly, he looked up, catching my stare. I froze, my cheeks burning like a bad sunburn. His mouth curled into a frown that held a hint of impatience.

"You should consider yourself lucky that I'm still here. I'm the least patient person in this world. I'm not even kidding."

I stared at him, refusing the urge to look away from his hard gaze.

"I'll think about all you've said. Thank you."

"I already gave you enough time to think about it," he said with a sigh. "You have five seconds to think about it."

"What?"

"One."

"What can you possibly expect me to think about in five seconds?"

"Two."

"This is just insane."

"Three."

I glared at him, trying to think about the important things and the implications of my decisions.

"Four."

What should I do? Take it? Earning ten times what I earn at Jose's would help me a great deal. I'd live comfortably, without fear of lacking anything I need.

"Five."

"I'll do it."

"We've sorted that out. You start today. Get your stuff ready. My chauffeur will get everything into the car.

The more he talked, the more crazy he sounded. "What do you mean?" I asked.

"Get your things ready, ma'am. You start working right away. I'll be downstairs."

Before I could say anything else, he slammed the door shut. The smell of his cologne lingering for a long time after his exit.

I picked up my phone and dialed Lila, my best friend. She picked up on the first ring.

"Guess who just walked into my place and offered me a thousand-dollar job?"

"What are you talking about, Andriana?" Lila asked softly, her voice edged with amusement.

"Just guess!"

"I swear, if you're only pulling my leg, I'll pay you back. Because over here, it's one in the morning. You've gotta be telling me the truth."

Lila moved out of the country right after college for her master's, but we didn't let the distance affect our friendship. It was hard sometimes, especially with the time difference, but I was glad we were able to work through it together.

"Alex Rocco. Check him online."

"Are you kidding me? I know Alex. I've heard about him, dumbhead."

I chuckled, pacing around the room, unsure of what to do next.

I heard her shifting positions and knew she was heading toward her computer. After a few moments, her voice echoed through the air.

"My goodness, still as handsome as ever."

"Okay, after yesterday's events, he knocked on my door this morning, asking me to work as his private chef."

"Alex was part of the bad guys at the restaurant?"

"Not part of the bad guys, per say. I'll give you the full details later, but right now, what should I do?" I paced around the room, thinking of the best decision to make.

"You have the time to think about it."

"That's the thing. I had five seconds. And now, he told me to get my things ready."

She was quiet for a while. "Where is he?"

"Outside, I guess, waiting for me to get my things ready."

"What do you think? I'm as confused as you are. But there's one thing I'm sure of; a man as influential as that wouldn't want to do anything that'll tarnish his image."

"Hello?" I heard a strange voice call out.

I ran toward the window and peeked out. A uniformed chauffeur, all crisp lines and a polite smile, stood by the door. I pulled the door open to tell him to tell his boss to be patient or leave, when I remembered the captivating salary he offered me.

"Give me a minute."

I adjusted the phone to my ear. "I'll take the job, Lila. I'll call you back."

"Be careful, Andriana. Stay smart."

"Roger that."

I rushed into my room, throwing clothes into my mini travel bag. I had no idea what to take along, so I just kept on throwing different things into the bag. By the time I was done, it was already past noon. I wondered why no one had come to knock on the door.

I grabbed my bags in both hands and rushed out the door, looking out to see if the car was still parked outside. Luckily for me, the chauffeur was standing patiently in front of the car.

"I'm so sorry I kept you waiting for so long. It was all so sudden. I didn't know what to pack."

I peered into the tinted window but couldn't tell if Alex was in there or not.

"Mr. Rocco left a long time ago," the chauffeur said as if reading my mind while he helped me drop my bags into the booth.

"Oh."

He smiled at me. "He doesn't joke with his time."

I shrugged. "I guess that's all. What's the next step?" I asked, my gaze landing on the sleek black car gleaming under the afternoon sun. It looked less like a car and more like a luxurious spaceship from a sci-fi movie.

He opened the door for me, and my mouth almost fell open as I looked into the immaculate interior of the car.

"Careful on the step, miss." he said gently, looking indecisive about whether to hold my shoulders or not.

Hesitantly, I placed my feet on the carpet, the plushness sinking softly beneath my weight. The air was cool and smelled faintly of leather and something fresh. The seats looked impossibly comfortable, wild, and inviting, unlike any others I'd ever seen. A tiny voice in my head whispered, *Don't mess anything up, Andriana.*

As I settled into the cool embrace of the seat, the chauffeur closed the door with a soft thud, the sound sealing me into this world of polished luxury. I sank deeper into the seat, a nervous chuckle escaping my lips. Maybe this wasn't such a bad idea.

I faced the chauffeur after a while, determined to ask him all of the questions that had been bugging me.

"Hello."

"Hello, ma'am. You can call me Steven." He smiled.

"Okay, there are a lot of questions I want to ask you. Can I go ahead?"

He shrugged. "It depends on the kind of questions you want to ask. I might not be able to answer them all."

I nodded. That was fair.

"What's it like living in Alex Rocco's apartment?"

He met my gaze through the mirror. "The apartment is, to put it mildly, a penthouse. It's very large."

"Oh." I nodded slowly. "Thank you, Steven, but I mean, how does he treat his guests? His workers? How does he treat those working under him?"

He shrugged. "He doesn't interact with us. Apart from us doing our jobs for him, he has no interaction whatsoever with us."

"That's fair, I think?"

He chuckled. "I guess so."

"Great."

"I also have a question for you," he said after a while.

"Go on."

"I'm sorry if I'm being too nosy, but Mr. Alex has never brought a stranger home since I've known him. You must be very dear to him."

My heart skipped a beat. Was I being kidnapped by Alex Rocco?

"How long have you known him?"

He thought about it for a while, his gaze fixed on the road.

"Ten years."

"Uh?" I choked out the words, and my breath caught in my throat, leading to a deep bout of coughing.

"Here," he said, handing me a bottle of water. "It'll help with the cough."

I stared at the water suspiciously, deciding not to drink it. In many of these movies, the water was poisoned with substances, especially when the victim was about to get kidnapped.

"No, thank you." I smiled at him, clearing my throat. "I'm fine."

He nodded, casting a worried glance in my direction. "Maybe I'm asking too many questions. Pardon my ignorance."

I ignored him. "Are you saying you've known him for ten years and he has never brought a single person into the house?"

He nodded. "It's just us, the same old workers. So this is like a shock to me."

I remained silent for the rest of the journey. I only sat up when I noticed the car turning toward the gliding gate in front of us. When the penthouse came into view, my mouth fell open.

The first thought that came into my mind as I looked around the luxurious house was to video call Lila, but that would make me look crazy.

"Welcome to our home, ma'am," Steven said as he opened the passenger door.

My initial worry hit me as soon as I stepped out of the car. There were a few workers walking around, and they were throwing really surprised glances at me.

"See? I told you," Steven whispered to me.

Shut up, man, I thought but didn't say.

"Come with me. Let me show you your room."

I nodded slowly. "He already told me what room he wanted you to be in," Steven added. I wasn't sure why he decided that was an important thing to say.

As we walked through the silent corridor, I started to chuckle. There was nothing to be scared about. I survived all these years alone without any fear, so where was this strange emotion coming from?

Steven glanced at me before stopping in front of a door. "Here."

I nodded. "Thank you, Steven. You've been very helpful."

"If you need anything, you can put a call through to any of the staff or just press the button by the side of the bed."

It looked like Mr. Steven didn't know I was also a staff member.

I chuckled. "That won't be necessary, Steven. I'm also a staff member. I should, in fact, get into business as soon as possible."

He laughed. "Nice try, ma'am. The staff quarters are on the other side of the building."

He winked at me as he turned to leave. "Show me the staff quarters, Steven."

He paused midway through the corridor. "I think you should settle in first. You've had a really stressful day."

There was no way I was going to be living here like one of the big guys while the other workers stayed in their quarters.

"Take me to the staff quarters, Steven." He looked confused as he led me out of the building toward the staff quarters.

I immediately regretted my decision when I stepped into the building. It was a direct contrast to the comfortable feeling of the main building. This place looked haunted.

"We don't turn on the light here because Mark, the laundry guy, has issues with his eyesight, and bright light makes him really uncomfortable."

I nodded, walking down the hallway with him. "It's really cold in here," I muttered.

He nodded. "The men prefer it this way, I'm not sure why."

Woah.

"Are there any women here?"

"Not really, no. Martha left last month. She worked here for five years. She was the housekeeper."

I swallowed the lump that was forming in my throat. I should've just stayed where he asked me to stay. Now I couldn't back down.

"Where was the room she stayed in?" I asked, my voice coming out quietly this time around. He looked at me pitifully before pointing to a door behind me.

I opened the door and looked inside the room. It had a single bed, and from where I stood, I could feel how chilly it was.

"Thank you, Steven. I won't need your services any longer."

"I don't know about..."

I smiled at him, shutting the door quietly.

I could do this. I grew up alone without any family. I navigated the ups and downs of life alone with no help from anyone, and I wasn't about to start asking for help now. Living in the main building while the other workers had a place to stay didn't sit well with me. If I could work at Jose's for that long, I could survive anywhere.

Steven knocked a few moments later to hand my bags to me. He still had the same worried expression on his face.

The sound of my phone ringing chimed through the air, and I smiled at him. "Thank you very much."

I shut the door before he could say anything else, grabbing my phone from the bed. It was Mia.

"Girl! Why weren't you at work today?" Mia's high-pitched voice echoed through the room. "And I hope you got home safely?"

I sighed. "I'm fine, Mia. Let's just say it had something to do with what happened yesterday. I just couldn't bear to be there this morning. I'm sorry I didn't tell you. How was work today?"

She chuckled. "Do you really think I'll go back there after what happened yesterday? I'm chilling at Luca's house right now. I can't deal with Jose anymore."

"He must be so furious right now. I've blocked him from calling my phone."

She laughed. "I did the same thing too. Let him attend to his customers by himself."

"At least we'll have enough time to rest."

"I'll come over this weekend. You know what to do."

I laid down on the bed, pulling the blanket over my head. "I'm not at home, Mia. I went out."

"Alright, just let me know when you'll be back, or you can give me a call."

"Okay, take care of yourself."

"You too, Andriana."

I tossed and turned after we ended the call, thinking of the choice I made. A salary ten times more than what I was paid at Jose's was enough confirmation that I made the right choice. I nestled beneath the mound of plush blankets, finally feeling the beginning of sleep tugging at my eyelids. A sigh of contentment escaped my lips, and soon I drifted toward a peaceful oblivion.

A few moments later, a single jarring thump sounded against the door. I bolted upright, my heart hammering a frantic tattoo against my ribs. The thump wasn't a polite knock; it was a fist pounding with urgency. Sleep, once so close, now felt like a lifetime away.

"Who is that?" My voice sounded so unfamiliar.

"Hello, ma'am. The boss says I should let you know he's ready to eat now!"

Oh my God! I thought.

CHAPTER FOUR

ALEX

NONE OF MY EMPLOYEES had ever disobeyed my instructions. It had been a smooth ride since they'd all started here, so I wondered why, today of all days, when I had the worst day, Steven decided it was a great idea to do the exact opposite of what I clearly told him to do.

"I asked you a question, Steven. Where is my guest?"

"The staff quarters, sir."

I remained silent. This was always my next move whenever something pissed me off. Silence made me control myself better.

"I'm sorry, sir. She insisted on staying there, and there was nothing I could do."

I nodded. There was no point in transferring my anger to the innocent man.

"You can leave."

"Thank you, sir." He turned briskly and hurried out of the room. Blade was testing my patience really badly. In his quest for revenge, he had totally forgotten the policies guiding the mafia. And as much as

I didn't want to involve the other gang members in all of this, it was better if I made a quick, smart decision as soon as possible before he exposed us all.

"Boss," Enzo said, appearing by the door.

I nodded in his direction. "What's the update?"

He nodded affirmatively. "We have a deal with them. That's really massive for us." His mouth almost curled into a smile, but Enzo never smiled. Instead, he handed me a file.

"It contains everything you need to know about the meeting; construction starts in a week."

I nodded. "Good job."

The door to the room was pushed open, and the girl from the restaurant rushed in, looking lost.

Enzo was already charging toward her when he suddenly realized who she was. He glanced at me, surprised to find her in the house.

"Go back and knock," he said to her, glaring at her.

"And why should I do that?" She met his gaze, watching him like he was insane. "You can get your point across without being condescending. Who are you?"

Enzo turned to me, his face burning with anger.

"Good evening, sir," she said to me, ignoring him.

"You should go back out there and knock."

She nodded without saying an extra word and walked out the door. She knocked a few seconds later.

"What is she doing here? In your private home?" Enzo asked with a worried expression on his face.

"I'll discuss that with you later," I said to him, turning toward the door.

"Come in."

She walked in slowly, her gaze crossing from me to Enzo.

"Your mama didn't teach you how to knock?" he asked.

She didn't respond.

"Where's my meal?" I asked instead, not wanting to sound mean on her first day of work. She had plenty of time to get used to all of this.

She glanced at me. "I didn't know I was supposed to make dinner for you tonight."

"And why's that?" I asked, crossing my arms.

She shrugged. "I don't know, no one told me anything."

"Why are you in the staff quarters?" I asked, studying her. I never really noticed her until now. She was dressed in a pink baggy shirt with white pants, and her hair fell in loose strands across her face. She looked really pretty. I wondered why I never noticed that.

"Steven directed me to a room in here. I was sure he was making a mistake, so I asked him to take me to the staff quarters instead."

"You were sure he was making a mistake?" I asked, watching her.

She nodded.

"Well, I didn't think you were that smart," Enzo stated with an amused hint in his voice. She narrowed her eyes at him.

"I'm a thousand times smarter than you, respectfully."

Enzo scoffed at her. "I can see that."

She shrugged.

"The room was meant for you, and if there's one thing I won't tolerate in this house, it's disobedience."

She nodded, looking away from me. "Yes, sir."

"If you had stayed in the room as instructed, you'd have seen a piece of paper informing you of all you're supposed to do for the day and all you need to know about your stay here."

"I'm sorry."

"Now get your stuff together and go back in there."

She looked like she was going to argue, but instead, she turned on her heels and walked out of the room.

Enzo turned to me after she left. "What are you doing?"

"What do you mean?"

"You want her to stay in here with us? Like a spy?"

"Can we talk about this some other time? I'm tired. I need to rest. Blade is getting out of hand."

"It's not safe to have the girl in here with us."

"Where would you have her be?" I asked "She's not safe in her house. You were clamoring for me to keep her safe. What changed?"

"To keep her safe," Enzo replied. "Not to bring her into the midst of the chaos."

"Oh, c'mon. You know she's safe here."

"It just doesn't seem right," Enzo continued. "We've never brought anyone in here."

There was a soft bang on the door, and we both turned toward it.

"Come in," I said.

She pulled her bags in with her, and Enzo pointed toward the hallway with his fingers. A lot needed to be done, and the earlier I started it, the better.

"Would you still like to eat French fries tonight?" she asked, peering in a few moments later. She had most definitely gone through the papers in her room.

I glanced at my wristwatch; it was ten o'clock. But that was her duty here, to cook.

"Yes, please."

She turned toward Enzo. "Can you show me the way to the kitchen, please?"

"There are about four kitchens in this house. You're standing inside one. This is the last living room arena, and it comes with a kitchen."

He pointed toward the back of the living room, and her eyes shone in realization.

"You're not as smart as you think," Enzo muttered. "And by the way, you should cook here because I don't have the time to show you around tonight."

She walked toward the kitchen area without saying another word. My phone beeped in my pocket, and I saw a text from Nappy, one of the gang members.

"We won't be working alongside you anymore. We've got a better offer," the message read.

"Shit."

Enzo turned to me while subtly throwing a cautious glance at the chef working behind me.

"Double shots; make it strong," I said to him, my voice hard. This was something I found really annoying. We'd made a deal already. You just couldn't back out after transactions had been made. I felt my anger rising, and I turned toward Enzo, who was hurriedly trying to fix me a cup of coffee.

"What's up?" he asked as he handed the cup to me.

I swirled the dark liquid in my cup. Nappy was testing me. That was very obvious. He knew I'd gotten a bit laidback from these whole operations since my company got successful, so he was trying to see what I would do. But this was where he'd gotten it wrong because, for the first time ever, I'd involved my business in mafia activities. I didn't expect so much from them, but definitely not this blatant disrespect.

Nappy texted and said he was no longer interested in the deal—after we'd gotten materials for them from the company's funds.

Enzo's eyes darted around the room. "Maybe you could reason with him a bit more, boss?"

My lips curled into a humorless smile. "Reason? Sure. That's exactly what I plan to do. Ring Steven and tell him to get the car ready. We're going to visit."

Enzo's lips curled into a knowing smile. "Now you're talking."

He hurried to the other side of the room, where he dialed Steven's number and told him what to do.

I downed the expresso in one bitter gulp, the sting a welcome jolt to my system. I walked to the kitchen counter and then slammed the cup on it, leaving a dark stain on the shiny Formica.

"Let's go collect what's ours, Enzo," I said, my voice as hard as steel.

"I'm almost done with your meal," the chef girl said, meeting my gaze in an annoying way.

"Fuck you and your meal."

If she was pissed, it didn't show in her facial features. Smart. Because the last thing I wanted right now was to transfer my aggression to the innocent chef working for me.

"Eat it," I said to her, grabbing my wallet and heading to the door.

——-

The hinges of the apartment door screamed their protest as I pushed through, the weight of the night clinging to me like a second skin. The air hung thick, with the stale scent of gunpowder and cigarettes clinging to my clothes and my mood.

I expected darkness to greet me. The lights were usually out by the time I stumbled in after "business." Instead, it shone brightly against the night, a direct contrast to my dark, brooding mood.

I moved farther into the living room, prepared to snap at whoever was still working there at this ungodly hour of the night, when I caught sight of the restaurant girl. She seemed to be fast asleep, a book in her hands. Then suddenly, she turned a page, her lips moving silently as she read on.

I remained where I was by the front of the door, my gaze fixed on her. The sight of her, so calm and untouched by the harsh world I inhabited, was a balm to my soul. This right here was what life should be like. Not the constant struggle, negativity, and violence that consisted of my daily routine. I would literally kill to have one day of peaceful life to myself.

"What the hell are you still doing here?" I asked her.

She turned her head slowly toward me, her eyes opening slowly in recognition.

"Oh, hello, boss." She got up and dropped the book gently onto the table by her side.

I remained silent, waiting for the answer to my question. My eyes went over her body in one swift movement. She was dressed in blue nightwear that suited her perfectly. Her hair was pulled up in a loose ponytail. She just looked really pretty.

"I believe I asked you a question, girl."

"Andriana, that's my name."

I narrowed my eyes. "Don't play with me; answer my fucking question."

She looked nervous for a second, but it was quickly replaced by a smile.

"I've actually forgotten the last question you asked."

I tried counting to five like I always did in delicate times to avoid doing something I'd regret.

"What. Are. You. Doing. Here?"

"Oh." She chuckled slightly. "Just reading."

"Did you actually read the content of that paper in your room?" I asked.

"Yes, I did," she replied.

I watched her, hoping she'd remember the part where it was clearly stated that "The light should be out by nine."

"And?" she asked. "Maybe I should go through the paper again." She turned toward her room.

"I didn't tell you to leave."

She started to laugh softly. "Were you ever in the army?"

"When you get to your room, go through that piece of paper again. I wouldn't want to repeat myself."

"Okay, I'm sorry about that, sir. I'll go through it again. Oh my God." She took a step toward me and stopped when she got close to me. "You have a blood stain on your face. Are you injured?"

On a good day, I wouldn't have explained myself to her or anyone, but I didn't want her to suspect any of my activities, so I nodded instead.

"Leave now," I told her. "This is where I stay at night before bed. You should read that stuff again."

"Have you eaten tonight?" she said, as if I never spoke.

I turned to her. "And why are you asking me that? What's that supposed to mean? Let me get this straight."

She nodded.

"You don't get to ask me personal questions," I continued. "Just try to be by yourself in this house and avoid trouble."

"But I'm your cook." A smile formed at the edge of her lips as she watched me. "How do I get to know if you've eaten or not?"

"I'll let you know if I need anything."

She nodded, picking up her book. "One last question: What's my schedule for tomorrow?"

I sighed, rubbing my hands against my head. "When you get to the room, pick up that paper and go through the content again."

"Why does everything keep leading back to the paper?"

When I didn't say anything more, she turned around and walked inside her room.

A few moments later, I was back in the living room. The lights were off, and I just sat there, thinking and planning. It was my normal routine.

Nappy. I shook my head as my mind went back to the events of tonight. It was easy. Don't play with fire if you don't want it to burn you. I tried to get the thoughts off my mind, but they just kept coming in. It was like my punishment.

"Fuck it!" I sat up, trying to find something to keep my mind busy.

"Excuse me."

I jumped to my feet, arms prepared to fight when I saw Andriana staring at me like I was sick.

"What the hell are you doing here?" I asked her.

"I can't sleep. What do you think could be the problem?"

She propped herself on the chair she had left a few minutes ago.

"If you'd like to stay here, refrain from asking me silly questions."

She nodded. "I'll try."

I leaned back against the sofa, staring straight ahead. After a while, her voice echoed through the silence. "Is this what you do all night? Everyday? Just looking straight ahead. I thought you had something fun going on here when you said you stayed here most nights."

Silence.

"I'll just keep quiet. Sorry."

"What's your definition of *fun*?"

We were both shocked by my question. I was more shocked than she was, since I didn't usually indulge in small talk.

"You know, something that provides joy or amusement. Like reading, cooking, or even watching a movie."

"Hmm."

She sighed, and after a moment, I heard her flip another page of the book she was reading.

"You consider reading a fun activity?" I had my back turned to her, but I knew she was paying attention to me. I knew it from the way she looked at me, more like she was trying to read me. The way she read her books.

"Yes," she said.

"So how come you couldn't read all that was in the paper?"

She laughed softly, and I felt myself relaxing a bit more. I had already started smiling before I realized what I was doing. So back to Mr. Hard Face.

"What about you? Do you find reading fun?" she asked.

Another bout of silence.

"I used to, but now I don't have the time," I finally said.

She was quiet for a long while, so quiet I thought she had fallen asleep. "Can I ask you a question?"

For a fleeting moment, a flicker of something dark crossed my face. When I didn't respond, she took it as a go-ahead.

"The tough guy from Jose's, I can't really remember his name—Blade or something. What's your relationship with him?"

CHAPTER FIVE

ANDRIANA

"So tell me everything!" Lila urged as soon as I answered the video call. "What's it like working for Alex Rocco?"

I sighed, leaning against the bed frame. I could see her excitement through the computer screen. "It's just..." I paused. "I don't know. It doesn't even feel like I'm working a real job."

"Well, you just started yesterday. Give it some time."

I nodded. "I guess so."

"Is he friendly? Hmm, scrap that. He doesn't even look friendly in photos."

I chuckled. "He's not. He's just the typical boss, but oh my God." I lowered my voice by several octaves. "He's freaking handsome!"

Lila laughed excitedly, clapping her hands. "Oh God, you're so lucky. Can you describe him?"

"Pervert." We both burst into laughter.

"You're such a killjoy," she muttered, laughing softly.

"Hmm. I guess you don't have to work this morning?" I asked her.

"Nope. My next shift isn't until three in the afternoon."

"Oh, great."

"Don't you find it odd that there's nothing about his personal life online?"

I was quiet for a while. "Maybe that's just how he wants it to be."

She nodded. "On a lighter note, what's your schedule like this morning?"

I jumped to my feet. "There's something I was supposed to read regarding that."

I grabbed the paper from the table and walked back to the bed, facing my laptop. Lila was watching me excitedly.

"So, it's a list of dos and don'ts. And also, this morning, I'm supposed to make breakfast by eight?!"

"You're in deep shit," Lila said, her eyes widening in horror. "It's almost eight."

"I have to go now. I'll call you later. Love you!"

I dashed out of the room before she could respond, making my way into the kitchen. The house was as silent as a graveyard, so my movements echoed through the walls.

I decided to make toast with some scrambled eggs for breakfast. By the time I was done with it, it was almost eight-thirty, but thankfully, neither of them was out.

"Good morning, miss," I heard someone say and turned to see Steven walking into the living room.

"Oh, hello."

He smiled at me, sniffing the air. "This place smells sweet."

I chuckled. "Thanks, Steve."

"Steve? I like that."

We both heard approaching footsteps, and by the time I turned back toward Steven, he was already making his way out the door.

Alex appeared by the doorway, all dressed in his suit and tie. My mouth went dry. There was absolutely no way one person could be this handsome. It was impossible. I tried to look away from him, but my eyes seemed to have other plans. He was way older than me, but I still couldn't stop myself from feeling attracted to him.

"Good morning, sir," I finally muttered as he headed toward the door.

"My name's Alex," was all he said, walking past me.

"Huh?" When I noticed he wasn't going to say anything more, I stepped forward. "Breakfast is ready."

"I'm late. Eat it."

Before I could say anything else, he was out of the house. Why did he employ me as his cook if he wasn't going to eat my food?"

I sat on the chair, feeling pissed. There was no way I was going to remain here, just eating his food without actually feeling like I was working to earn it.

Enzo appeared by the door, watching me. "Good morning," I muttered, standing. "I made breakfast."

He paused, unsure of what to say.

"Why do I have a feeling that you both don't want to eat my food?" I continued.

"That's insane. Why are you employed here as a cook if we weren't going to eat your meals?"

I shrugged. "That's what it seems like."

He smiled. It was the first time I had seen him smile since I got here. I stared at him suspiciously.

"What did you make?" he asked.

"Toast with some scrambled eggs."

"Hmm. Have you eaten?"

I shook my head. "I made breakfast for you both, not me."

"Let's eat." He walked to the table and sat. "What are you waiting for?"

I sauntered over to the table, bringing out two plates and setting the food on top.

"Thanks," he said. He pulled a plate toward himself and just kept looking at me.

"What?" I asked.

"You have to eat first."

"Why? Do you suspect I poisoned your meal?"

He rolled his eyes. "Now that you've said it, is that what you have in mind? To poison us?" His eyes glinted with amusement, and I started to laugh.

"Please don't do that to me ever again." I took a bite of my food and turned to him. "You must be a very bad guy."

"Why?"

I shrugged. "Only people who do bad things expect bad things to happen to them."

"Really?" He looked really interested in what I was saying. "How so?"

"It's simple." I took a bite of my bread. "I wouldn't have been scared of you poisoning me; it just wouldn't cross my mind."

"Because you're a good person?"

I turned to him. "I'm not a bad person."

"The opposite of *bad* is *good*," he said.

I shrugged. "Say whatever you want, but I meant what I said."

"You're indirectly saying I'm a bad person?"

"Directly." I met his gaze. "I know for sure that you're not a good person."

He still hadn't taken a bite of his meal. It was like he was waiting for me to start reacting to the food before he ate from his. After what felt like a lifetime, he took a bite.

"Who is Blade? Is he a friend of yours or Alex's?"

He looked at me. "You call him Alex?"

I shrugged, meeting his gaze. "He told me to refer to him as Alex."

"Oh."

Silence.

"You heard the name that night at the restaurant, right?"

I shook my head. "No, I have my sources."

The look he gave me next made me retract my statement. "Just kidding. I heard it that night. Where else would I hear it?"

"Be careful of the things you say around here," he said with a smile.

"Why did that sound like a threat?"

"Did it?"

I nodded. "Yup."

"I'm not really familiar with that guy. Alex needed some manpower on his site earlier that day, so we paid them for their services and took them out later on for dinner."

Uh? Then why was Blade acting like a gang leader or something?

He looked at me. "Why do you look so confused?"

"He seemed a little bit in control, like he knew something he shouldn't know. Are you sure he hasn't accidentally seen something he shouldn't have?"

He chuckled. "You're so—" he paused. "Funny."

"No one has ever told me that. I don't think I am."

"Then maybe I'm mistaken." He winked at me, picking up both our plates from the table and bringing them to the sink.

"Aren't you going out with Alex this morning? I thought you were his personal assistant?"

"He told you that?"

I shook my head. "No, I just figured it out. Am I wrong?"

"No. And I'm not going out with him today. He's out for personal reasons."

I nodded. "So I'm guessing today is your free day?"

"Isn't that what weekends are for?"

"Oh." I burst into laughter. "I've actually lost track of time."

"It happens."

"Can you show me around the house?" I asked him when he started heading toward the door. I made my most pitiful face at him.

"Fine, let's go."

"Really?" I didn't expect him to be so friendly.

"Don't make me regret it."

I jumped excitedly, trying to catch up with him as he walked out the door.

"There's really nothing much for you to see," he said, stopping in front of a door. "These are all just empty rooms. That room over there is Alex's room. The one directly opposite it is mine."

Alex's room was just a short walking distance from mine, so I was pretty safe.

"This is the second kitchen."

"Wow." I stepped into the room, my mouth opening wide in amusement. "This is where I'll be making my meals now."

"Hmm."

We walked down a little bit more, and he showed me several other rooms: the library, store, bathroom, second living room, and many other places.

Enzo was showing me around the compound when Alex's car pulled into the driveway.

"How was it?" Enzo asked as soon as he approached us, leading him into the house.

I didn't know what to say, so I just watched them both as they walked into the house. I realized I still hadn't gone through the entire content of the paper Alex gave me, so I passed through the back exit Enzo showed me and found my way into my room.

I picked up the paper and went through it carefully this time around, making sure not to miss any detail. I had nothing to do until mid-afternoon, so I picked up my laptop to study some more.

But curiosity had the best of me, and I found myself typing "Alex Rocco." I studied cybersecurity and computer science, so getting people's information was easy.

Should I really do this? I thought to myself. I erased his name from the screen. If he didn't want anyone to know about his personal life, he had his reasons.

"Alex Rocco," I muttered as I typed his name into the screen several moments later. There was nothing much to see, just the usual stuff that was all over the internet, so I delved deeper. When he was just ten years old, his parents were killed in an apparent assassination, and the Marcel family raised him. Woah. No siblings, no relatives. Just like me. At least we had something in common.

I sighed. No relationships whatsoever, no kids, no scandals. Now that's a very smooth record.

"Hmm. What does Alex Rocco do for a living?" I muttered, typing the letters on my keyboard.

CEO to Rocco's Construction. Hmm. Fair.

What else could I check? Hmm. I placed a finger on my chin, trying to think of something, but nothing came to mind.

"How come there's no single picture of any of his girlfriends? At forty years old, he definitely should've had a good number of girlfriends," I said to myself, deep in thought.

I dragged the laptop close to me, searching to see if I'd find something more personal.

"Voila!" I sat upright. I was staring at the picture of his last girlfriend. The picture was taken exactly six months ago. She wasn't pretty. Why was he with someone so basic-looking? I felt bad that I thought that way about her, so I cleared his name from my screen and closed the laptop.

Enzo. What was his surname? Richards? No.

I sat upright again, opening my laptop. It was easier to get a lot of information about Alex through his personal assistant. Soon, I was staring at Enzo's picture on my screen. He had the same profile as Alex. Smart. There was really nothing much to see except for his birthday, which was in two days' time, so I closed the laptop, not ready to make any extra findings on him.

There was a slight knock on the door, and I turned to the door, surprised.

"Who's there?"

"I'm here to clean the room."

I was going to tell whoever it was not to bother me, but I didn't want to cause any trouble for the other staff, so I picked up my phone and walked out of the room. A man was standing outside the door with his cleaning supplies.

"Hello." I waved at him, earning a smile from him.

"Hello," he replied.

Alex was seated in the living room, receiving a call, when I walked in.

"Yes, I'm coming out for lunch in a few minutes," he said to the person on the other end.

I suppressed the urge to look at him, so I just picked up my phone instead, doing nothing exactly.

"Alright, bye."

Neither of us said anything even after he ended the call, but my mind was filled with a thousand questions. Why did they employ me if they had no intention of eating what I made? Unless there was something else they weren't telling me.

I just couldn't sit down all day long and, at the end of the month, receive ten times what I was earning at Jose's while working my ass off. Something was definitely going on.

"Why did you employ me here as a cook if you had no plan to eat my food?"

He turned to me. "Who says I have no plan to eat your food?"

"I've been here for three days now, and not once have you eaten what I cooked."

He shrugged. "Just see it as nothing."

I shook my head. "So why am I here? Why are you paying me ten times what I was being paid at Jose's if you won't be needing my services?"

He sighed, shifting uncomfortably. "See it as a gift."

"I won't do that. If you don't need my services, I should leave. I feel like a charity cause."

"But you've been cooking since you got here, or am I wrong?"

"Cooking for myself. I can't just remain idle. I need to do something with my time."

"Then why don't you take culinary classes online? At least that way, you'd finally be called a chef when you're done."

"What?"

"I've seen one already. When you're ready, let me know. I'll pay whatever you need for the class."

"This is exactly what I don't want. Why are you doing all that for me? You barely even know me."

He stared at me, his gaze piercing deep into my heart. I didn't like the way he made me feel.

"You're not used to receiving help from others, huh?"

"That's not what this is about. There's something you're not telling me. I know that."

He remained silent; his attention fixed straight ahead. I wondered why he always did that, just stared at nothing.

"I'm supposed to make lunch for you now. Should I go ahead with it?"

"Do what you're supposed to do, Andriana."

It was the first time he mentioned my name, and I wanted him to say it again.

"But what's the point of cooking and wasting all this food if you aren't going to eat it?"

He turned to me. "Have you been throwing them away?"

I shook my head. "I eat it."

"Then it's not a waste." His eyes scanned over my whole body in one quick movement. It was so fast that it seemed almost unbelievable, but I knew what I saw. Did he find me attractive? I knew the answer to that even without hearing from him.

Alex went out a few minutes later while I was still making lunch, but this time around, I didn't let it get to me. I'd keep trying all my baking and culinary skills with the ingredients available. It would be a win-win.

I was plating the food when Enzo walked into the kitchen. "Why do you have that look on your face?"

I turned to him. "It's a new dish. I'll need an honest review from you." I pushed him a plate.

"Oh." He rubbed his hands together. "I can definitely do that. Where's yours?"

"I haven't dished it yet. Tell me how it tastes."

I had a feeling he was being serious about the fact that I could poison him, so I reached for the food to taste it first, but instead, he slapped my hand away.

"Leave it."

He took a spoonful and faced me. "It's perfect."

"Why am I finding it hard to believe you?"

He shrugged. "You asked for my honest opinion; that's it."

I jumped excitedly, dancing around the kitchen. Even though I didn't know how I suddenly got so used to Enzo, he made me feel a lot more comfortable than anyone else. I was still dancing around excitedly when my eyes clashed with Alex's. I froze, mid-spin. My heart was hammering frantically against my chest. He glanced from me to Enzo before walking into his room.

Mortification flooded my cheeks. All my confidence and my carefree abandon evaporated like mist. I hadn't realized how uncoordinated my behavior could've appeared to him. I glanced at Enzo, who continued eating like nothing was wrong.

"I'm so embarrassed," I said, taking a seat opposite him.

"Why?" He looked at me. I shrugged, looking down.

"He's acting strange," I said.

He dragged a piece of chicken with his teeth, pulling on it like his life depended on it.

I chuckled when he grabbed the next piece. "You like eating chicken?"

He shrugged. "Who doesn't?"

I suddenly remembered the chicken barbecue I made at my apartment a few days ago. "I made chicken barbecue some days ago. It's in my fridge at home. I hope it doesn't go bad."

He paused. "Are you kidding?"

I shook my head. "I'm dead serious."

"Tell Alex about this, and I'll go get it for you."

"Uh? He's probably in his room right now. I wouldn't want to annoy him more."

"He's in the library, the one I showed you yesterday."

"There's another one?"

He shrugged. "Go on."

"I don't think this is a good idea. He'll be so mad I disturbed his quiet time for some damned chicken."

"Just go. He doesn't care about all you're thinking. Just tell him what you want and leave."

I nodded, standing up from my seat and walking down the hallway after making a "he'll kill me" sign at Enzo. I took a deep breath when I got to the door, thinking about my decision for the umpteenth time.

"Who is there?" His voice echoed through the hallway, sending shivers down my spine. How the hell did he know I was standing here?

"It's Andriana." I said. "There's something I need to talk to you about."

There was something else I had wanted to discuss with him before this, so I'd bring it up before talking about the chicken.

I hope I don't get kicked out.

CHAPTER SIX

ALEX

I HAD TOLD ANDRIANA to come back in three hours, which she did, but I didn't answer the door. Now I felt like a proper douchebag. I stood up from my study, feeling hungry and tired. I came home earlier to eat lunch, but the sight of Andriana and Enzo bonding so well rubbed me the wrong way.

I stopped when I got to her door and contemplated what I was about to do. It was way past bedtime. I glanced at my wristwatch. It was 11 p.m.

"Hello," I called out, in a voice that even I almost couldn't hear. But the door was pulled open a few seconds later, and Andriana stood by the door, a surprised look on her face.

"Alex?" She shifted to the side. "Do you want to come in?"

I shrugged, stepping into her room. It had this soft, feminine lavender scent.

She sat on the bed and faced me, her nightgown hugging her body tightly. I cleared my throat.

"You wanted to see me," I said.

She nodded. "Yes, please." She placed a finger on her chin, watching me with mixed emotions. "I made barbecued chicken the day you came to my house, and then I forgot to pack it along with me." She looked away, ducking her head in embarrassment.

I almost laughed at the sheer sincerity of it all. "So what do you want?" I asked.

She looked at me. "I want to go back to my place and take it, and also get some of my other things."

"Enzo will get them for you."

"They're personal things."

"Enzo will get the ones that are not private, and you can buy anything else you'll need this evening. I'll ask Steven to drive you to the mall."

The house wasn't safe for her to return to right now. Blade was still searching frantically for her, so she needed to just lay low.

"What?"

I shrugged. "That should solve it, right?"

"Yes, but—"

I cut her off. "I guess that's all."

"No," she said sharply.

I crossed my arms. "Go on."

"Do you celebrate birthday parties?"

"I believe so."

She nodded. "Enzo's birthday is coming up tomorrow, and I was hoping we could celebrate his birthday, like a surprise party."

"A surprise party?"

She nodded. "It's totally up to you. I don't have a say in anything going on in this house. But he has made this place really easy for me; that's why I thought about doing something like that. It's totally up to you to decide."

I sighed. "Like what?"

"Just a surprise party." She looked at me hopefully.

"Like pretending not to know tomorrow is his birthday and then surprising him later on?"

"Yes, yes." She nodded excitedly.

"What do we need for that? Just a couple of gifts?"

She nodded. "You could invite some of his friends over, you know, to make it more interesting."

"I don't like random strangers coming into my home."

"We could use another place, like a friend's apartment. A hotel."

"And all of this is supposed to happen tomorrow?"

She nodded. "It's not so difficult."

"What do you need?"

She jumped to her feet. "First, can we go to the mall right now?"

"We? Oh no, no, I don't go around like that. I'm sure you must know I try to live a very private life."

"Is it because of your status?" She hurried over to her bags, searching frantically for something.

"Here." She handed me a cap. "This should do right, and then a face mask. You can never go wrong with that."

"I'm only doing this because you think it's going to make Enzo happy. He has been a great person, and I really hope this will show him how grateful I am."

"That's so sweet."

"I'll be waiting in the car. If I don't see you in five minutes, forget about all of this."

She nodded, running back to her bags to grab some other things.

"Wait. Where's Enzo? If he sees us going out together, he'll get suspicious."

"He's out for personal business, and he won't be back until tomorrow evening."

"Perfect."

She came down a few minutes later, dressed in baggy shorts and a white shirt.

"What about Steven?" she asked.

"It's just the two of us."

She nodded, rushing into the car. "Thank you."

The ride to the mall was very fast and quick, and before I knew it, we were on our way back home.

"Okay, one last thing," Andriana said, looking at me.

"Go on."

"You'll have to send messages to Enzo's closest friends, informing them about the surprise party."

I shook my head. "That's where we're going to have a problem."

"You said you'd do it if it'd show your gratitude to him."

I narrowed my eyes at her, and she laughed. "It's just a very short message. And you don't have to send it one at a time; you can send it once, like a broadcast."

I glanced at her before fixing my gaze on the road.

"I could compose something really quick for you," she offered.

"Go on."

"Hi, Marco, we'll be hosting a surprise party for Enzo tomorrow night. Your presence will be greatly appreciated at an unknown venue. How about that? Easy and simple. I don't know the venue yet."

It was not my thing, and I had the strongest desire not to involve myself in it, but it was the least I could do right now.

"What's in that little bag of yours?" Andriana asked on our way into the house. "It's so small."

"Do you want to know?"

She shook her head. "No, I'm just thinking out loud."

I copied and pasted what she said and sent it to Enzo's five friends. My phone beeped a few moments later. It was a text from one of them.

"Alex? Can I call to confirm this? Or is this a silly attempt to kidnap me?" the message read.

Another message came in almost immediately: "Why am I finding it so hard to believe this?"

I turned to Andriana, who was walking toward her room already.

"None of them believe me," I said to her, laughing softly. "It's just so out of my character."

She laughed. "Really? What are they saying?"

I turned my screen toward her, and she grabbed my phone, laughing softly as she went through the messages. "So are you going to call them now? It's not many, just five of them."

"They'll be there."

She made a face at me before turning into the hallway. "Thank you for doing this, Alex." Before I could reply, she had already left.

———

Enzo nodded slowly as he approached me, which meant the mission was successful. I shook his hands happily; this was why I could trust him with anything. He never disappointed.

"Good job, Enzo. Good job."

He nodded.

"Let's go get some drinks to celebrate," I said to him, walking to the car. This was all going according to plan. His friends were already situated at the hotel, with Andriana waiting to welcome him with whatever they planned. I had no interest.

"Did you hear from Nappy?" Enzo asked on our way.

"He's being a good boy," I said. "He should've known better than to play with fire."

He nodded. "That's good. And what about Andriana? I'm surprised to realize I miss that girl."

I shrugged. "Great, I guess. You both seem really close."

"Close?" He shook his head. "I wouldn't say close, but she's good company, and I actually love spending time with her."

"Good for you. I thought you didn't want her here." I glanced at him.

"Well, I'm glad she's here. Her presence has brightened the house a little bit. Your presence in that house is like a dark cloud brooding over us."

"Wow," I scoffed, deciding that was enough conversation for the day and facing my attention on the road.

"Do you have a target here?" Enzo asked as we got out of the car and I led him to the hotel door.

"Keep quiet." I placed my hands on my lips.

He looked so confused. I almost laughed.

"Why didn't you tell me we had another mission?" he whispered, watching me like I was insane. "Have you informed the other guys?"

"Oh, just keep quiet." I didn't want anyone wondering what he was talking about from the other end of the door.

"Go on, open it."

He placed his hands in his back pocket, reaching out for something. I frowned. "Oh, c'mon, Enzo, what the hell are you doing?"

"My rifle. Why do you keep questioning me?" He frowned, looking really pissed.

At this moment, I could barely hold back laughter. "It's not a mission. There are innocent people at the back of that door. Behave yourself." We were both whispering.

"Oh." He pulled the door open, and they all jumped excitedly, singing the "Happy Birthday" song to him.

"Oh my God!" He looked around, his face shining with joy. "I can't believe this."

"Happy birthday, man." I said to him as his friends bombarded him with gifts."

"Why, thank you, Alex. This is such a pleasant surprise."

He caught sight of Andriana and laughed. "You too. Oh my God!"

She handed him her gift, but he pulled her into his arms instead, patting her back softly.

"Thank you," he told her.

After a while, Andriana walked up to me. "Can we leave now?" she asked. "Are you ready to leave?"

I looked around. "But the party is just starting."

She nodded. "I know. I'm not really a fan of parties."

Deciding not to say anything more, I informed Enzo we were leaving.

Neither of us said anything until we got home. "Thank you," she muttered softly as she walked into the hallway.

"Andriana?"

She took a few steps back, watching me quietly.

"Are you okay?"

"Oh." She laughed softly. "I'm good, I just get tired of parties easily."

Her laughter faded as she turned to me, her gaze locking with mine. The air crackled with unspoken words, with a sudden awareness that felt both thrilling and terrifying. I shifted closer, the space between us shrinking with each hesitant step. Her scent, a mix of lavender and something warm and uniquely hers, filled my senses.

"Andriana." My voice sounded rough, and then slowly, almost imperceptibly, she leaned in. And just when I thought I would shut down and walk away, I let out a low sigh and pulled her to me. It wasn't a sweet kiss; it was hard and demanding, and her little moans were driving me crazy. I only had time to draw a quick breath before her hands fisted my hair, and my mouth crushed down on hers.

CHAPTER SEVEN

ANDRIANA

I TOSSED AND TURNED on my bed the next morning, not wanting to face Alex. Why did we let that happen?

Oh my God.

I sat upright, thinking of what to do. Why don't I just video call Lila and let her know what happened? She picked up on the third ring.

"What the hell, Andriana? I was bathing." She still had the towel tied around her body.

"Well, you shouldn't be bathing right now."

"What happened?" she asked with a chuckle.

"We kissed," I whispered, covering my eyes in shame.

"Uh? What the hell, Andriana?"

I nodded. "I know. I feel the exact same way." I explained everything that happened, and she sighed after I was done.

"So what's your next move?"

I shook my head. "I don't even know. I'm so confused."

We were both silent for a while.

"Okay, okay. Enough of all this. How was the kiss?"

I narrowed my eyes on her. "Lila!"

She laughed. "C'mon, bring it on. This is a safe space."

"Is this really a safe space?" I asked softly, my mouth curving into a smile.

She nodded. "Yes, my friend. Tell me about the kiss."

I sighed dramatically, leaning back on the bed frame. "It was heavenly. It was the best kiss I've ever had."

"Was it better than that one kiss?"

I nodded. "It's literally the best kiss of my lifetime."

She chuckled. "You're such a fool."

"Lila, it felt like I was already in paradise. He kissed me with so much gentleness, so much care." My hands went to my lips automatically, and Lila burst into laughter, shaking her head as she laughed.

"Wake up. Are you sure this wasn't a dream?"

"No. I'm dead serious."

"Hmm."

I heard approaching footsteps and placed a finger on my lips, asking her to keep quiet.

"Andriana?" Steven called.

I kept quiet, pretending not to be awake. "The boss wants to see you..." he paused. "Right now, Andriana."

Lila made a face at me through the screen, and I groaned silently. I heard retreating footsteps a few moments later.

"Bye." She waved at me. "You can handle this; it's easy, just pretend like it never happened. Don't ever bring it up."

I nodded. "Okay."

"Andriana?"

"Hmm?"

"Don't bring it up for any reason. Don't do that. I'm repeating this because I know you."

"Oh, please. Bye, talk to you later." I closed the laptop and made my way out of the room and into the living room.

Alex was seated in his favorite position, going through his phone.

"Good morning," I said.

"Breakfast is supposed to be ready by 8 a.m." He turned to me, his gaze blank.

"I know. I'm sorry. I woke up late."

He sighed. "Get started."

He was acting like we didn't just lock lips with each other in this same spot several hours ago. He was such a jerk. I made pancakes and paired them with coffee because I wanted to leave as fast as I could. When I was done, he faced me.

"Where's mine?" he asked.

I made just enough for myself because I thought he wasn't going to eat, as usual.

I placed the food on the plate and poured him a cup of coffee.

"I'm done. Your food is on the table." I said to him, turning to leave.

"Aren't you eating?"

"No."

"Why's that?"

"I don't feel like eating anything. I'm okay."

He nodded. "Fine."

I walked back to my room, desperately wishing Enzo would just walk in right now. It was as if he read my mind because, as soon as I turned toward my room, I heard Enzo's voice coming from the living room. I tiptoed back to the door, trying to figure out what was going on.

"There's trouble," Enzo said to Alex. I couldn't see either of them, but that wasn't my concern as long as I could hear them clearly.

"What's the problem?"

"Code nine."

Code nine? Why were they talking in codes?

"What the hell? How's that even possible?" Alex asked, his voice sharp.

"I don't know. I had to rush down here when I got the call."

"Get the items ready. We'll have to operate tonight. Where are the other gang members?"

Huh?

I moved away, my heart beating frantically against my chest. What the hell were they talking about?

"Franko and the rest are aware, and they're getting everything ready."

"Where's Andriana?" Alex asked suddenly. My heart raced frantically as I looked down the hall leading to my room. I wouldn't make it. "She just left."

"What? Just now?" I heard Enzo's voice approaching and did the quickest thing I could think of: I pretended to just be walking in. We bumped into each other, and I jumped in surprise when I saw him by the door. He squinted his eyes at me.

"Andriana!" Enzo said. "I was just asking Alex for you." He looked at me suspiciously.

"Oh. How are you?" I asked him.

"Good. Did you make anything for me?" Enzo asked as I made my way back inside. Alex still hadn't touched his meal.

"What would you like to eat?"

He shrugged. "Anything that wouldn't stress you."

"What do you want, Enzo?"

His gaze went from me to Alex, before finally settling on me. "I'll have the same thing he's eating."

I nodded, making my way to the kitchen.

"You can have mine, Enzo. I'm not hungry," Alex said, without looking at anyone.

I dropped the bowl back into the cabinet, turned off the gas cooker, and walked out. My heart was still beating when I shut the door to my room. I grabbed my laptop from my bed and turned on the Wi-Fi. Something was definitely going on in here, and the earlier I figured it out, the better.

Gang members? An operation tonight? Something was definitely going on.

I called my roommate from college, who now worked for the Secret Service. She was lucky enough to find a good job immediately after college—the perks of having a wealthy living parent.

"Hi, Camilla."

"Andriana!" she called out excitedly. "It's been a while. I'm so glad you called."

"I need a favor from you." I went straight to the point, not ready for any form of conversation.

"Woah, this is pretty serious. Go on. If it's something I can do, I'll help you out."

"Thank you. Can you help me check out someone very influential?"

She was quiet for a moment. "Who is it?"

"Alex Rocco."

"I shouldn't be doing this, Andriana. You know that. I'm only doing this because of how dear you are to me."

I rolled my eyes. "Noted, thank you."

She was quiet for a while before her voice echoed through the line again.

"There's really nothing much to see here. Just the usual."

"Can I know the usual? Can you tell me what you can see?" I sounded desperate, but I didn't care.

"CEO of Rocco's Construction. Orphaned. Nothing else."

"Can you help me delve deeper? Like, are there any scandals? Criminal records?"

She laughed. "Criminal records? Alex Rocco is clear of all these, my dear friend."

I sighed.

"Is everything okay?" she asked.

I nodded before muttering a quick *yes* when I realized she couldn't see me.

"There's one thing, though, Andriana."

"What?"

"A very smooth record almost always means the person has something hiding."

Woah, I thought to myself. I could feel my heart beating frantically again.

"But you've seen nothing, Camilla?"

"No."

"Thank you." I ended the call and jumped out of bed, packing my stuff into my bag. Something was definitely going on, and I couldn't figure it out when I was right in the middle of the storm.

CHAPTER EIGHT

ALEX

"START THE FUCKING CAR, Steven!"

Enzo turned to me, his gaze hard. "We got this boss."

"No, we don't, and the earlier you stop acting like everything is going well, the better. Get the men ready."

He nodded, casting a worried glance at me. A gang member was killed this afternoon. He was found dead in his apartment. This was Blade's handiwork, and the earlier I handled this bullshit, the better it would be for all of us.

"Fuck it!" Enzo cursed, hitting the car seat violently. "Rick was such a great guy."

I looked out of the window. He was one of my favorites. Blade had just toyed with the wrong one.

"He killed just one of my men. We'll take down three."

Enzo started to shake his head. "No, boss. That would cause a whole lot of trouble."

I stared at him, trying to calm myself down. "You sound like a fool. Since when did you start caring about trouble?"

He looked away. "I just want us to handle this differently."

"Exactly the way I'm going to handle it," I said, turning to the driver. "Steven!"

He looked at me through the rearview mirror. "Yes, sir?"

"We have an operation tonight, which I'm sure you already know about. Be prepared. Be alert."

He nodded. "Roger that, sir."

"You have three addresses with you. Stop at each house according to how it was sent to you."

"Yes, sir."

I tapped my jacket to make sure I still had my weapon with me. I didn't like to fight with a gun, but if it was important tonight, so be it.

"Stay in the fucking car, Enzo, if you're going to keep acting like a bitch. You're beginning to piss me off."

"I'm on your side. I just don't want you in the middle of this."

"Then act like it."

"We're three minutes from the first address, sir," Steven stated, his voice hard.

Enzo nodded. "Let's fucking go!"

———

For the first time in many years, I failed an operation.

I stumbled into the apartment, my normally slicked-back hair a greasy mess. All I could think about was the fact that I failed an operation. A meticulously planned attack went south faster than a greased pig on ice.

Something was definitely going on. "Fuck it!" I flung the books on the table right in front of me. "Fucking bullshit."

Enzo walked in at that exact moment, his face dull. "I'm sorry, boss."

It was best I didn't say anything, even though all I wanted was to blame him for all that happened tonight.

"Just leave, Enzo."

He threw one last glance at me before turning around and walking out the door. The fact that we didn't get any of Blade's men made my blood boil. I grabbed my keys from the table. "I'll do it on my own."

Steven cornered me on my way out, his face still stained with blood. "Get yourself together, Steven. Don't forget we have a visitor in the house."

"Let me give you a ride, boss. Where are you going?"

"Tend to your injury. Don't bother with me," I said.

Steven was going to say something else, but stopped when he noticed my hard glare.

I unlocked the car and settled in, different things running through my mind. If I couldn't handle things with the men around, I'd have to do it by myself. I was starting the ignition when I heard a rapid banging on the window. I rolled down the tinted glass, staring into my right-hand man's worried eyes.

"I'm coming with you," Enzo said.

I shook my head. "Not now, Enzo. I'm going for a ride."

He was quiet for a moment. "This is the first time we've ever lost a fight, boss, and it's because we didn't plan it as well as you thought we did." He sighed. "We acted based on our emotions for the first time, and that's why this happened. Don't beat yourself up about this."

Without uttering another word, I stepped out of the car and walked back into the living room, deciding not to think about any of this for the rest of the night.

"Would you like anything, boss? Beer? Water? Any drink?" Enzo asked, walking toward me a few minutes later. I looked around the house, suddenly remembering I hadn't seen Andriana in a long while.

"Where's that girl?" I asked.

"Probably in her room," Enzo said. "Do you need her to cook for you?"

"Give me a shot of tequila, please," I said.

"Roger that," Enzo said.

"And tell her to come prepare dinner," I continued. "I wonder why she won't do her fucking job."

Enzo looked at me while pouring the drink, his features uncertain.

"What's the problem?" I asked him.

He shook his head.

"You clearly have something on your mind," I said. "Go on."

He shrugged. "I don't know. You've never eaten any food she cooked. I'm just wondering why you're always bothered when she doesn't cook."

"She is being paid to cook. Whether I eat or not is none of her business. I just need her to do her job."

"Did something happen this morning?" Enzo asked, throwing a nervous glance at me as he approached with the drink.

"What are you talking about?" I asked, my gaze turning hard as I swiped through the pictures I received of Ricky, gasping for breath in his own pool of blood.

"Never mind, boss."

"Answer my fucking question now, Enzo. You know I'm not in for all of that."

He nodded. "When I got in this morning, it felt very uncomfortable with the both of you."

"What are you getting at now?"

He shook his head. "Nothing. It's just a random thought."

"Get out, Enzo. I'm in a really bad mood right now. You have to be very careful with what you say. I'm sure you know that by now."

"Yes, I do." He turned to the door. "I'll go now."

"Call that girl out before you leave."

He turned to the other exit and appeared with her a few minutes later. She was in her sleeping wear and had a book in her hand.

"What took you both so long?"

"I'll leave now," Enzo said, walking to the door. When I didn't respond, he unlocked the door and bolted out of the room. I didn't blame him. I'm a very hard nut to crack when I'm in a bad mood.

"You called me?" Andriana asked, leaning against the door frame.

I tried to take my mind away from that one reckless act that happened last night, but as she stared at me, my mind kept going back to that very moment. She tasted sweet. And all day long, I hadn't been able to get that one moment out of my mind. I hissed, getting annoyed as I realized what I was thinking about yet again.

"Of course I did. Don't you have a task for tonight?"

"I'm not hungry."

"Who gives a shit if you're hungry or not?"

She shrugged. "I cook for myself all the time, so I might as well decide when to cook and when not to cook."

I narrowed my eyes at her. "You don't have that liberty in this house. No one gave you the freedom to do as you wish."

She looked away from me, pressing her lips together. Those goddamned lips—lush, pink, and soft. Images from last night flooded my brain, and I almost let out a frustrated growl.

"Go and prepare dinner," I told her.

"I'm only going to prepare dinner if you're going to eat."

I sighed. "That's an order. If you're going to remain in this house, then you'll have to obey my instructions. And if you know you can't do that anymore, I'm afraid you'll have to leave."

She stared at me for a long while, her chest rising and falling.

"Have I made myself clear?" I asked.

"Why do you want me to cook if you're not going to eat? I don't get it. Do you want the food to just go to waste? Or is this some sort of power thing?"

"Watch your mouth now, Andriana."

"But it's just unreasonable. I've been cooking for myself since I got here, and you want to pay me by the end of the month for just eating all your food?"

She had a point, but I didn't care. She was here to do as I commanded, or leave.

"I won't be going back and forth with you," I told her. "It's up to you. Your job is to cook, and whether someone eats it or not is none of your business."

"Okay."

"Good, now get to work."

"Do you have anything you want me to cook, sir?" Her inflection on the last word made a mockery of it, and I almost said something I knew I'd later regret, but instead, I turned away from her. "You're the cook. Do whatever you want."

"Great."

She dashed into the kitchen, bringing out a few items from the cabinet. A beep from my phone dragged my attention away from her.

It said, "Blade is currently at a restaurant: Jose's. His reason for being there is not yet known."

Oh God.

My eyes darted to Andriana. Blade had probably searched the whole city for her. She didn't know how lucky she was to be here. I suddenly felt pity for her as I watched her. Her once peaceful life would be cut short if she wasn't careful.

She narrowed her eyes at me as she lifted up two flavors of jam. "Which one do you prefer?"

"I'm indifferent. Just do your thing."

She sighed, still looking confused, as she dropped them on the table. "The strawberry flavor is fine."

"Hmm."

She picked up the other flavor and opened it while holding my gaze. "I'm the cook. I know what's best."

After a while, she faced me. "Dinner is ready. I guess I'm done for the night. Goodnight."

"Hmm."

She stopped when she got to the door. "Is everything okay?"

"I told you: no personal questions."

"You don't look happy tonight." She shifted uncomfortably, leaning her body against the door frame. "It's not like you've ever had a happy face, but I know there's something really bothering you tonight. Tell me about it. It'll make you feel better."

"Why do you care if I feel better or not? Do you really care, or are you just trying to get some information out of me?"

She sighed. "You're so difficult."

"Just leave. I don't like people being around me."

She took the chair opposite me instead. "Just talk to me. You know, I used to be a therapist when I was still in college."

I had no interest whatsoever in what she was saying, but her last statement caught my attention. "So what happened? Did you give someone the wrong advice?"

"Oh lord, I don't even want to remember it." She covered her eyes with both hands. "Someone took my advice and got into trouble. I gave her my honest opinion. I just don't know how it all went wrong. She and her friends were after me for a week. I had to skip classes for a full week. Since then, I don't care what could be going on in your life; I'll keep my opinion to myself."

She looked so serious, yelling her college tales, that I didn't know when I started to laugh. The thought of her running around college made everything worse. I guess this was not the first time she'd had to run for her life. Only this time, she wasn't aware she was running.

"This is like the first time you've laughed since I got here. You're always in a tough mood. Like a soldier."

She walked to the kitchen then came back to me with a full plate of food. I felt my stomach churn at the sight of the food.

"Can you tell me why you're always in such a foul mood?" she asked between bites of her meal.

"Hmm." I looked away from her, fixing my gaze on the ground instead. I should just order something. This was one of the times I wished she would suddenly talk about me not eating any meal she had prepared since she got here.

"This chicken is very tender." She glanced at me while pulling on a piece of chicken.

"Hmm," was all I said.

"You're missing a great deal by not eating my food," she continued. "I'm a really great cook."

"Hmm."

She dropped the plate on the table and faced me. "There's something odd about you, about the way you act. I just can't put my finger on it yet."

"Hmm."

She smiled. "Can you tell me about yourself? Anything?"

"Leave."

She blinked. "What?"

"Leave, right now." I punctuated my words with a sharpness I only used when I needed to get my point across as soon as possible. Any attraction I'd felt for her crumbled into ash as I watched her.

"Did I say something wrong?" she asked, but she scurried to her feet as Enzo walked in. "I hate him," she said, facing Enzo while pointing to me. "Your boss, he's so rude and annoying. I can't deal with him anymore."

Before Enzo could say anything, she turned around and dashed out of the living room.

Enzo cleared his throat. "I'll leave now."

"Please do. And tell the rest of the men that no one comes in here until they're told to do so."

"Okay, boss."

I let out a loud sigh after Enzo left. What an absolute mess this day turned out to be. Ricky was gone, and Blade was still somewhere around, living his life. I smiled briefly. "Not for long, Blade."

I felt my stomach churn once more, and I glanced at the time. It was way past working hours, so I headed over to the kitchen, hoping to get a few crumbs of what she had cooked earlier. The mere thought of sneaking around my own kitchen irked me.

I was lifting the lid off the pot on the cooker when I caught sight of her watching me.

"What the hell?" I barked, jumping in surprise. In all my years of being in the mafia, not one single person had ever caught me off guard. This was one of the thousands of reasons why I couldn't trust her.

"Are you hungry?" she asked with a smirk.

"What the hell are you doing here?" I asked, folding my hands against my chest.

"I didn't want the food to go to waste, so I came out to eat it," she replied.

I shifted for her to get whatever she wanted.

"Are you certain it wasn't the food you were about to eat?" she asked. "I could leave it and go back in. I just don't want it to get bad."

The smirk on her face was so annoying that I wanted nothing more than to say something that would get it off her face.

"I was just about to make something for myself," I said. I didn't like cooking, so I never did, but if it would take this impending shame away, then so be it.

She grabbed my hands as I made to turn on the stove, and I felt my entire body react with so much emotion that I yanked my hands away from her.

"What would you like to eat? I'll make it for you. You can stay here if you don't trust me."

I was going to say no, but my stomach chose that moment to make the most awkward sound, so I took a step back.

"There are different types of noodles in that cabinet over there. You can make any one you like."

She nodded before placing a pot on the burner. The microwave made a loud bang a few seconds later, and I snapped out of my thoughts. Andriana threw me a concerned glance.

"Here, have this before the pasta is ready." She pushed a plate of salad over to me, and I almost dug in the moment I took a whiff of it.

"Thank you," I said gruffly, picking up the spoon.

I watched her as she cooked, different thoughts running through my mind. Undoubtedly, I was attracted to her. She was beautiful, smart, and daring. Of course I was attracted to her. And that was the main reason why I should steer clear of her.

Attractions like these for us folks in the mafia only meant danger for the affected party. It never ended well. Even something as simple as a fling would usually end up with the person being killed. And if there was one thing I hated more than anything else, it was the death of the innocent.

So I was attracted to her, but that was all it would ever be.

"Here." She stretched a plate of food to me.

"Thank you." The aroma alone sent me into a frenzy.

We ate the meal in silence, neither of us uttering a single word until she had washed and dried both plates and was on her way back to the room.

"Wait." I suddenly felt a twinge of guilt thinking about the way I had treated her since she started working here. It would serve us both well if we were on the same side. She leaned against the door, her gaze fixed on me.

I took a step toward her so we were only a few inches apart. I had no idea what I was doing, but I knew at this moment that I was drawn to her more than I could ever imagine.

"Er, this is really awkward," she said.

We were so close that I could smell her perfume—the sweet lavender scent I could never get used to. I'd never seen her eyes like that before; they were the perfect shade of brown. It was like staring into the depths of the sun.

I felt my organ throb, and my hands clenched into a fist.

"Goodnight." My breath came out in a harsh exhale, and a small shiver rolled down her body. I could see her nipples clearly through her silk nightgown. Maybe it was just my own imagination, but judging from Andriana's flushed cheeks, I wasn't the only one aware of the charged air between us.

I took a step back. This was why I didn't want to get close to her in the first place. I didn't want any baseless feelings to come between us. Just when I made up my mind to leave, she placed her hands on my shoulders and pulled me forward, so we were only a few inches apart.

CHAPTER NINE

ANDRIANA

I T TOOK EVERY OUNCE of self-control I had not to pounce on him and give him the best kiss of his life. Here he was acting all prim and proper, and my entire body was raw with hunger. Hunger for him. I wasn't one to fawn over men. In fact, I'd been celibate for as long as I could remember. But there was something about him. This was masculine energy.

"There's something on your shirt," I said instead, dusting off nothing in particular from his shirt.

"Goodnight, Andriana," he said, before walking out of the room. I remained at that same spot long after he left, my heart racing.

This was wrong on so many levels. He was my boss, and he was also about seventeen years older than me. But that didn't change anything about the way I felt; it actually made me feel more aroused.

"Oh lord, help me." I eased off the door, my heart still racing as I walked to my room. I picked up my laptop once inside the room, ready to call Lila, but I decided not to. I already had an idea of what she would say: *Don't have any form of relationship with him, Andriana.*

It'll only get complicated. We've seen this play out so many times before. I'm sure you know better.

I desperately wanted to talk to someone else, but I had a limited number of people in my life, so I just paced around the room in frustration. Apart from Lila, I had no one else to talk to. No family, no friends. What a boring life!

As if the universe were listening to me, my phone started to ring. I dashed over to it with the speed of light. Well, not as fast, but fast enough to pick up my phone before it stopped ringing. It was Mia.

"Hey, Mama," I said.

"Andriana!" She sounded worried, like something was wrong. My heart skipped a beat as I sat on the bed.

"What's the problem, Mia? Are you okay?"

"I'm okay. Are you okay?"

"Yes. Talk to me."

"Haven't you heard?"

I was getting really impatient now. "Heard what?"

"Jose's restaurant was burned down tonight. No one knows who did it. It's all over the news. Aren't you online?"

"Oh my God!" I said. "I had no idea. How's Jose?"

"He looked so different and so distant when he was interviewed. He couldn't even talk."

"Maybe it was a kitchen mishap."

She sighed. "Who knows? It's so unfortunate. I just feel so bad for him. Even though he was a total jerk to his workers, I know how hard he struggled to build that place. I feel so bad."

I nodded. "I don't even know what to say. I've had him blocked ever since that day."

"Me too," Mia said.

We were both quiet for a while. "Where have you been, girl? It's like you disappeared from the fucking Earth."

I chuckled. "Just chilling with a few friends."

She laughed. "I'll take that to mean you don't want me to know where you are, because even Jose knows you don't have any other friends around."

We both laughed. "I'm good, Mia. Thanks for reaching out. I'll keep in touch."

She sighed. "Please do. I know you don't have many people around you. I love hearing from you."

"That's so sweet. Thank you, Mia. I'll keep that in mind."

"Have a good night's rest," she said.

"You too, Mia."

It took several hours after that before I finally fell asleep. And I had a dream that I saw the man from the restaurant, Blade, chasing me around with a shotgun.

———-

I woke up the next morning feeling worse than I did the night before. I hadn't woken up in such a bad mood in ages, and it took me a minute to remember why. The restaurant. In fact, all the events of last night.

I glanced at the time as I rolled around in bed. It was almost three in the afternoon. I jumped in panic. I was supposed to cook breakfast by eight. Normally, Alex would've had someone come knock on my door. I wondered why that didn't happen today.

My suspicions were confirmed when I went out to the living room a few moments later. The house was dead silent. I felt my heart skip a beat at the thought that I was the only one in the house.

"Nope, nope. Not happening," I said to myself, making my way outside, heading toward the staff room.

"Good day."

I turned around to see the laundry man watching me. "Oh, hello. Have you seen Steven this morning?"

"He went out with the boss," came his quick, short reply, like he wasn't interested in any form of conversation, especially with me.

"And Enzo?" I prodded, not minding his unfriendly attitude.

"Enzo works with the boss. They're almost always at the same place, at all times. I hope I've answered your questions."

I looked around worriedly. I knew I was acting paranoid, but I couldn't help it.

"What's the matter? Do you need anything?"

I nodded. "Do you have his number?"

"Who? Steven?"

"Either Alex or Enzo."

He looked at me like I was insane but didn't say anything. "Give me your phone. I'll dial it in."

"Oh, thanks."

After a few seconds, he handed the phone back to me. "I only gave you Enzo's number. You have to work hard to get the boss's number, just like the rest of us."

Normally, I'd have ignored him and gone inside, but I didn't want to be in there all by myself.

"You had to work to get the boss's number?"

He nodded, looking more interested in our conversation. "Not like *work*, per se, but we had to show our loyalty. You just got here; you still have time."

"Hmm."

"Yeah. Don't you have anything to do? Like cooking or something?" he asked.

"Oh." I would've stopped at that, but I didn't particularly like him, so I continued, "I don't cook all the time."

He frowned. "Why not?"

"Because," I said, throwing my hands in the air. "Just because."

He sighed. "Well, if you'll excuse me, some of us actually have things to do."

I eyed him as he walked away. What an annoying man. Since I had nothing else to do outside, I made my way back into the living room, feeling a lot worse than I did when I woke up.

It just felt like I wasn't making any progress in my life. Lila was over there, studying for her master's. Camilla, on the other hand, landed a high-paying job with the Secret Service, and here I was, walking around a stranger's house doing absolutely nothing in hopes of collecting a salary by the end of the month.

I made my way into the room. It was best I leave. Maybe that way, I'd be able to get myself together and actually do something great with my life. My bags were already packed. It wasn't the first time I'd thought about leaving. But I couldn't leave now, not without having one final glance at Alex and even Enzo.

They didn't come back until later that night. I was in the living room, fast asleep, when I heard retreating footsteps in the hallway.

"Hey, sleepy baby," Enzo said, making his way inside. "Did you miss me?"

I smiled brightly. "Surprisingly, yes. I missed you and your annoying boss."

Alex chose that moment to walk in. He stopped by the door when he saw me and Enzo talking.

"Just kidding." I smiled at him, genuinely happy to see him. It was my last moment with them. I just hoped Alex wouldn't spoil it with his mood swings. I didn't want to scare him off by talking too much, so I kept quiet as he settled on a chair close to the window.

"Did you watch the news today?" Enzo asked, watching me quietly.

I had an idea what he was going to talk about but pretended not to. "Uh?"

"Did you watch the news at any time during the day? Or even this evening?"

I shook my head. "No."

"Oh." He glanced at Alex, who showed no interest whatsoever in our conversation.

"So that means you haven't heard what happened at Jose's?"

I sat upright, concern etched on my face. I should take a role in acting.

"What happened?" I asked.

"It got burned; no one knows what happened yet. It could've been a reckless mistake from any of the staff."

"My God." My hands flew to my mouth. "I can't believe this. How did this even happen? Poor Jose."

He shook his head. "Here, have this. Eat this instead of going through the long process of making dinner. We've eaten." He pointed to Alex, who was now barking out orders to his construction workers.

"Oh, thank you, Enzo," I said.

"Not me. Alex bought three plates."

I made a surprised face at him, and we both chuckled. Alex was so unpredictable. It was impossible to know his next move.

"We had a successful contract today. We've been going back and forth for a while now, but we hit our goal today," Enzo whispered, a huge smile on his face.

"That's impressive," I said. Enzo reminded me of Lila in so many ways. They were both great friends. And even though Enzo was just like a personal assistant to Alex, I could see how much he genuinely cared for him. I was going to miss them both so much.

I grabbed the bag Enzo handed me from the table and faced Enzo. "Good night," I said.

"Why are you so eager to leave tonight?" Enzo narrowed his eyes on me.

I shrugged. "Three is a crowd."

Alex was still arguing with the person on the other end of the line. I pitied whoever was at the receiving end of all of this.

"See ya tomorrow, then," Enzo said, patting my shoulders softly.

"Hey, why are you being so nice to me tonight? You're going to make me cry."

"Huh? Are you on your period? Why are you so emotional?" Enzo teased.

I slapped his arms playfully, earning a dramatic yelp from him.

"Goodnight." He blew a kiss at me.

As I made my way to my room, I couldn't help but feel guilty for what I was about to do. But I knew it was the best option I had. I just couldn't remain here, unsure of what was going on around the house. A part of me knew there was something odd going on, but I just couldn't put my finger on it yet.

Steven mentioned that no one came into the house, Enzo talked about gangs and operations, and Alex himself acted like there was something up his sleeve. I could only solve the mystery from outside the house, not while I was still within the house.

I contemplated calling Lila before I left, but changed my mind. It was best if I just kept this to myself. I'd wait till everyone had gone to bed before leaving.

A few minutes later, my laptop began to beep. I raised it up to see that it was Lila calling.

"I have to leave tonight, Lila, so I'll call you once I'm back home."

"What? Are you okay? Did something happen?"

I sighed. "Yes, everything is fine. But I don't feel like a worker here. I rarely cook; I mostly eat and sleep."

She chuckled. "Are you crazy? That sounds cool. Maybe they don't eat much. You're supposed to enjoy it while it lasts."

I shook my head. "You know I don't like things like this."

She laughed. "I remembered one time in college when that woman paid you to look after her child, and she was always taking him along with her whenever she was going out."

"Oh, that woman!" We both started laughing. I left and never returned. I hated feeling like a burden to people.

"Does Alex Rocco know about this?"

I shook my head. "No, I haven't told anyone. Once I'm sure they're all asleep, I'll leave."

"Hmm," she murmured

I shrugged.

"So, after this? What next?" she asked. "You left Jose's already. What will you be doing? Because I hate it when you don't have a job. You're always cranky and sad."

"I'll figure out something."

She looked like she wanted to argue, but instead, she just stared at me. "I hope you're making the right choice, Andriana. He's paying you so much, just for you to make such a reckless decision. Many people would jump on this opportunity."

"Hmm," was all I said.

"Is he harassing you? Is he being mean? Tell me the truth," she prodded.

"No."

"I know he's older than you, and you might feel uncomfortable if he ever suggests something like that. I'll understand if that's the case."

"No, Lila. Please, excuse me. I'll call you back later, okay?"

She was still shouting on the other end when I hung up.

After that, I decided to leave. There was no point in lingering when I had already made up my mind to leave. I dropped the food Enzo gave me inside my already-packed bag and decided to go through the secret exit Enzo mistakenly showed me. He hadn't meant to show me that day. I noticed it from the disappointment on his face after he told me but didn't say anything more.

I snuck out of the room, making sure no one was walking through the passage as I tiptoed down to the secret exit. Fortunately for me, it didn't require a key. I held my bag tightly and went into the dark, long hallway leading to God knows where. By the time I got to the end of the hallway, there was another door. I said a quick prayer, hoping it wouldn't need a key. Thankfully, it didn't. But unfortunately, someone was guarding the gate leading out.

"Who's there?" the gateman barked, walking toward me.

I laughed. "It's just me. Hello." I smiled cheerfully, hoping to leave as soon as possible.

"What do you want?" he continued.

"Open the gate. I'm leaving," I replied.

"Why didn't you pass the main gate?" He looked at me with suspicion.

"Secret business," I whispered.

He was quiet for a while. "Why do I find it hard to believe you?"

I shrugged. "If anything goes wrong, you'll have yourself to blame. The boss sent me, and it's a matter of urgency."

"I'll call him. I need to confirm before letting you out."

"I wouldn't call right now if I were you. He's in a really bad mood. But do as you wish."

He sighed. "I hope you're not playing pranks on me, miss. I really hope so."

"Have a good night, sir." I waved at him as I walked out of the building, but I started to regret my decision the moment I stepped out of the gate. There was no one waiting for me at the house, no friends, no family. I also had no job to fall back on, so what was all the trouble for?

I walked for about an hour before I saw a cab willing to take me home. It was way past midnight at this point.

"What's a young, beautiful woman like you doing out at this time of night?" the driver asked me.

"Can you just drive me home?"

He shrugged, glancing at me from the mirror. "Just go into your house and lock the door the moment I drop you off. It's not safe for you or anyone else. I'll wait outside until you're inside the house."

"Why? Thank you very much." I smiled brightly at him. It had been a long time since I saw a genuine gentleman. These days, the men out here were so bad that I wondered who raised them.

True to his word, he waited till I was inside the house before leaving. I breathed a sigh of relief as I dropped my bag on the bed.

"I missed you so much," I said out loud, sniffing the air dramatically as I made my way to the bathroom. I had just put on my night clothes when I noticed the shadow of a man on my doorstep. My eyes opened in horror. Who the hell was that? How did the person know I was here? Maybe it was that driver; it had to be him.

Men!

A few seconds later, I heard the clanging of keys, and my heart started to pound. "Who's there? Go away!"

"Shut up and open the fucking door!"

"Alex?" I jumped off the bed, hurriedly making my way to the door.

"Alex?" I called out uncertainly.

"Open the goddamn door."

I pulled the latch, unlocking the door, and he came into the room, his eyes scanning the room urgently before landing on me.

"Why do you think it was a great idea to leave the house at this time of night?" His voice was calm, and it reminded me of the silence before a storm.

I didn't hear what he was saying. I was too preoccupied staring at the gorgeous man who was standing right in front of me.

"Will you fucking answer me?" he said.

"Huh? I had to leave. I felt like a burden. I needed to do something with my life."

"Then why didn't you tell me?" He folded his arms, watching me.

"I'm sorry." I didn't know when the words left my mouth. "I was just so confused."

When he didn't say anything else, I looked away from him. He was staring at me with so much raw, unapologetic intensity that I felt naked.

"Do you know you scared everyone in that house?"

"I did? That's surprising."

He narrowed his eyes at me. "Don't fucking play with me, Andriana."

I threw my hands in the air and turned in the direction of the bed, but Alex held my hand and pulled me back to him in one quick move.

We both stared at each other, our breaths rising and falling in sync. I wanted him so badly that I knew I'd do whatever he wanted.

"Kiss me," I said softly.

"Fuck, come here." He grabbed my jaw with his arms and crushed his lips on mine, kissing me with a fierce desperation that took my breath away.

Alex picked me up and carried me to the bed, where he dropped me carefully. I looked at him, my eyes half closed, as he smothered me with kisses.

"Alex..."

"Take off your gown."

My heart pounded against my chest as he watched me, his gaze dark with lust. I reached behind me and did as I was told, keeping my eyes on him the entire time. Now I had on just my underwear, and I ducked my head sideways in embarrassment when I felt his gaze rake over my body.

"Good girl."

A part of me knew this shouldn't be happening. This was Alex, caring today and hard tomorrow, but I couldn't help it. I was drawn to him more than I'd ever been to anyone. The mere sight of him watching me only in my underwear turned me on more than I could've ever imagined.

He was still fully dressed in a black woolly sweater and black pants while I lay on the bed, almost naked, watching him with pleading eyes.

"You're so beautiful, Andriana. You make me feel things I never want to..." his voice trailed off as he pinched my nipples, earning a soft moan from me.

"Oh God, Andriana." He took one long look at me before lowering his head and capturing my nipples in his mouth.

"Fuck." I placed my hand on his head, caressing his hair softly as he worked wonders on me. I'd never felt this way before. It all felt so surreal. I wanted more; I wanted him to fuck me like a common whore.

I wanted him so bad. He pulled my nipple so hard that I moaned loudly, arching my body against him.

"Good girl."

He fisted my hair with one hand and used the other to unbuckle his pants. His cock sprang out, thick and hard, the swollen head dripping with precum. My eyes widened as I took in the sight of it. Could that really go all the way into my pussy? Does it get tighter if it hasn't been actively engaged for a long time?

I wrapped my hands around him, closing my eyes when I heard his soft groan.

"Andriana..."

Before he could say anything more, I flicked my tongue over the head of his dick and sucked up the beads of precum before finally taking him in my mouth. I sucked and pulled, feeling so much more aroused as Alex caressed my hair, his groans coming out more intently.

"That's it!" he growled, then turned me around in one swift movement. Now I lay on my back while he hovered over me, his chest rising and falling.

"Take off your underwear."

I did as instructed, my gaze never leaving his as I pulled them down. His eyes got darker as I lay stark naked before him.

"Spread your legs."

"Huh?" I ducked my head shyly. *Spread what?*

He took off his sweater as swiftly as possible and leaned against me, kissing every part of my body. I turned around, my pleading and whining growing louder and louder as he kissed me.

"Spread your legs for me, baby."

Baby? Heat scalded me from head to toe, but I did as he asked, my face burning with shame.

He positioned the tip of his dick at my entrance and drove into me with one deep thrust.

"Oh God, Alex." I struggled to keep my eyes open as he thrust slowly into me. I could feel every inch of his dick in me as he went in and out.

"Please, faster," I begged.

Alex's hot breath fanned my cheeks as he reached around to pinch my nipples. "Be patient, princess." He kissed my lips softly, letting out a soft groan as he continued his movements. I was getting relaxed when he suddenly slammed into me with a vicious thrust.

"Oh lord," I moaned as he kept going. In and out. Harder and faster. My eyes were half closed as he fucked in and out of my pussy.

"Alex, oh lord. I need to..."

He kissed me one more time as he pounded into me, and my body trembled violently as my orgasm crashed over me. Alex went on, his movements becoming jerkier, and I knew he was also about to come. A second later, he came with a quiet grunt before sliding out of me.

"Wow." I blinked, looking a little confused.

Alex gave me a kiss before picking me up from the bed and carrying me to the bathroom. "Let's have a shower, baby."

He was still calling me *baby*?

After taking our shower, we had round after round of sex, and then Alex fell asleep while enveloping me in a tight embrace. I slept with a smile on my face. This was easily the best night of my life.

CHAPTER TEN

ALEX

I WOKE UP THE next morning in a better mood than I'd been in a long while. I swept my gaze over Andriana's naked body and felt my organ thicken up in my pants. No matter what my heart wanted, yesterday was just a fulfillment of our desires. That was all it could be. Nothing more.

She yawned softly before her eyes fluttered open and clashed with mine. She sat upright, ducking her head shyly.

"Hi," she said.

I smiled at her. "How was your night?" I meant that genuinely, but considering the way her whole body turned red, I knew she had something else in mind.

I caressed her nipples softly, sucking on each one. Her moan sent warning signals into my brain, but I couldn't stop; I was fucking attracted to her. The way her petite body fit perfectly with mine, the way she was clinging to me, everything was driving me crazy. And never had a woman had such enormous power over me.

"Touch me," she said softly, placing soft kisses all over my body.

"Andriana," I breathed before crushing my lips on hers. We sucked on each other's lips, biting and pulling like we hadn't just had sex a thousand times the night before.

"I want you so bad," I muttered against her neck, my fingers making their way into her pussy, which was dripping wet already. But I knew this would lead us both nowhere. I couldn't get into a relationship with her, and Andriana wasn't the type who would be used just for her body.

"Please," she moaned, her eyes closing briefly as the passion built within her. "I'm coming." She shook violently in my arms as I increased the rhythm of my fingers, thrusting into her as fast as I could.

"Alex!" She shattered in my arms, her body going rigid as she came violently.

"I'll be in the living room. Get ready," I said as soon as I knew she could hear me. And before she could say anything else, I walked out of the room.

A few minutes later, after having her bath and doing some other stuff I didn't know about, she appeared by the doorway, already dressed.

"Can we leave now?" I asked.

She shook her head. "Alex, I left for a reason."

"You can't stay here." Every minute we'd spent here since yesterday had been carefully monitored by my men, who were keeping watch. No sneaky movements had been discovered so far, but I knew it was only a matter of time before word got around that she was in here.

"Why can't I stay here? It's my house. It might not be as luxurious as yours, but it's enough for me."

"That's not what I'm talking about," I said. "You have a job at my place, and I want you back at work."

She chuckled softly. "I wasn't working at your place, Alex. You know it."

"So, what do you want?" I asked her.

"A real job."

"I'll get you a respectable job, Andriana, but first I need you back at home."

She crossed her arms across her chest. "Why?"

"You're my cook."

"But you've not been eating what I cook."

"That stopped the first day I tasted your food," I countered.

She narrowed her eyes. "Hmph."

"Can we leave now?" I tried again.

She was quiet for a while. "I'm only accepting this offer on the basis that you'll provide a better job for me, and in the meantime, you eat any food I prepare."

"Correct."

She glared at me. "Okay, give me a minute; let me grab my things."

The ride back home was very quiet. Neither of us said anything as Steven drove us down the familiar pathway leading up to the house.

We were almost home when my phone started to ring. I glanced over at Andriana, contemplating whether to pick up the call or not.

"Hello?"

"There's been an attack at a nursing home for older patients, and several folks have been killed. We'll need you to look into this as soon as possible. Get the names of those involved."

"Do you have an idea why this happened?" I asked.

There was a brief silence. "We believe they had a target in mind."

"Thank you. I'll get back to you as soon as possible."

"Thank you."

Another attack. This was the third attack in three days, all happening to various innocent people.

Andriana glanced at me as soon as I ended the call. "Why didn't Enzo come along with you last night? He should go everywhere with you since he's your personal assistant."

"I guess he should've."

Her face turned a bright shade of red, and she muttered something inaudible just as Steven pulled up to the house. I held out my hands as she made to get out of the car, but she brushed them off, throwing a glare at me before storming into the house.

"Hello, boss." Enzo nodded at me as I walked in.

"How was today's business?" I asked him. "I should schedule a meeting with them. It's been a while since I visited the company."

He nodded. "It went well."

I explained the call I received earlier to him, and we both pondered on the next step to take. Some months back I would've jumped into action, but the success of my company had really taken my mind off anything that had to do with the mafia.

"There's somewhere I need to be tonight, but before we go into that, there's something I need you to take care of," I said to Enzo.

He leaned closer to me. "Go on."

I handed him a file. "Hand this over to Skye."

"Who's Skye?"

"The address and everything you need to know about your journey have already been sent to Steven. I'll just need you to hand this over to him."

"All right, so how can I be sure that this Skye and not some random guy is the one receiving the file?"

"No one else received Skye's files. Be rest assured, this is going to be received by him."

He nodded and stood. "This place you need to be tonight, may I know where it is?"

"Just go, Enzo. Don't bother yourself with anything else. The file with you is equally important."

He nodded. "Aye, captain."

"Enzo!" I called out just as he turned to leave.

"Sir?"

"That file with you," I said, and he nodded, glancing at it. "It must not be tampered with. I'll need you to watch it carefully."

"Of course, boss." And with that, he was out the door. I stretched my legs on the sofa, prepared to have the most uncomfortable nap of the day. I found it difficult to sleep at noon; it just never worked out for me.

"Boss?" Enzo opened the door slowly, peering in.

"What's the problem, Enzo?"

"I know this might sound silly, but can I see Andriana before I leave, just for one second?"

"What the hell are you talking about?" I sat upright, watching him like he was insane. This was an important document in his hands, and he was talking about seeing Andriana for God knows what.

"Leave," I told him.

"Enzo? Do you need anything?" Andriana asked, coming out from the other side of the room.

He cocked his head against the door. "I made lunch the same way you taught me that night. Try it and tell me what you think about it when I'm back."

He didn't wait for her to reply; he just turned around and walked out the door.

"He's such a sweetheart." Andriana beamed at me, chuckling softly.

"There's something I need you to do for me." I crossed my arms, watching her as she looked at me with interest.

"Good." She rushed over to me, taking a seat by my side. "Tell me."

I sighed. This was a dangerous path I was treading, but I'd thought about it all day, and this was the best way to get a solution.

"There's a party I was invited to tonight, and I want you to come with me."

"Okay?" she said tentatively.

"It's a masked party. You'll need to be very careful, so you don't reveal your identity."

"Wow, that sounds fun."

I shifted closer to her. "No, it's not. It's a really dangerous place. We need to catch a bad guy; he was involved in the incident that took the lives of about eight elderly people."

"Why are you in charge of that? Isn't that the job of a detective? Or Secret Service?"

"Are you doing this or not?" I asked.

She looked uncertain for a while as she pondered what I said. "So what exactly do you need me for in all of this?"

"Good," I said. "I'll need you to try to get some important information out of this guy. Do you think you could do that?"

"Yes."

"So we won't go in the same car. As a matter of fact, we don't know each other."

"Do I even know you?" she said, playing along.

"Good, good. So you'll find a way to get any bit of information out of him."

"Any?"

"Any. He's certainly not going to tell you he committed murder, but we just need bits and pieces of information. We'll find out answers from these clues."

"I understand."

"I don't know if you've noticed, but you're not very observant. The dress you'll be wearing and everything else has been sent to your room. We'll leave tonight by nine."

"In my room?" She stood up, dashing out of the room.

"I certainly hope you try to be more observant once you get there," I called after her. "It's really important for the job!"

———-

"A nice party, isn't it?" someone asked, walking toward me.

"Hmm." I'd recognize that voice from anywhere. I took a sip of my drink, ignoring Blade as he stood by my side.

"Alex, Alex."

We both had our masks on, but we knew each other well enough to decipher each other's faces through the facade.

"It's been a while," Blade said. "I haven't heard from you since what happened to Ricky. God bless his soul."

I clenched my fist. Now wasn't the right time to be moved by Blade's reckless words.

"Amen," was my only reply.

He chuckled, taking a long sip from the drink he was having.

"That girl. Where is she?"

"What are you talking about?"

"Hmm. Let's not play games now, Alex. You're not a coward. I know she's with you."

"I have no idea what you're talking about, and the earlier you move past what happened several weeks back, the better it is for you."

"I told you to stop using that tone with me, boss," he said with his mocking voice, which I recognized from the countless times we'd been together.

The voice irked me beyond relief.

"I'm my own boss now, Alex," Blade continued. "And we both know I have more power and more men to fall back on than you do."

"Good for you," I said.

"You know the most annoying part of all this?" He didn't wait for me to talk. "It's the fact that you think you're too good to indulge in all of this now. And that's a lie! That's a fucking lie. We all learned from you; you brought us in and inspired us. You can't chicken out." He laughed once more, setting his empty glass on the table opposite us. "About that girl. I'll find her. And when I do, I'm sure you know what'll happen to her. For now, goodbye."

I scanned the bar after he left, looking for Andriana. She had been right in front of me, talking with her target, before Blade approached me. Where could she be?

I had to be very careful. I knew it. Anyone could be monitoring my movements. My phone beeped, and I picked it up to see it was a text from Andriana.

Thank goodness.

Her message said, "Got what I want. I'm out of here. Please inform the driver of my arrival. I think I'm being followed."

I quickly called the driver in charge, but he wasn't picking up his phone, making me wish I had used Steven instead. She was on her way out, and the goddamned driver wasn't picking up his phone.

If she used my car, if there was anyone monitoring my movements, they'd know what we were up to.

Shit.

I tried the driver's number again, and thankfully, he picked up.

"Just one job, and look at the mess you've made," I told the driver.

"I've picked her up. We're on our way out," was all he said.

"Give her the phone."

"I'm with him," she said into the phone. "We're heading home."

Great, I thought to myself.

I walked out of the building, my mission accomplished.

Andriana was in the living room when I got back, and I almost pulled her into my arms. But the look on her face was rather different.

"How was it?" I asked her. "Tell me what you know."

She shrugged. "He was drunk, so getting information out of him was the easiest thing in the world."

"It was only easy because you're a woman. He let his guard down."

"Hmm."

"Well? Tell me already." I was growing extremely impatient with each passing second.

She handed me a small piece of hardware. "Here, I had it recorded. Everything he said is here. He talked about the mafia or something. I really don't care; it's in there."

"Nice job. Why do you look so down?" I asked, watching her carefully. "Is everything okay?"

She shook her head. "Have you been feeling like someone has been spying on you? Telling your business to the bad guys?"

I shrugged. "Of course I have. I'm working on it. I've asked Enzo to—"

"It's Enzo." She looked down, her eyes glassy.

"What the hell are you talking about?" I narrowed my eyes at her. "You don't have anything else to say. You should just leave. Trying to paint him as the bad guy to prove to me that you did a nice job is just tacky and outright stupid."

She sighed. "After that man told me all about the murder incident, I asked him what he thought about you. He was so drunk at this point because I kept handing him drinks. It was then that he told me Enzo was his spy."

"What?" My heart broke into a million pieces. "That's impossible. Get me something I can use to listen to this."

She pushed her laptop over to me. "Here, use this."

I picked up the flash drive and connected it to the laptop. She kept quiet as I listened intently to the entire conversation they had together, my heart shattering even more when I heard his revelation about Enzo.

"This could be a lie for all I know. Enzo would never do this to me." I've had my fair share of betrayal in my life. So if this were true, it wouldn't be new to me, but I loved Enzo like a brother. He was the family I never had. Why would he do this to me?

"That motherfucker was lying," I said. "He's such a fool."

She shook her head. "When I got home, I did some searching. Enzo has been sending crucial information via email to him for several days now."

"What do you mean you did some searching?"

She shrugged. "I studied cybersecurity in college. I also have a friend who currently works in the Secret Service. We traced phone calls and conversations between the both of them."

"Enzo?" I couldn't believe it. Enzo was more than a personal assistant to me, and he knew it. This one hurt me so much.

"What are you going to do about it? He's been giving out private information about your company to several others too," she continued. "Over a hundred thousand dollars have been sent into an unofficial account over the last couple of days."

"He must've known about this," I said. "He won't be coming back."

"How? He had no idea that man exposed his lies."

If anyone told me Enzo would have done this to me, I would've sworn with anything I had that he wouldn't. I sat down dejectedly on the sofa, my heart racing.

Never trust anyone Al, in this gang. No one can be trusted. No one, not even your own family. My father's voice echoed through my head as the reality of what happened dawned on me.

Andriana threw me an apologetic smile. "Everything is going to be fine. You've got this."

No, everything was just about to get bad.

CHAPTER ELEVEN

ANDRIANA

"You're joking," I said to Lila. I pulled out the packs of pasta in the cabinet, checking to see which one I wanted.

Lila smiled, gazing at me fondly through the laptop screen.

"Why are you looking so intently at me?" I asked her.

"I've missed you so much, Andriana. I miss you. I miss home. And it's just so lonely over here."

I never thought about what life was like for Lila over there, and I felt bad as she watched me, her eyes glassy with tears.

"My goodness, Lila. I think you're just overwhelmed with studies right now. Do you think you could take a break? Like, come back here for a few weeks to relax?"

"I don't even know." She sniffed. "This is crazy."

"It's fine, Lila. I'm here for you. Just be yourself."

She chuckled. "How's Alex Rocco coping with the whole betrayal thing?"

I sighed. "He's hardly around. I think the workload on him now that Enzo is no longer there is just so much. So he'll need a lot of time to get things right."

She shook her head. "It must've really hurt him, you know, considering how close they were."

I nodded. "He doesn't act like anything happened, but I know deep down that he misses his friend and wishes that things turned out differently."

"Wow."

It was just work, home, and back to work for him now. He spent no time on small talk with me or anyone else around the house. Enzo was such a big fool for betraying him, and I missed the idiot so much.

"Why are you smiling?" Lila asked, chuckling softly.

"You wouldn't believe me if I told you."

"Tell me."

"Enzo."

"Life is just so unpredictable." She shook her head.

I leaned closer to the laptop, looking around carefully. "I'm not entirely comfortable here." I sighed, cleaning my hands with a napkin. "There's strange activity going on. I can't really tell what it is yet, but I'm very certain of it."

"Like? Criminal activity? Is he a thief? A drug dealer?" She frowned.

"No, no." I chuckled and picked up a bottle of white wine, one of the most important ingredients for the meal I was making. "None of that. More like a detective, but not approved by the government. Remember that night he told me to get some information out of that man?"

"And you did it! Walked straight into the danger zone. I didn't know you had it in you. Hmm."

"Shut up."

She chuckled, adjusting her bag on her shoulder. It was a parting gift I gave to her. "I have to go now, Andie. I'll call you later tonight or whenever."

"Stay safe, baby."

Now back to making lunch. Thankfully, Alex had been eating all the food I prepared. It made everything a lot easier. The door screeched open, and he appeared by the doorway, his eyes scanning the room briefly.

"Hi." I waved at him as he walked in. He nodded in my direction, his face unsmiling. As usual. We never talked about the night we had sex. It just never came up in any of our conversations, only on some nights when he stared at me with so much raw, undiluted hunger that I knew it flashed through his mind as well. Like right now.

"Lunch is almost ready," I said, pointing awkwardly at the pot on fire.

"Hmm."

Last night, I wrote down a list of fun places I intended to go to, and staring at this strikingly gorgeous man in front of me, I realized there was no one else I wanted to go with but him. That was a tough one, but it wouldn't hurt to try.

"Erm." I cleared my throat, shifting uncomfortably when his gaze landed on me.

"Is there a problem?" he asked.

"I wrote down a list of fun activities I want to try. Um, I was hoping you'd—you know—accompany me?"

"No," came his quick, short reply. I sighed. That hurt a great deal.

"Okay."

After a while, he glanced at me, his expression stoic. "When do you want to go? I'm a very busy man. I have a very tight schedule."

"Tomorrow. Saturdays are the perfect time for activities like this."

"I don't know how safe it is, but I'll think about it." He had a worry line on his face as he looked away from me.

"Safe?" I chuckled. Obviously, he had never been to any fun place his entire life. "It's the safest place we could ever be."

"Hmm. Let's see how it goes," he said.

I didn't like that statement. It sounded uncertain. I'd prefer for him to tell me he had no interest in going with me, instead of raising my hopes and then disappointing me tomorrow morning.

"We'll leave by 10 a.m. tomorrow," I said.

This time around, he didn't respond to me, and that was all I needed to know that the conversation was over.

"Uh, just let me know when you're ready to eat lunch," I told him.

He nodded briefly, and I turned around and made my way to my room. This was one of the times I really missed Enzo. I imagined the way he would've made a face at Alex if he was in there, and I groaned. "Such a fool."

I took a final glance at myself in the mirror, adjusting a loosened strand of hair as I prepared to leave. I'm my own woman, and I didn't need a man to make me feel like my life was complete. I'd go out there and have the best time of my entire life. Fuck Alex and his sour mood. With one final glance around the room, I turned around and walked out.

Alex was seated in the living room all dressed when I went out; he had on a blue woolen sweater with black pants. He looked extremely handsome just sitting there. Existing.

"Busy as usual," I muttered, throwing him a glare as I headed toward the door. He always had somewhere to go.

"You said 10 a.m."

"Uh?" I glanced at my wristwatch. It was several minutes past eleven.

He repeated, "You said we were leaving by 10 a.m."

What? I stopped myself from beaming with excitement. Was he coming along with me?

"I didn't know you were coming along with me. You didn't sound so certain yesterday afternoon."

He shook his head. "You need to learn to keep to your word. It's very difficult, but you should learn."

I chuckled. "Noted. So are you coming or something?" I couldn't hold back the smile any longer. His face twitched, like he was trying not to laugh, but instead, he grabbed his car key from the table and pointed to the door.

"Are you driving?" I asked as we headed toward the garage. A fleet of cars was parked in it. This particular part of the house was where I got my daily motivations from. Imagine being so rich that you had to walk through a fleet of cars before deciding on which one to go with. I followed him awkwardly, wondering which car we'd go with today.

"Get in." He stopped in front of a magnificent-looking car and pulled the door open.

"Thank you." It looked like an entirely different place in here. I sniffed in the rich scent of the car, leaning back against the seat. If we just drove around town in this, I'd have a fun day too.

"So where are we headed?" Alex asked, climbing into the front seat. Oh great. It was just the two of us.

"Let me check the address real quick," I said as he started the car's ignition.

"Okay, I have three places in mind: a zoo, a museum, and a cinema. But I want us to go to the zoo first."

"Hmm."

"Have you ever been to a zoo?" I asked.

"No."

"Okay, great."

We arrived in no time, and soon we were walking through the entrance of the building. "Stay by my side," Alex muttered, glancing at me.

"Please, don't make me laugh. It's totally safe here."

He glanced at me, and his expression was unreadable. "Just stay by my side, Andriana. We need to be together." He paused, looking around. "You know, I'm not really familiar with this place."

"Neither am I. Free yourself, and let's have fun!"

The tour guide was saying something while we were talking, so we missed a good chunk of what he said. I glared at Alex. "Just try to have fun. That's why you're here."

He scoffed, adjusting his cap. "Let's hope so."

"The first animal we'll be showing you is the crocodile, so follow me over here." The tour guide signaled for us to follow him.

"Haven't you seen a crocodile before?" Alex asked me as I beamed with excitement.

"No, have you?"

"Several times."

"Show off," I said.

He glanced at me with a funny expression on his face.

"This is the crocodile pond." With a big smile on his face, the tour guide pointed at a small pond.

"But there are no crocodiles in here," someone said, looking around the pond.

He nodded. "The crocodiles are probably inside the water. They are good at hiding beneath the surface of the pond."

"So does that mean we can't see any crocodiles? I can't take pictures?" someone else asked with a frown.

I peered into the pond, my earlier excitement clearing up. "That's just plain stupid," I hissed as everyone started murmuring. Alex chose that moment to smile at me.

"Just stop smiling," I told him.

He turned to the tour guide. "There should be a way to get these crocodiles to come to the surface of the water."

"There are still a lot of other animals that we haven't seen," the tour guide said.

"If there's a way, we want to see the crocodiles! That's why we're here."

The tour guide smiled briefly. "It's really not that—"

"Just throw something they can eat on the surface of the water, and watch them all scurry outside," Alex said as he looked inside the pond. "They're probably hungry. Is this a private zoo?"

The guide nodded, looking away uncomfortably. "We feed them once a day for now because of limited funds. We hope to increase their feeding as time goes on, you know, when we have a lot more funds."

"Wow," someone said.

"This is just crazy," I said in agreement.

"Let's get the hell out of here," I heard another person say.

"Feed them. Let the people see the crocodiles. And let me know what that'll cost. I'll pay for it," Alex said to the guide, unsmiling.

"Are you sure about this?" the guide asked.

He nodded, and the men yelled out orders to a group of boys by the corner. Sooner than expected, they flung their meals into the pond, and a bunch of crocodiles scurried up to the surface of the water, earning a bunch of excited screams from the crowd. I captured a few pictures, smiling with joy as I looked on. At least I had one picture to share with Lila.

"You know you can partner with us." The tour guide was saying this to Alex as we all took pictures. "I know you; you're Alex Rocco."

I smiled. I really loved business-minded people.

After a while, the tour guide left us to explore the zoo ourselves.

"Look over there! I'm thirsty. Let's get something to eat or drink," Alex said to me, heading toward a mini marketplace. We got a coconut drink, which was just a coconut with a straw in it. It looked so fancy that I almost forgot I had to drink from it.

"Do you want me to take a picture of you?" Alex said to me.

Did I just hear that right? I thought to myself.

"Huh?" I said.

He shrugged. "I could take a picture of you having a sip from the drink. You know, as a keepsake."

"Why, I'd love that! Thank you."

I made a few poses with the coconut and beamed with a smile as I went through the pictures. They were perfect!

"Now it's your turn."

He laughed. "In your dreams."

I raised my phone to capture his face, but he reached for my phone. Thankfully, I swerved my arms fast enough.

"Just smile," I said.

He didn't, so I took a picture of him with a scowl on his face.

We were just moving down a hill when a group of monkeys charged at us, pointing at the coconut in my hand. I jumped in fear, flinging the coconut in my hands away. The monkeys rushed over to it, grabbing it and taking sips out of it.

"My coconut!" I turned around to see Alex fighting off a bunch of monkeys.

"Just give them the fucking coconut." I laughed when he held on tightly to the fruit.

"They're just fucking bullies!" He laughed as he waved them off, turning around in their midst. After a while, when it was obvious they weren't going to have their way, they left him alone, going in search of their next victim.

"He took mine away." I made a sad face, pointing at one of the monkeys.

"Do you want another one?" Alex asked me.

"What? No." I chuckled. "I'm just kidding."

After a few more minutes, we'd gone through every part of the zoo. Alex finally agreed to take pictures with a few of the larger animals. He seemed more alive by the time we were heading out of the zoo. And unlike his usual frown, he had a peculiar smile on his face.

"Now let's go to the next place, the cinema!" I said.

"Let's find somewhere to eat first. Aren't you hungry?"

I shrugged. "A bit. Let's try out this new Nigerian restaurant in town."

He glanced at me. "Are you kidding?" He let out a short laugh.

I shook my head. "I've been wanting to go there for a while now."

"How do you know you're going to like it?" he asked.

"It doesn't hurt to try."

He threw me an amused glance. "Okay."

The restaurant owner came out to welcome us herself, and it was the sweetest thing. She talked about the various foods they had and what she thought we'd like. Alex glanced at me after she was done, and I laughed.

"Can we have your best dish?" he asked her, looking really excited about all that was happening.

She chuckled. "They're all our best dishes," she said in a really thick Nigerian accent.

"Can we have the most requested dish?"

She nodded. "This you can have. That would be jollof rice and turkey."

I glanced at Alex. "I've heard of that before."

He nodded. "It's a pretty popular dish. We'll have that."

I squealed excitedly, earning a smile from Alex.

"Please don't tell me you've had a Nigerian meal before?"

He shook his head. "Actually, no."

"Great!"

The waiters appeared a few minutes later with a large tray of food, and I felt my stomach churn as I got a whiff. I glanced at Alex after they had left, and he laughed, staring down at the food in front of him.

"Shall we?" I asked.

He had already started eating before I finished asking. I waited for him to have a spoonful before asking how it tasted. But I didn't need an answer from him because the moment he took the first spoonful, he reached out for the second one immediately.

"Does it really taste that good?" I asked.

By the time we were leaving the restaurant, we had ordered two more times and even requested an extra plate for us to go home with. Alex was in a much more relaxed mood as we headed to the cinema, humming along to the sound from the radio. But a single phone conversation a few minutes later turned everything around.

"Andriana?"

"Huh?"

"Steven is on his way. He'll take you home from here. There's some important business I have to do."

CHAPTER TWELVE

ALEX

I DASHED INTO THE pale white building I had gotten used to from all my years of working actively in the mafia. It was the spot where we usually reported every single activity of the day to the boss, the commander-in-chief. It had been a while since I'd been here. And I didn't regret that decision one bit.

Now, staring into the eyes of the many men watching me, I knew they thought me an infidel. Why else would I want to leave the mafia if not for a successful career and a promising future?

"Alex!"

I turned sharply toward the one in charge now, Ferd Marcel. Technically, I was the next leader in line, but since I didn't want anything to do with the mafia anymore, someone else had to be in charge.

"You know more than anyone else here that you're bonded to this group and everything that it entails. There's no going back in this group; it's do or die," Ferd said with a glare in my direction. "You can't decide to be with us or against us. None of us are given that choice."

I turned to him. "At no point did I ever mention leaving the mafia. I only took a step back. I needed to focus on myself and my well-being, and that's what I'm doing."

"Do you really think we are fools here? You know, Alex, you were raised by the don, who trained you like his own son and even gave you command before he passed away, rather than me, the next in line. Yet here you are, believing you have a say in all of this." He laughed.

The rest of the gang murmured among themselves. "I'm giving you one day to get yourself together and get back to business. This is just a warning, but after that, you know what we're capable of doing."

"No one gets to boss me around, Ferd. I make my own rules. I'm the boss before anyone else."

He laughed long and hard, his face turning into a scowl. "That was before you gave up your position, man. Now you're just like the rest of the gang members without any rank. Now you're going to hustle for a spot at the top."

"Hmm."

"You know the rules, champ," Blade started, walking forward. "I'm the second-in-command now, just in case you've not heard."

"No love interests." His eyes glinted mischievously. "The gang provides a spouse for everyone when it's time. We do this to ensure the continuity of our group," he said with a laugh. "You already know this, so who am I to lecture you?"

I clenched my hands in a fist when he pulled Enzo out of the crowd.

"Every single bit of information regarding your company is here with us; one reckless move and it's down the drain. Thanks to our man here."

Enzo looked down.

"Be fucking proud of yourself, man!" Blade snapped, raising his jaw. "You did that shit!"

"That's good to know, guys. I'll take my leave now." I turned around, ready to leave.

"We have a job we want you involved in this weekend," Ferd stated suddenly.

"What kind of job?" Before Marcel died, he made sure the gang was running smoothly. He never indulged in activities that cost the lives of the innocent. He was a bad guy just like the rest of us, but one thing I liked about him was the fact that he made sure he didn't get involved with the innocent.

Now that he was gone and Ferd had taken over, they didn't care who got killed in their reckless acts. And apart from the fact that this was a dangerous and wicked game to play, I had a reputation I needed to maintain, and I couldn't afford to continue such a thing any longer.

"The usual job," Ferd said.

"What kind of job, Ferd?"

"Stop talking back to the don!" Blade fired, his breathing hard. I threw one last glance at them all before turning around and walking out.

——

Steven was at the entrance of the house when I arrived. He hurried over to me the moment he saw me, and I knew something was wrong.

"What's the problem, Steven?"

He glanced at the house. "She's asking questions. I'm afraid she's going to leave."

I ignored him, making my way into the house. If she wanted to leave, then so be it. I'd tried my best to keep her safe. But if she persisted and demanded to leave, then that was her fault. She was seated in the living room when I walked in.

"What was all that about?" she asked the moment she saw me.

"What are you talking about?"

"Don't fucking play smart with me."

"What are you talking about?" I asked again.

She frowned. "There's something wrong. I can feel it. I know it, and you know it too."

I stared at her long and hard. There was no point in hiding my real identity any longer since she was so curious to know what was going on. She should be able to live with the consequences of her actions.

"I'm in the mafia. Apart from being the CEO of Rocco's Construction, I also belong to the leading mafia group in the country."

She laughed. "Don't be such a fool. I'm being serious right now, and I need an answer from you."

When I didn't say anything more, she took several steps back. "Are you fucking serious?"

I stared at her, not saying anything more. It was up to her to decide what she wanted to do with what she knew now.

"You're part of the people killing several innocent civilians in the streets? What?" she yelled.

That was what Ferd and the rest of the gang members had turned it into for the last couple of months.

"I don't indulge in the killing of the innocent."

Her hands flew to her mouth. "You're a monster! I'm leaving!" She raced in the direction of the room, and I followed her.

"You can't leave Andriana; your life is in danger."

"Don't fucking come near me! I'm not in any danger, you fucking piece of shit! Liar!"

"You're going to get killed once you leave this house, Andriana. Your life is in danger."

"What?" She stared at me in horror. "What are you talking about?"

"The other night at the restaurant, the first day we met. That guy that kept harassing you is one of the most dangerous mafia members out there, and he has made it his mission to kill you as some sort of revenge. It's best you remain here, where you're safe."

She sniffed. "What?"

"Andriana I—"

"You're a monster! An animal. All these innocent people are dying, and you've been the mastermind behind it."

I shook my head, my heart breaking into a million pieces as she yelled those words at me.

"Jose's restaurant wasn't just some kitchen hazard, right? It was your mafia guys? Right?"

"Andriana, you need to listen to me."

"Answer my question, monster! Was it those guys that burned down that place?"

I nodded, and she burst into tears, running into her room and slamming the door. There was no point trying to talk things through with her, as she wasn't even giving me a chance to speak. If the only option included keeping her here forcefully, then I had no choice but to do that, because the moment she stepped foot outside of this building, that would be the end.

"Steven!" I dashed toward the entrance of the house. He hurried over to me, the same worried expression on his face.

"Tell all the security guards that I said Andriana is not allowed to leave this building for any reason today."

"Yes, sir!" He turned to leave.

"Or any other day," I added.

He glanced at me. "She's not allowed to leave this house for any reason?"

"You heard me correctly."

He sighed before running toward the security guards. He had stayed long enough with me to know that I had told her my true identity.

Andriana didn't leave her room for the rest of the day, and I didn't bother disturbing her. It was up to her to decide if she wanted to hear me out or not. I knew being in the mafia wasn't a respectable job or something to be proud of, but that was where I belonged, and there was nothing I could do at this point to fix it.

It wasn't until the middle of the next day that she finally came out of her room. She looked so lost as she stood in front of me that I almost reached out to her. But I was equally as pissed with her as she was with me.

"Why are you involved in the mafia? And why do they want to kill me?"

All the anger I felt from earlier evaporated into thin air as she uttered those words.

"Come." I patted the seat close to me, and I sighed when she took the seat opposite me instead.

"I can hear you clearly from here," she muttered, curling up into a comfortable position. I moved toward her, sitting on the little bit of space available.

"I grew up in a mafia family. I had no idea who my real parents were. The mafia boss raised me since I was a little kid, and that was all I grew up to know. After he died, I had no interest whatsoever in anything that had to do with the gang, but the rest of the group wasn't having it."

She glanced at me, her eyes glassy with tears.

"They insisted I take over from my father and continue the legacy he had built. I wouldn't have had so much of a problem with it, but the bad guys had now infiltrated the group and turned it into a bad group, killing both the innocent and guilty," I continued. "Now bringing you into this—the night at the restaurant, Blade saw me protecting you as a challenge, and he has since sworn to harm you when he sees you. That's why I employed you to work with me; it's to keep you safe from harm."

"So do I keep hiding forever? How do I get out of all this?"

"You just have to lay low in the meantime and stay here with me. Don't be stubborn and leave here without my knowledge."

"This is just crazy," she said. "God, what have I gotten myself into?"

"I'm so sorry," I told her.

She glanced at me. "It's not totally your fault. From what you just described, you're also trying to get yourself out of there."

We both fell silent. It had been a lot different with my father around. I was able to skip activities I didn't want to do, but now that he was no longer there, that couldn't happen anymore. I had to do what was expected of me.

"What do you want to do?" She turned to me, watching me intently.

"I'm still thinking about it. It's something I need to plan well."

She nodded. "I'm sorry for reacting that way. You've been nothing but kind to me."

"It's okay. I deserved it."

She smiled at me. "Don't beat yourself up too much about this. We'll figure it out together. As long as you don't want a part in this game any longer, we'll find a way."

I smiled at her. It wasn't as easy as she thought, but I wasn't going to say that to her. Planning to leave the mafia was like a death sentence.

"Now, what would you like to eat? Have you had anything to eat?"

"I'm not sure I want to eat anything right now," I said.

"Not while I'm around, boss," she said as she chuckled and headed into the kitchen.

I narrowed my eyes on her.

"Are you sure you're not that hungry?" she persisted.

I just continued looking at her as she walked away.

"What?" She chuckled. "That's just crazy."

A day had passed, and Ferd's voice kept echoing through my mind. They could do anything they wanted now. But since Enzo had already exposed most of my secrets to them, it was time I started making sure of my own safety.

"Get your things ready, Andriana. We'll have to leave this house."

"Huh?" The spoon she was holding fell to the ground as she dashed over to me.

"When? Why? Is it because of what Enzo already knows?"

"Yes, it's not safe in here anymore. Get your things together. We have another place we can go."

She looked around fondly. "What about the other staff? And all the cars? How do you transfer them all to the new place?"

"We'll probably leave the cars behind. First, we have to get out of here. I'll inform the others about this."

She nodded. "We leave today?"

"Yes, right now."

She looked at me. "Don't you have anything to pack? Clothes? I don't know anything."

"No, my things are over there too."

"Oh." She nodded softly. "I packed all my stuff yesterday too."

I narrowed my eyes at her. "Did you try to leave during the night?"

"What? No." She let out a short laugh. "Who would let me out of the house?"

It was clear that she attempted to leave, but the security guards stopped her.

"Get your things and let's go, Andriana."

She dashed inside the room and appeared a few seconds later with her bag. "I'm all set."

"Great." I picked up my car keys.

"Do you think it's a great idea to go with these guys? What if they betray you again?"

I'd been thinking about it for a while now. Either of these men could be used to get at me. It was best if I went through this alone.

"We'll go alone."

"We're not being selfish. We're actually saving ourselves," she muttered, following me out the door.

Steven hurried to us when he saw us heading out. "What car are we taking, sir?"

"Don't worry about this, Steven. I'll be driving. I need to get Andriana somewhere safe."

He nodded. "And what about you? Are you coming back here?"

"Of course. Where else would I go?"

"Okay, great. Bye, miss." He waved at Andriana, who was already settled inside the car.

"Where are we headed?" she asked as we pulled out of the driveway.

"Wait and see."

She let out another short laugh. "I can't believe I'm caught in the middle of this."

My phone started to ring, and I glanced at the screen, wondering who was calling. It was Ferd, as expected. I ignored the call.

"Is that from the mafia group?" she asked quietly, looking around the street worriedly.

"Yes. It's okay. You're safe with me."

She nodded. "I'm just a bit tense right now," she said while glancing at me. "I'm about to use my earphones. I listen to music when I'm troubled."

"Go ahead."

She put the earphones in and turned her face to the window. Almost immediately, I heard a beep from my phone. I picked it up to see a text from Ferd.

The message read, "Who in God's name do you have with you? Blade is going nuts, planning how to get the girl you have with you. Come back to the gang, and let's get all of this over with. You know the danger that lurks if you fail to listen to us."

CHAPTER THIRTEEN

ANDRIANA

A LEX AND I DIDN'T talk again after I put my earphones in several hours ago. The ride to the house had been quiet and charged. I knew there was something on his mind with the way he kept his attention on the road all through the journey, but decided not to say anything concerning it. Right now, I had just woken up from a long nap and felt the need to walk around the new place.

It was totally different from the penthouse, as this was just a little bungalow with a few workers lurking around, but I liked it a bit more than the penthouse. It felt a lot more homey in here, unlike the dark, brooding air surrounding the penthouse.

"Good day, ma'am."

I turned around to see one of the workers standing behind me. "Oh, hi."

"I'm Sandy. I just wanted you to know me. I'm the housekeeper."

"Great. Nice to meet you, Sandy." I smiled at her even though I wished it would just be me and Alex in here. I had no trust in any other person, considering that even the last person Alex thought would betray him was the one who did.

"Have you seen the boss?" I asked.

She nodded. "He went out shortly after you both arrived."

"And he's not back yet?"

She looked around uncertainly. "I don't think so. I would have noticed."

"Alright, thanks."

I made my way into the living room and was looking around the mildly decorated apartment when I heard Alex's voice. Life was just so unpredictable, who would've thought I would be several miles away from my apartment with a man I barely even knew, running for my life?

He paused slightly when he entered the living room and saw me, but didn't say anything.

"Hi," I said.

He nodded at me, his gaze fixed on his phone. It was obvious he was in no mood to talk, so I continued what I was doing before he came in, looking at the art pieces hung up in different corners around the room.

Alex's phone made a slight beep, and he jumped to his feet some seconds later.

"I'll be right back," he said gruffly, walking past me. I held his hand.

"Take it easy on yourself, Alex. You're not a robot."

"Hm." He pressed my hands softly, and without muttering a single word, he turned around and walked out the door. I picked up my phone to call Lila after he left, but I could not move an inch when Alex appeared by the doorway.

"Enzo was involved in an accident."

"My goodness!" My hands flew to my mouth, and fear enveloped me. "Where? How?"

"I have no idea right now. None of the gang members are there with him. He's all alone. I'm only going there to sort things out with the doctor for him and probably assign him a caregiver."

"Oh my God."

He looked so unbothered, but I knew he felt the same way I did. Enzo was nice to us all. Well, until he wasn't.

"Can I come with you?"

"What? No way. Just forget about it."

"But you said I'm safe when I'm with you." I pouted my lips, hoping my charms would work for him, but instead, his eyebrows creased and he frowned.

"Just forget about it," he said.

"Oh, I'll dress like a man. I've practiced it a couple of times, and no one suspected a thing."

"Don't push it, Andriana. That's dangerous territory. We can think no one is there, only to get there and find out that there are spies all around the place."

"Give me five minutes. I'll be right back."

He started to shake his head disapprovingly as I turned in the direction of my room.

"Please. Just five minutes. If I'm not back by then, you can leave."

I knew he would leave with the way he arched his back against the wall. It didn't seem like a comfortable position, so I knew I stood no chance.

Once inside my room, I changed into my "bro shirt," as Lila would always call it: an extra-large top. Then I straightened my hair into a tight little bun before putting on my cap. I made sure my face was also bare and dry before walking out of the room. But something still felt odd about my camouflage. I looked at myself once again before realization hit me.

"Oh yeah! No bra." I dashed into the room and yanked it off my chest while putting on a tight singlet instead. "Perfect," I muttered on my way out.

Alex's face was now plastered into a permanent frown, and as he saw me, his frown deepened.

"Are you out of your mind, Andriana?"

"What? No one would know. I've tried this several times. What do you think?" I turned around slowly. "Please let me go with you. I really want to see him too."

"Let's go, but behave yourself, and do as I say without asking unnecessary questions."

"Noted."

The drive to the clinic was very fast, and soon we were heading inside the hospital.

"I'll go and meet the doctor now." He pointed toward a door but stopped hesitantly.

"Wait." He walked toward the door and peeped in before turning to me. "You can go in. I need to settle some things with the doctor."

"What if Enzo informs the bad guys about my presence here?" I asked him as he turned to leave.

"If he wanted to, he would've told them long before now. Don't worry," he said as he smiled at me. I could swear that was the first time he smiled today. "You're safe in here. I have people keeping watch. Just lock the door and enjoy your time here." He patted my shoulders softly and turned toward the doctor's office.

I remained hesitant to enter the room after Alex left. If it wasn't something very serious, Alex wouldn't have told me. Was he badly injured? Like, beyond recognition? I knew Alex would be out at any moment, so I opened the door slowly and peered in. Our eyes clashed almost immediately.

"Oh, Enzo." I dashed into the room as my eyes scanned his entire body. He didn't have any physical injuries, so I hoped it wasn't something extremely bad. He just stared at me, his face blank. No facial expression, nothing.

"Are you okay?" I watched him, my heart breaking into a million pieces. What was the problem?

"Andriana!" Alex's voice echoed in the hospital room, and I jumped back in fear. "I told you to lock the fucking door!"

I turned back, surprised to find the door wide open. I thought I locked it. "I thought—I thought I locked it." My voice shook.

He placed his hands on his head. "I shouldn't have listened to you. I shouldn't have brought you here. You just won't get it. Any mistake, and you're gone, Andriana! These people don't fucking care."

My heart was racing frantically now, and I knew I was only a few seconds away from bursting into tears. This was all too much for me to handle.

"I'm sorry. I totally forgot." I turned to Enzo once again before glancing at Alex. "What's wrong with him? He seems okay, but I don't know. Can he hear me?"

"He can definitely hear you. We just don't know if he can speak yet, or if he's not willing to speak due to the whole situation."

"What's going on?" I asked.

"He's paralyzed."

My hands flew to my mouth, and I tried to keep my emotions to myself because Enzo kept staring at me like he was listening to our conversation and watching us. I didn't know what to do.

"Oh no." I tried wiping off the tears that were falling from my eyes. "No, no."

Alex sighed. "We have to go now, Andriana."

"And leave him like this? He'll be so lonely."

"I've paid someone who will care for him, and the doctors and nurses are still here doing their jobs. He'll get better. Hopefully. But we have to leave now."

I turned to him, ready to pour out my mind to him, but a glance in Enzo's direction was enough to make me shut up.

"Let's go," he continued.

I walked to Enzo. "You'll be fine, don't worry. Keep your head up. It might take a while, but you'll get through this, Enzo." I kissed his forehead gently. "I'll bring you food very soon."

I stood up slowly before whispering in his ear. "Once I'm able to convince your grumpy boss, I'll bring you something really special."

His facial expression didn't change, but I hoped he could hear me. It was better if he could hear people. Being paralyzed and unable to hear or speak must feel like prison. I wouldn't wish that even on my enemy.

"Let's go now." Alex was already heading out of the door when I caught up with him.

"You didn't even tell him anything."

He ignored me, his attention was focused on the hospital door ahead of us. "I'll need you to go over to the car alone. I'll be right behind you."

I nodded, moving away from him swiftly, my mind racing. For how long was I going to keep doing this? I almost raced to the parking lot, eager to get into the car and out of the way of danger.

When I finally got into the car, I breathed a sigh of relief. I hadn't told Lila about all of this because I knew how worried she would be, but it felt like I was going through all of this alone. Alex wasn't acting like someone I could talk to, and Enzo...

I looked out of the window as Alex entered the car and started the engine.

You're all alone in this world, Andriana, I told myself. *All alone.*

———

By the time we got home, it was way past midnight. I couldn't call Lila, and I wasn't in a really great mood. The whole day had greatly affected my mood, and I wanted nothing more than to curl up in bed and just cry my eyes out.

"Do you want me to cook dinner for you?" I asked, coming out to the living room after having my bath. It was dark, and I couldn't see him clearly, so I turned on the light. Surprisingly, he wasn't there. Alex was almost always in the living room. I think he hated staying inside a bedroom. I decided to knock on his room door since he wasn't in the living room.

After knocking twice and getting no response, I started heading back to my room, but then his door opened and he appeared by the door, shirtless.

"How long have you been here? I was bathing."

I swallowed as my eyes raked his body. "Oh, not so long."

"Do you want anything?"

I looked down. I wanted comfort. I needed to be treated like a baby. This was one of the times I wished I had a partner.

"No," I said, shaking my head. "I was going to ask if you wanted me to make dinner for you."

He frowned. "Tonight? No way. Why would you want to make me dinner at this time of the night?"

"Oh, okay. Goodnight then."

"Are you okay?"

I nodded. "I'm fine."

"You're not. Come." He held out his hand.

"No, really, Alex."

He shook his head and pulled me into the room. It was the first time I was in his room, and I looked around in awe. It was dark. Extremely dark. The only thing I could see was the reflection coming from the sky through the window.

"Why is it so dark in here?"

He didn't say anything. He just led me toward the bed. I glanced uncertainly at him, but this was what I had dreamed of all day. Cuddling next to someone. But Alex was nowhere close to a partner or family.

I climbed into bed, shifting a few inches from him. "Come here, Andriana."

I moved over to him, and he pulled me into his arms.

"What's on your mind?" he asked.

It looked like he knew just the way I was feeling. I snuggled close to him until there was no space left.

"This is just what I need. I'll be fine."

He nodded. "I understand."

"You do?"

He was silent for a while, and I thought he wasn't going to say anything. "I grew up without my parents or siblings. I totally understand how you feel."

I tried moving away from him, but his grip was so firm on me that it was impossible. "You know I don't have any family, right? How did you find out?"

"The same way you find out things about other people," he responded.

"Why were you checking up on my private life without my consent?"

He laughed softly. It sounded so strange but beautiful. I wished he would laugh more often.

"Do you feel bad about it?" he asked.

"No."

"I see," he said.

"What else did you see?" I continued.

Silence.

"Alex?"

"Nothing much. That was it."

I had a feeling he was lying, but I decided not to say anything else about it.

"Do you think Enzo is going to get better soon? I'm worried about him."

"Hopefully."

"He really broke my heart today. He's such a fool."

We were both quiet after that, until he started to caress my neck softly. "You're safe with me. You just need to trust me."

I tried to calm my racing heart, but it wasn't working.

"Do you trust me?" he asked.

"I—I do."

He kissed my neck softly. "I'll never let any harm come your way as long as I'm alive."

I didn't know why he was making all these statements, but it was making me feel things.

"But you act like you don't care about me."

"If I didn't care about you, you would be dead by now."

I slapped his arms away, and he rolled me over so that I was on top of him, facing him. "Have you read anything about the mafia before?"

I shook my head. I'd never thought about it until now.

"You should," he said. "It'll help you understand a lot of things about me."

I nodded and felt my heart flutter when he kissed me all over my face. I kissed his lips in return, moaning softly as he caressed my breast. He pulled up my gown in one swift movement, and I lay there, stark naked, watching him, filled with pleasure as his lips found my nipples. Thankfully, the room was dark. I arched my body toward him, begging to be touched. He touched me with so much love and so much expertise.

He suddenly stopped and reached for a remote. "What's that for?" I asked breathlessly, missing the feel of his hands on my skin.

"It's to turn on the light."

Before I could protest, the lights in the room came on, shining brightly in the dark.

"Alex!" I tried to get the duvet so I could cover my body, but he held my hand.

"Stop."

He was looking at me with so much admiration that I had to look away from him.

"You look so beautiful."

He kissed me from my cheeks all the way to my stomach and was going lower and lower when he suddenly looked up at me. By this time, I was greatly aroused. I wanted nothing more than to have him inside of me.

"Spread your legs for me, mama."

I couldn't. I sucked in a deep breath as he chuckled softly and leaned his body against mine. "Do it."

He was watching me like I was the best thing in the world. I just couldn't imagine showing him all of me while he just watched. There was no hiding here because the light was shining brightly.

"C'mon now, baby." He pulled my nipple softly, and I moaned. "Open up for me."

He pulled on the other as I was still thinking about what he was saying. I spread my legs slowly when he started to kiss my lower belly.

"Oh, Alex."

"Now touch yourself."

"What?"

"Do it." He sucked my nipples, pulling them softly as he worshiped my body.

Despite my blush, I didn't take my eyes off him as I caressed my body, squeezing and pinching my nipples before one hand slid between my legs. Soon, I was whimpering in pleasure, my mouth falling open and my breath turning shallow as I fingered myself.

Alex stood there, devouring my body with his eyes. His gaze was fierce, arousing, and destructive. I couldn't take it any longer, and I could feel myself on the brink of bliss.

"Stop," he said.

"What? No, I can't." My eyes closed slightly as my body tensed in anticipation, and suddenly Alex pulled my hands out.

"Oh, Alex." I laughed softly.

He lowered his head and gently scraped his teeth over my clit before sucking on it. Between that and the finger fucking, I was dripping down my thighs.

"Fuck me," I muttered softly.

He chuckled. "You have such a dirty mouth for your quiet personality."

I ducked my head shyly. "I know."

He positioned his dick into my entrance and slammed into me in one deep thrust.

"Andriana, you're so sweet," he muttered, fucking me with reckless disregard. My moans became screams. I didn't care who heard me, and nothing else mattered more than what my body was currently feeling.

"Alex, oh God, I need—"

He smiled, slamming his dick into me. He pinched my nipples and fucked into me with a thrust so hard that I exploded. My mouth opened and closed in a soundless scream. He came right after with a loud grunt, pulling me into his arms in a tight embrace. This right here was all I wanted. Just me and Alex. I felt my heart swell with an emotion I couldn't really express as I watched him. Nothing made sense when it came to both of us. But then again, nothing had made sense in my life since Alex Rocco came into it.

CHAPTER
FOURTEEN

ALEX

"GOOD MORNING, ALEX!" ANDRIANA breezed into the living room with a large smile on her face.

"Morning," I said without looking up from my phone. "You woke up late. I would like pancakes for breakfast."

"Uh, okay." She walked out of the room without another word.

I was acting stupid, and I knew it, but I didn't want my feelings to get in the way of my personal life. Having a relationship with Andriana only meant danger to her. It couldn't go on for long without something going terribly wrong.

The more I drew away from her, the closer we got.

"Breakfast is ready," she said softly, peering into the room a few minutes later. "It's on the dining table already."

"Great. You can leave."

Her smile faded. "Did I do anything wrong?"

"Leave, Andriana. I have a very busy day today, and I don't want any form of distraction."

"What?" She made to say something else, but instead, she threw one last glance at me before dashing out of the room.

"Target One spotted at the casino, boss. Should we go ahead with the operation?" I heard through the phone.

"Go on with it," I responded.

I dropped my phone on the table and made my way to the dining table. Since I couldn't leave the mafia, I might as well run it the way I pleased. The bad guys had been running the gang for about a year now, and things had gone terribly wrong. It was high time I took my place back.

After my meal, I called Ferd, letting him know my intentions. I knew he wasn't happy with the idea, as it meant he had to step down from his most cherished position.

"I thought you had no interest whatsoever in returning to the gang."

"I changed my mind."

"You don't get to change your mind whenever you like, Alex. You know this. I'll think about what you just said."

"I'm not telling you this so you can make a decision, Ferdinand. The next time, I'll be coming to the gang meeting, and I expect you to welcome me the way a boss is welcomed."

I ended the call and prepared myself for the day. I had a meeting with the workers at the construction site, and I also had a few more people I had to see about my return to the gang. Andriana was busy on her laptop as I made my way out. Neither of us said anything to each other on my way out. As much as I wanted more between the both of us, it was best we didn't get attached to each other.

———

"Alex Rocco!" Ricardo beamed happily as he ushered me into his office. "It's been awhile."

Ricardo was a very close friend of my father, and I hadn't seen him for a long time. He opened his fridge and gave it a cursory scan before turning back to me.

"To what do I owe this visit? Would you like a bottle of beer?"

I shook my head. "No, it's fine. I have so many other places to go before the end of the day."

He nodded. "What's going on, son?"

"Nothing much. I just stopped by to see you, you know? It's been a while."

He chuckled. "You haven't been doing your job properly, Alex. I've been hearing rumors."

"I took time off."

"You know you can't do that, Alex. Now look at what's happening. Or haven't you heard what's going on?"

I nodded. "I'll be back at the base in no time."

"You tread on dangerous ground, Alex. The longer you take a break from the game, the more enemies you have."

I nodded. "Thanks, Ricardo. Tell me, how have you been?"

He narrowed his eyes on me. "I'm an old man. I'm more concerned about you. You need to get your head back in the game, Alex. This is a matter of life and death."

I nodded.

"And who's this lady they're all talking about? No one has seen you with one, but they're sure you have a lady with you."

"Just rumors."

He watched me, his eyes unwavering. "Be careful, Alex. You know you're not a part of the Marcel family, and you've got more haters than you know."

"Great. How's Nina?"

"She's good."

"I'll take my leave now. I was driving by before I decided to visit."

He nodded. "Thanks for visiting. I'll see you later."

My phone beeped on my way out the door. "Who's on the line?"

"Enzo is in a really critical situation right now. The doctors are trying their best to revive him."

"What happened? I thought he had gotten better yesterday."

"I don't know; he suddenly started showing some unusual symptoms. I called the doctors to inform them, and right now, I really don't know what's going on."

"I'll be right there."

"Okay."

A text from my phone caught my attention: "They're overpowering us, boss! We're running out of men. We need help."

"Goddamn it!" I hissed, wondering where to go next. Enzo was in a very critical position, but the men I sent on an assignment were in the middle of a crisis.

"I'll be right there," I texted.

I sent my men to go after those who killed those elderly people. It was sheer wickedness, and I couldn't sit back and watch them do as they liked. When I got back to the group tomorrow, I would bring them out. The only person we didn't have solid evidence for was Blade. But after what he did to Ricky, his days were numbered.

By the time I got to them, they had completed the mission.

"Where are they?"

"Locked in the other room."

"You know the plan. Stick to it. When I call you out tomorrow, throw them out."

"Roger that, sir."

"Nice job, guys. I'm really impressed."

I couldn't wait to see Blade's reaction tomorrow upon finding out who the new boss is. I'd let him have his way for too long.

"See you soon."

They nodded.

"This isn't going to be easy for you, Alex. The group has now been separated," someone said as I turned to leave.

"What do you mean?"

"Since Ferd has his own men now, Blade is also trying to be in charge. So the group has now been divided," another person answered.

"It's not going to be easy. It's going to turn into a fight."

I sighed. "Thanks for informing me about this, guys."

They nodded. "It's the least we can do to save the group. Blade has turned it into a murder game."

I glanced at my watch; it was way past midnight.

"Alright, guys, see you tomorrow." I shook hands with them.

Andriana wasn't in the living room when I got into the house, which was surprising because that was her usual spot. She was probably still mad about this morning, and she had every reason to be. I couldn't keep giving her mixed signals. It was totally wrong.

"Andriana," I called out, making my way to her room.

No response.

"Open up. Let's talk."

I tried the knob and was surprised when it came open. I peered into the room. "Andriana?"

She wasn't there. I dashed out of the apartment.

"Susan!"

She rushed toward me, her face etched with concern. "Where is she?"

"She went to meet a friend."

"What friend?"

She shifted back uncomfortably. "I have no idea, but when she was leaving, she told us she wanted to go and see her friend."

"What the hell?" I grabbed my car keys from the table and dashed to my car.

"She'll be back soon. She's been gone for a while now, sir."

"And none of you thought it wise to call me?"

I was driving out of the house and down the road when I saw her with a man laughing hysterically. I could feel my temper rising as I watched them. What the hell did she think she was doing, frolicking around with random men? My intention was to wait till they were done talking, but the moment the man touched her shoulders, I turned the car around and parked right in front of them.

"Get in the car, Andriana!"

She looked confused for a moment until she realized it was me.

"What do you mean?" She frowned.

"Get in the car, right now."

The guy kept glancing from Andriana to me. "Anna, what's the problem? Who is this?"

"Please give me a minute," she said to him before walking over to me.

"What the hell do you think you're doing, Alex?" she whispered.

"Who is that? And why are you out here in the open with him?"

"Oh, please." She waved her hands dismissively. "You have no right to do this. Just go away."

"Who is he?"

"I don't think I owe you any explanation regarding this, Alex."

"I'm not here to exchange words with you. We're going home together, right now."

"Don't create a scene here, Alex. Just leave."

"Anna, what's the problem?" he asked again.

"Who are you? And what are you doing here?" I barked, getting out of the car.

"I'm—I'm just here..." his voice trailed off when he noticed my glare.

"I'll see you later, Andriana! You both are acting so weird."

"Nathan, wait."

"Sort things out with whoever this is and give me a call. I don't want any trouble," he said before turning around and walking away.

"Let's go," I said to her.

"Leave." She frowned. "If you don't want any problems, just leave."

"I can't leave you here all alone."

"Don't fucking play with me, Alex! Leave."

I looked around, and thankfully, not many people were going around the block.

"Now, let's get in the car and head out. We can argue about this later, when we get home."

"There's no home, Alex. Get the hell out of my sight!"

"Why are you so pissed? Did I just break your little relationship?"

"Now Alex, don't piss me off more than this."

I had never seen her so mad before. "If he was your boyfriend, then you should've just told me. I asked you."

"Whether he's my boyfriend or not is none of your business. My private life is none of your business. You're not my man."

"Get in the car right now, Andriana."

"Or what?" She narrowed her eyes on me.

"Watch me do it."

"You're such a dickhead," she muttered before pulling the door open and entering the car. "You think you can talk to anyone however you like."

"I just want you to be safe."

"That's the lie you tell yourself all the time, but this isn't because you want me to be safe."

"Okay then, what's it about then?" I asked her, maneuvering the car around.

"I can't wait to find my way out of all of this. You're insane, with no sense of boundaries."

"This is what I get for trying to help you? You're such an ungrateful person."

She shrugged. "You were not helping me, Alex. I was perfectly fine. Ask yourself what this is."

I nodded, bringing the car to a halt. "You should've just told me he was your man. If you had, I would have given you both the privacy you needed."

She stared at me as I turned off the ignition. "You're just jealous. Get yourself together, Alex."

"This is the last time I'm going to say this. If you feel that I'm just keeping you here for no reason and you want to be going around with different men, just let me know. You pack your things and get the hell out of my house."

"You're so—" Her voice shook softly as tears slid down her face. She tried to wipe them off with the backs of her hands, but the more she wiped them off, the more tears dropped down.

Even though I knew I was acting ridiculous, the image of her laughing with that guy made me mad, and I lost all control of my feelings.

"I'm sorry," I said.

She glanced at me. "Why are you telling me that?"

I shrugged. "I should have handled it differently. Stop crying."

"Okay."

"Who was he?"

She narrowed her eyes on me. "He's Lila's brother. Let's just say he's a friend of mine." She sniffed, casting an accusing glance at me.

"Am I supposed to know who Lila is?"

She shrugged. "Lila's a friend of mine."

"Oh."

We both fell silent, neither of us making an attempt to get out of the car.

"Don't you have any friends? I mean, apart from Enzo, I've never seen anyone else with you."

"Maybe I don't."

"Talk to me."

"You can't keep friends while in the mafia, Andriana. Your friends are your mafia brothers."

She adjusted herself to a comfortable position. "Really? Why so?"

"Enzo is a good example. They'll expose you. You can't trust anybody."

"Not even your family?"

I laughed shortly. "Yes, not even them."

"What kind of life is that? That's not a good life to live. That's why you all are always grumpy and, I don't know, depressed."

"You think I'm depressed?" I laughed, watching her.

"No, but you're definitely not happy. You're somewhere in between."

"Hm."

"You don't have friends or family, so how are you coping? You just spend the whole day with yourself. You don't call friends? What a boring life."

"I have you."

"I can confidently tell you that you don't." She chuckled.

"Ah, I see."

"Tell me."

"That's the way I live my life. It's great when you get used to it."

"No, it's not," she said firmly, shaking her head.

"Talking from experience?"

She inched closer to me. "I grew up alone, in case you didn't know, and I understand what it means to be lonely."

"You grew up alone?" I asked, watching her quietly.

She nodded, stepping out of the car. "I was all alone until I got to college, so I know you were lying when you said you got used to it. No one ever gets used to loneliness."

I got down from the car also, walking slowly beside her on our way into the house.

"That's the difference, Andriana. I wasn't feeling lonely."

She scoffed, and before she could say anything else, I lifted her against my shoulder, earning a surprised yelp from her.

"Put me down, Alex! I'm still mad at you. You can't be doing that."

"No! Tell me you've forgiven me."

She pressed her lips together. "No."

I spun her around, laughing briefly when she started to scream.

"Say it."

She laughed. "I've forgiven you, Alex."

"Good." I dropped her slowly, and we both watched each other quietly.

"I'm sorry, Andriana. As a member of the gang, I'm not allowed to have a relationship outside of the gang. It's dangerous, especially to the lady, if I go ahead and they find out."

"Why are you telling me this?" she asked, her eyes boring into mine.

I caressed her cheeks softly. "I'm really attracted to you, Andriana. I try to fight it off sometimes, only to keep you safe. I need you to understand that."

"I do, and that's why I want you to make up your mind. We can't be together, so there's no point of—"

"Shh." I placed a finger on her lips. "I can't stay away from you. I'm too drawn to you to do that."

She sighed. "Then what do you want from me? A secret relationship?"

I actually wasn't sure what I wanted right now. There were a lot of hindrances to our relationship. She was twenty-three, and I was forty. It was absolutely unheard of, but I just couldn't stay away from her. The more I tried to keep away, the more drawn I was.

"Why are you staring at me that way?"

"Come here." I pulled her into my arms. "I'm here for you."

She raised her head to catch my gaze. Neither of us said anything. A beep from my phone caught my attention a few seconds later. She eased off me so I could go through the phone.

A message read, "Blade and his guys are desperately trailing one of your lady's friends. We're still trying to figure out who at the moment, so we can step in."

CHAPTER FIFTEEN

ANDRIANA

THE MOMENT ALEX'S FACE creased into a frown, I knew something was wrong and that it had to do with the mafia gang.

"What's the problem?" I asked.

He shook his head. "Nothing. I have to leave now, Andriana. Important business."

I glanced at the time. It was several hours into the night. "Can't it be postponed till tomorrow morning? It's late."

He shook his head, reaching for his keys. "No, I have to go now. See you soon."

My heart started to pound as he turned to leave. "Please stay safe," I said.

"Of course," he said, pulling the door open. "Don't leave here, Andriana. I've told you a million times that these people are actively searching for you."

"Okay."

He shook his head. "Stay in here, and if you need anything, ring me up or send me a text. I'll have it delivered to you."

"Okay."

He nodded once at me before stepping out of the house.

"What are you doing, Andriana?" I said out loud, falling into the chair after he had left. "Use your head!"

After a while of trying to figure out what was going on in my life, I picked up my phone and made a video call to Lila.

"I've been waiting for your call. Start talking!" She frowned. I knew Nathan must've told her something.

"I'm totally sorry, Lila. It was just a misunderstanding."

"Okay, go on. I'm listening because Nathan explained a lot to me."

"What did he say?"

She explained all that happened earlier, and I sighed. "It's true, but it was just a misunderstanding, Alex was just worried about me."

"Uh? Now I'm worried about you." She sighed. "He has no right to do that. Or are you in a relationship?"

"No."

"So talk to me. What was all that for? I'm worried about you. I know you've been keeping a lot of things from me. Just talk to me."

"Lila, he's in the mafia."

Her hands flew to her mouth. "What? Your life is in danger, Andriana. Find a way to get the hell out of there."'

"Just chill, Lila, and let me explain."

"Chill? You must be out of your mind. That guy is dangerous."

"Not really," I explained everything that had been going on to her from the moment Alex told me who he was.

"Look at the danger he has put you in, and now you're running around with him." She started to pace around her room.

"It was the other guy, Blade."

"Why are you taking his side? Do you even realize the kind of trouble you're in?"

"You're only making matters worse, Lila. I've gone through all these stages already. Right now, I'm just hoping Alex figures something out as soon as possible."

"Wow. So help me understand what's going on. Are you dating now?"

"No."

"So, why did he act that way to Nathan? Why is he being jealous and protective if you're not in a relationship?"

"He likes me, Lila. Don't be dumb."

"He likes you? Isn't he, like, forty?"

"Can I call you back?"

"No, Andriana, you cannot. Stay on the line and listen to me."

"I'll call you back." I ended the call without waiting for a response from her. Lila was a hard nut to crack sometimes.

Heck! I thought. *What am I even going to do?*

"Andriana! Hide!"

My heart skipped a beat. Did I just hear that correctly? I made my way to the window to see what was going on outside and gasped when I saw a bunch of men outside fighting off the bodyguards.

"Oh my God. Oh Lord." I ran back to my room and hid under the bed, cussing when I realized I had forgotten my phone in the living room.

A few minutes later, the door leading into my room was forced open, and I winced in horror.

"No one is here!" someone yelled.

"Check all the corners of this building." I could see him from beneath the bed as he walked around the room, opening cupboards and throwing things around.

"I know she's in here. Come out, lover girl! Let's make this smooth and snappy."

Lover girl?

"Hey, mama!" My eyes opened in horror when he bent down and smiled at me.

"Come on, come on."

I shook my head. "Get the hell out of here. I'm not coming out."

He frowned. "Now let's not make this painful for anyone. Don't make me hurt you. We don't want to hurt you," he said to me. "Guys! Target found. Get the vehicle ready."

I said a quick prayer as the man dragged me out from beneath the bed, hoping Alex would walk in right now and save the day.

"Follow me." He walked briskly ahead of me. I looked around, searching for something I could hit him with—anything to escape from this horrendous man.

"Don't even try to play smart," he said without looking back. "You'll regret it."

They pushed me inside the car and drove away from the house as I struggled to get away from them.

"Shut up, or I'll make you stop."

I looked at the faces of the men in the car and knew they weren't bluffing.

"Where are you taking me? Who are you? What did I do?" My entire body was shaking with fear now.

"Just shut up!" the man in front of me shouted, hitting my head with the back of his gun. And that was the last thing I heard before everything went black.

——

By the time I woke up, it was morning and my head was pounding. I placed my hands on my head to keep it steady. Pain shot through my body as I tried to adjust myself into a more comfortable position to see where I was.

"Now that you're awake, it's better to be quiet," I heard someone say.

"Uh? Who are you?" I squinted my eyes at him, trying to understand what was going on. The room was extremely dark. I could barely see the person talking.

"Here." He pushed a plate toward me. "Eat that."

I looked at the plate, which contained two small pieces of meat.

"Eat it," he said.

"No, thanks." I shook my head, instantly regretting the movement.

"That's the only thing you have to eat for the rest of the day, so you had better eat it."

I ignored him, leaning against the wall so I was more comfortable. My whole body ached with pain.

"Who are you?" I managed to ask again, turning to look at him.

"I told you, keep quiet," he said gruffly.

"I'll keep quiet, but can I know why I'm here? I need to know what's going on at least, before I die."

He glanced at me. "Who said you were going to die?"

"Then why am I here?"

"Oh my God, you made me do this!"

I watched in horror as he walked over to plaster tape over my mouth, then he tied my hands up.

"I can finally have some peace." He sighed, heading back to his seat.

The other men joined him some minutes later, and they all laughed and talked about random things, completely ignoring the fact that I was right behind them.

"Wait! Did you hear that?" someone asked suddenly.

"Hear what? There's nothing."

"Keep quiet!"

The room went silent immediately as they all tried to focus their attention.

"There's nothing."

"No, I heard something," the man muttered, looking more convinced. "Hey! You! Go out and confirm everything is in order."

"Yes, boss!"

I said a short prayer in my heart, hoping to God that it would be Alex. After a while, the same man turned to the rest of them. "Eric is not back yet. There's something going on."

The men jumped to their feet, cocking their guns as they walked toward the door. They all trudged out quietly, and I hoped whoever was out there was here to rescue me. After a few moments, I started to hear gunshots all around the place. I curled my body into a ball, hoping none of the bullets would hit me.

After what felt like a lifetime, the door was thrown open, and a shadow lurked in the doorway. I whispered softly, my heart beating frantically as the man pointed his gun at me.

Please, please don't shoot me.

"Hmph, hmph." My voice wasn't audible enough to be heard through the tape.

"Fuck you!" Alex appeared behind the man, and he hit him aggressively several times with the back of his gun until I was sure he had died. I was screaming behind the tape, but it was so muffled that no one could hear me.

"Andriana!" He ran to me, holding my hands softly. "I'm going to take off this tape now, but it might be a little painful."

I nodded as tears streamed down my cheeks. He removed it as carefully as he could, and then loosened the rope on my hands.

"I'm so sorry." He pulled me into his arms when he was done. "They did this to you?" he asked, caressing the spot where they hit me with the gun.

"Ouch." I touched his hands softly. "It's still sore. Don't touch it."
He nodded.

"Can we go now? I don't want to be here anymore," I said to him, placing my hands on my head to ease the pain. I wasn't sure I liked the way he was looking at me right now, like he really cared for me.

"Of course, let's go." He lifted me into his arms and carried me all the way to the driveway, where his car was parked.

"How did you find me here?" I asked on our way home.

"I have my ways, Andriana. Don't bother yourself about anything. Try to rest." He patted my hands softly before reaching for his phone and placing it on his ear.

"Vacate the area. She's out of there."

I glanced at him, and he smiled shortly. "These are the men who work with me now. They helped in rescuing you, Andriana."

"Thank you," I muttered.

He glanced at me. "You must be so hungry."

I nodded.

"I'll get you food," I heard him say from a distance. I was thinking of my life and how I got caught up in mafia activities. Mafia! Never in a million years would I have thought that I could be entangled in their lives like this.

"Do you know who did this?" My voice came out with a little quiver, and he looked at me with concern.

"No."

"Why do I feel like you're hiding something from me?"

He shrugged. "You need to eat, Andriana, and rest. Look at you."

I shook my head. "That's not what I asked you, Alex."

"I'll tell you, but only when I'm sure you're better, when you've eaten and had some rest."

I nodded, thinking about my life before I met Alex and how peaceful and quiet it had been compared to now. I was living, eating, and dining among criminals now. I sighed. But what could I do?

"Are we moving away from the house again?"

Alex glanced at me, his expression unreadable. "No, I've increased security in the house."

I looked out of the window. "Are they doing this just to get me?"

He shook his head. "No, they have their reasons."

"They want me. Don't try to make me feel better. I know it's me they want."

"I told you you're safe with me, Andriana. That's all that matters."

I tried hard to stop the tears from falling. He wasn't telling me everything, which bothered me a lot, because my life was in danger.

"What's the problem?" He glanced at me, his eyes filled with compassion.

"Nothing."

"Don't worry. When you eat and have some rest, everything will be alright. You're fine; you're not dead. I'm here for you, and I'm promising you that no harm is going to come to you. That's all that should matter, really."

I nodded, feeling a lot better than I did earlier.

"Would you like to have some jollof rice?" he asked, beaming at me.

I laughed shortly. "That'll do."

"Then let's go!" He rubbed my cheeks fondly. "You're safe with me, mama. Always know that."

I smiled at him. "Thank you."

He nodded. "You don't have to say that."

"How's Enzo? Were you able to see him yesterday?"

His eyes opened in realization, and my heart sank. "Is he okay?"

"He had an emergency yesterday, but I was too occupied with work, so I couldn't go. Since then, I haven't heard from them."

I sighed. "That means he's okay. If there was something wrong, I'm sure they would've reached out to you."

"I guess so."

"Can we see him later today?" I smiled at him. "Please."

"No, Andriana. It's not safe for you to be going around yet. When the time is right, you'll see him."

I nodded, suddenly remembering the workers at home. "How's everyone at home? Those men came in yesterday just hitting and fighting them."

"When I got home this morning, I found the house empty."

My hands flew to my mouth. "You must've been so terrified."

He scoffed. "Terrified? You must have the wrong impression of me. I had to think fast. Call them, ask questions."

"You got home this morning? And you were here even before it was bright."

"I had a very busy night."

I didn't want to imagine what a busy night meant for him, so I just looked out the window, trying to calm my nerves. All of this was beginning to be a part of my world now, and the earlier I found a balance, the better it would be for me.

"There's something I need you to do," Alex said, his gaze still fixed on the road.

"What is it? If it has anything to do with bringing these rascals down, then I'm all for it!"

This time, he brought the car to a stop and faced me. "That's my girl."

CHAPTER SIXTEEN: BUILDING TRUST AMID TURMOIL

ALEX

"I DON'T CARE HOW you want to do it. Get that girl out of there right this moment!"

I stuck my phone between my ear and shoulder so that I could grab a drink out of the fridge. "I want this over as soon as possible."

"Blade has the girl over in his house, Alex. It's almost impossible." Andre's voice seeped over the line.

"Blade has gotten away with a lot for the last couple of days. Enough of all that bullshit."

Andre sighed. "I have eyes on his girlfriend right now. Should I go ahead with the deal?"

"Get her and keep her hostage. No food, no drink," I said.

"Roger that."

I hung up without another word and turned to see Andriana watching me, her expression hard. "Who were you talking to? Who are you keeping hostage?"

It was the first time she was coming out of the room after the incident with the gang members this morning. She looked so stressed out that I wished I could just hold her close, but this was the life she was living, so the earlier she got used to it, the better.

"Don't worry about any of this. Just relax for now."

She shook her head. "What girl are you talking about? You said he should get the girl out of there as soon as possible."

"Were you listening to my conversation?"

She shrugged. "I've been here all along. I heard you clearly."

"Well, this is not a conversation I want to have with you."

She pushed herself off the door with an urgency that caught me by surprise. "Alex, my life is in danger because of you and your gang members. Tell me what is going on right now! I have a feeling it has something to do with someone I know."

"Feelings are not real, Andriana. There are real-life issues to deal with." I patted her shoulder gently. "Calm down."

"What the hell are you talking about? I heard you clearly. The bad guys have someone I know with them. All I want to know is who."

"I'll see you later, Andriana. I've got important issues to take care of."

She held my hands as I turned to leave. "If this has anything to do with me or any of my family or friends, I need to know."

I didn't exactly know which of her friends Blade had with him, as we were still trying to figure it all out, and I didn't want any more distractions from her before I embarked on my journey.

"He abducted a friend of yours yesterday afternoon. We have no idea who it is at the moment, but my men are working on it."

"What the hell are you talking about, Alex?" She shifted back slowly, holding on to the chair close to her for support. "What do you mean? Who does he have with him?"

I grabbed my car keys from the table and turned to her. "Try to remain calm. Everything will be sorted out.

She held up a finger. "I have a few friends around here, some of whom I'm not really close with. There's Mia, Nathan, and a couple of other people. Lila's not in the country at the moment. Oh my God, oh my God." She yanked her phone out of her pocket, and I grabbed it from her.

"What do you think you're doing?" I asked, glaring at her.

She sniffed back tears. "Calling my friends to check on them, of course. Give me back my phone!"

"You can't do that. It'll only cause suspicions to arise where there's nothing. Listen to me, Andriana."

"I'm not listening to you. Give me back my phone! I've had enough of all this." She slapped my arms, trying to get the phone out of my hand.

"Andriana, I want you to listen to me right now. Your friend will be okay. There are men currently trying to reach them. Just calm your nerves."

She glared at me, her chest rising and falling. "Give me my phone right now, Alex, or I'll call the cops."

We both stared at each other, neither of us moving.

"The phone, Alex." She stretched out her hand.

I handed it to her with a sigh. "Be careful with what you say, Andriana. Try not to draw attention to yourself."

"If there's anyone I'm drawing attention to, it's you and your god-damned mafia gang. My goodness!"

She typed frantically on her phone for a moment before placing the phone on her ear.

"Mia?" Her voice shook slightly. "Mia, are you okay? Where are you?"

"Oh, thank God. Can I call you back? No, no. Everything is okay. I'll call you right back."

She ended the call and sighed. "She's okay, she's okay, Andriana," she mumbled to herself, rocking gently. Her hands shook as she dialed another number.

"Andriana," I called, reaching out to her. She held out her hands.

"Nathan, how are you? Are you okay?" She paused, listening to what he was saying on the other end. "I know. I know. You have every reason to be upset with me. Where are you?" she said. "Since when?" She started to pace around the room. "Just relax, Nathan. I also spoke to her yesterday morning. I'm sure she's fine. I'll call you right back."

She sat with a sigh.

"Somethings wrong. I can feel it," she continued with a glance at me. "Stop looking at me like that, Alex! I'm going nuts here. I don't know what to do."

"You don't have to," I told her. "I'll figure out a way. That's why you have me."

She scoffed. "Bullshit."

"Stay right here," I said. "Don't go anywhere. I'll be right back."

She shook her head. "No, Alex. Enough of all this. I'll go wherever I want. If they want to kill me, then so be it. I can't keep hiding forever. You're requesting that I remain composed despite the fact that they have one of my friends with them?

"I'm asking you to keep calm because there's nothing you can do. So you should listen to whatever I tell you so you can also stay safe."

"Oh my goodness." She nodded slowly. "This is real life."

"Look, Andriana, I've told you a million times that you're safe with me."

"Stop telling me I'm safe with you when my friends and family are in danger. I'm not safe if they're not safe," she said. "What's the point of being safe if my friends and family are in danger? Hm, Mr. Mafia?"

My phone started to ring. It was Andre, the man I put in charge of finding the girl. "Give me a minute."

After a lengthy conversation with him, I turned to Andriana. "I have to go now."

"I'm coming with you." She jumped to her feet, grabbing her jacket by the door.

"No way." I laughed briefly and frowned when I realized she was serious. "Andriana."

She shook her head. "I'm not staying here all alone again. What if those guys come back for me?"

"I've increased security in the house. You're going to be safe. I promise you."

"But I don't want to stay without you. I only feel safe when you're with me." She looked around uncomfortably.

"It's dangerous having you out there right now, but you're safe here. Stay here." I held her shoulder, trying to make her understand me.

"I don't want to stay here alone," she continued as she watched me, looking really scared. But I didn't want to take chances with her. Anything could happen out there.

"You said you could protect me, right? Then do it. I'm going with you, and you can protect me from danger if you're truly a mafia leader."

I knew she was testing me, but those words hit me really hard.

She leaned forward so we were only a few meters apart from each other. "Or can you only protect me when I'm indoors?"

"Get in the car, and do as I say at all times."

She nodded. "I can do that."

"Good."

"You abducted someone related to Blade?" she asked me while we were driving down the road.

"His girlfriend. I'm going to put a call through to him very soon. Once he knows we're with the girl, he'll release your friend."

She sat back against the seat, looking lost. "I don't have many friends around here. I don't understand what's going on. Apart from Mia and Nathan, there's no other friend I think Blade can abduct."

I glanced at her. "What are you trying to say?"

She sighed. "I don't know. Something is off."

"Are you trying to say Blade doesn't have any of your friends?" I glanced at her.

"I don't know, Alex. It's just a random thought. My mind is just incredibly busy right now. I'm so confused."

"Don't worry. We'll figure this out."

"Your phone," she said, pointing to the dashboard. "It's ringing."

I couldn't hear the phone over the noise from the street. I picked it up before it went off.

"Hey, boss."

"Go on. I can hear you."

"We have the girl with us, but Blade still has the girl's friend with him. We've not been able to access the house, as it's fully secured."

"Great, I'll put a call through to Blade now. You know the usual. Once I've settled with him, I'll give you a call. Are you at the warehouse?"

"We went somewhere else. It looks like Blade has figured out our hideout."

"Where are you now? I don't want you to send me a text or even say it over the line in case this call is being monitored. Try to give me a hint."

He was quiet for a while before his voice shot through the air. "Andrew."

I didn't totally understand what he meant by that, but I could work with what I had in mind. Andrew was a part of the rivalry gang some years ago, and he exposed the group and got killed. His favorite spot had always been behind one of our most unused buildings. He claimed it made him relax and think more.

"What's going on?" Andriana glanced at me.

"We're heading over to the men. I'll put a call through to Blade, so he has an idea of what's going on. But first, I need to get to the girl."

She nodded, shaking her legs nervously. "I'm so nervous. I wish I could talk to my friend right now."

"Why not?"

She shrugged. "I don't want to distract you in any way."

"I've driven in way worse scenarios."

Lila's number didn't go through. Andriana kept trying, until we got to the venue and were on our way in.

"Put your phone down, Andriana. Phones are not allowed in."

She glanced at me. "Phones are not allowed in for everybody, or just me?"

"Everybody," I replied curtly.

She nodded.

The men were gathered in groups as we made our way in, and they jumped to their feet when they saw us.

"Where is she?" I asked.

Andre walked into an empty room and wheeled the girl out a few moments later. "Here she is, boss."

I walked toward her and scooted in front of her. "Hey, mama." Her face was covered in blood, and she was almost passing out as she held my hand.

"Please! Please, take me out of here. They want to kill me."

"Relax, lover girl!" Someone chuckled. "No one's killing you. You got involved in mafia activity, and now you face the consequences."

"Mafia activities?" she choked out, coughing out blood. "I don't know what you're talking about."

Andre looked at me. "She's lying. She works for Blade. As a matter of fact, she's one of his greatest hitmen."

She started to shake her head. "That's not true. I don't even know what he's talking about."

I squatted down so I could get a clearer view of her face. She met my gaze, a flicker of anger flashing through her eyes. I knew she was guilty of everything that was said about her.

"Who does Blade have with him? Tell me everything you know. Let's make this easier for everyone."

She sighed. "I told you that I have no idea what you're talking about."

Andre hit her head angrily with the back of his hand, and Andriana screamed in disbelief, looking at my face uncertainly. "We're not here to play. Talk now. Or face the consequences. You know this."

"Fuck you," she seethed, spitting at him. "And fuck you too." She turned to me, breathing hard.

"You're going to make this really hard for yourself, girl. What do you know? It's simple. Tell me, and I'll let you out of here immediately. I mean it."

"I don't know anything. I swear."

"Then what do you call this?" one of the men asked, raising her phone in the air.

"What's that?" I asked, watching him.

"Here's a text she sent to Blade yesterday. She was the one who abducted the girl on her way home."

She started to shake her head. "I don't know anything about this. Why don't you guys call Blade to confirm?"

"Don't worry. We know how to make you talk," Andre said, nodding at her.

"What's that? Please leave my personal life out of this. I already told you that I don't know anything."

"Here's a video of your son going to school this morning." He waved the phone at her, and she started to scream at the top of her lungs. "If anything happens to that boy, then the battle line has been drawn."

"You've killed thousands of innocent people, both kids and adults. Why is yours so special?"

She started to cry. "Please, leave my boy alone. I know nothing about this."

I glanced at Andriana, who looked around like she was in hell. She shook her head when she caught my gaze. I turned to the men. "Quiet, everyone."

The room fell silent immediately, and they all watched as I dialed a number on my phone.

"Hey, Alex, long time no see!" Blade's voice echoed through the room. I put the phone on speaker.

"Who do you have with you, Blade?"

He chuckled. "Straight to the point, Alex. As you know, I'm a very busy man, unlike you."

"Who do you have with you?"

He sighed. "Send that cook over, and all of this will stop. That's all I ask."

Silence.

"By the way, I have her friend with me, Lila, or whatever she's called."

"What? No!" Andriana screamed in shock. She shook her head in disbelief. "He can't have her with him. He's lying."

"Oh? So you have the bitch with you?" Blade laughed softly.

I turned to Andriana, my anger evident on my face. "I told you to keep quiet!"

"But he's lying. He doesn't have her with him."

Blade's voice echoed through the line as the men held Andriana back. "Just wait and see. I'm going to send a video of the girl now."

My phone beeped a few seconds later, and Andriana yanked herself free from the grip of the men and ran to me. "Let me see that." She grabbed the phone from my hands and peered into the screen, shaking her head in disbelief.

"Oh God, no, no, no." She handed me the phone, tears streaming down her cheeks. "No, no. He has her with him. Look what he's done to her! She's almost dead!"

The girl was drenched in a pool of blood, her face barely recognizable. I glanced at Andriana, who was bawling her eyes out now. I took a video of the girl we held captive and sent it to him. Blade called me a few minutes later.

"Kill her, Alex. I don't care about the fucking whore!" He chuckled. "I don't care about anyone, Alex. You can't use anyone to get at me."

"No, please. No!" The girl screamed, shaking her head.

"You bastard!" Andriana fell to the ground. "They have Lila with them. He has Lila with him, oh God."

"Send that cook over within the next few hours, or else I'll send a video of this bitch struggling for breath."

"No, Andriana! Don't come here! He'll kill you!" Lila's voice echoed through the phone.

"Shut the fuck up, bitch!" a cracking sound came through the line before it fell silent.

The other girl started to shake her head after the call ended. "Please don't kill me. Please don't kill me."

I had enough of Blade's recklessness. This had to stop.

Andriana jumped to her feet. "Did you see the way she looked? She's almost dead. Do something! I don't want my friend to die."

I shook my head. "I'm finding a solution to this, Andriana! What would you have me do? Send you over to him?"

She shrugged. "I should be there, not Lila! She's innocent in all of this. Send me to him, and let Lila go home and receive treatment. She'll die!"

There was no way I was sending her over to Blade. The thought of it annoyed me. I drew her toward me. "Listen to me, Andriana," I whispered, pulling her close, but she stopped me.

"No, Alex, I'm done with this. I'll find him myself and give myself to him."

"You'll do no such thing!"

"And who's going to stop me? I'm the problem here. You'll have a peaceful life with the mafia gang, and my friends and family will be safe. What other option is better than this? Send me to him!"

Her last statement echoed through my mind. The thought of losing her hadn't crossed my mind like this before, and it really unsettled me. I couldn't bear to lose her.

"We'll find a way. You're not going anywhere."

"Oh God! Okay then. What's the plan?" She wiped tears from her eyes, nodding her head.

I turned to the other men who were watching us quietly. My eyes caught sight of Blade's girlfriend, and I frowned. "Shoot her!"

"What? No!" Andriana screamed, holding my hands. "You can't shoot her; she's innocent in all of this."

I nodded once to the guys as I made my way out and into the building's mini-office. "Finish the job, guys, and let's plan our attack!"

Andriana's scream was the last thing I heard as I walked out of the building. It was a silent revolver, so I knew they had completed that part.

"I'm done! I'm done with all of this!" she yelled after me, running to catch up with me. I stopped halfway, turning back to see the other gang members behind me.

"I'm not going to try to stop you anymore, Andriana. Stay right here where you're safe, and let me find a solution to all of this. Or let Andre lead you out of here right now! I'm sick of your drama!" I pointed toward the exit. "Make your decision, now!"

CHAPTER SEVENTEEN: LIGHT IN THE DARKNESS

ANDRIANA

I HADN'T SEEN ALEX since he angrily left me a few hours ago at the entrance of his office, and I didn't care. Nothing was making sense anymore. That horrible man, Blade, was unstoppable—a ruthless, wicked animal. It was during moments like these that I wished I had superpowers I could use to eliminate bad people.

I wondered what Lila was doing in the area in the first place. Everything was so confusing. The video Blade sent resurfaced in my mind, and I winced, shutting my eyes in pain. She looked so bad. I tried to hope for the best, but I knew if she remained there for long, she wasn't going to make it.

This was all my fault. I felt like a traitor staying here where I was safe, while Lila was in the middle of the storm. I was all they needed for her to be set free. I was the one still keeping her in pain. I started to pace around the room, different ideas running through my mind.

"The boss asked me to give you this."

I turned to see one of the men walking to me, a bag in his hand. I eyed the bag skeptically, feeling really irritated. "What's in there?"

He shrugged. "Food."

I narrowed my eyes at him, feeling my anger resurfacing. "Go away, please." I didn't want to snap at him, so I just looked away, walking to the window and looking out into the street.

"I was asked to hand this over to you, it's an order. I can't take this back without delivering it to you."

Oh God, please give me the patience to handle this, I thought, and I turned to him. "Leave."

He dropped the food on a nearby table, and I shook my head. "With the food. I don't want it."

"Now listen." The man frowned, raising a warning finger at me. "I'm only being patient with you because I don't know what relationship you have with the boss, so don't make this any harder for either of us."

How in God's name did they expect me to eat while their fellow mafia brothers were torturing Lila? I wanted the ground to open up and swallow me. This was the lowest I'd ever been in my life.

"Just go away. I don't want any trouble either. I'm not hungry. I just want to be alone." I softened my gaze. "Please."

He sighed, taking a step toward the table. "I'll leave, but not without dropping this." He put the bag on the table and walked out of the room without saying another word.

My phone started to ring sometime after he left. I raised it to see who it was, and my heart caught when I saw Nathan's name on the screen. I had two options: ignore the call and pretend I didn't know what was going on, or answer it and lie to him. I groaned in frustration. This was getting messed up. The phone kept ringing until I was sure he desperately wanted to talk to me.

"What do I do? What should I do?" I muttered while pacing around the room restlessly.

"Hello?"

"Andriana! What the hell is going on? We've all been trying to reach you for hours now. Why aren't you picking up your calls?"

He sounded so pissed that my voice shook as I tried to speak. "I—I wasn't with my phone. I'm sorry. What's up?"

"We haven't been able to reach Lila. We were able to reach her friends from school, and they said she left two days ago. There's something wrong. I'm still trying to distract our parents from all of this, but it's only a matter of time before they figure out all of this. You know how fond they are of Lila."

I held the phone to my ear, my heart beating frantically against my chest.

"Andriana?"

"I can hear you." I wanted to tell him I had no idea where she was, but they had been like the family I never had. I couldn't bring myself to tell them a lie.

"Say something, Andriana, you're the only one she talks to. Do you have any idea where she is? Who has she been with? Anything? I just need to know she's fine. I'm so worried."

"I've been trying to get to her, Nathan. Once I'm able to reach her, I promise I'll give you a call. I'm also as confused as you are right now. I'm a total mess. I don't understand what's going on."

He was quiet for a while. "Are you okay, Andriana? You know I'm like a big brother to you, and if anything is bothering you, tell me."

I shook my head, trying to hold back tears, but I couldn't help it. Soon, I was sobbing.

"Andriana." His voice held a softer note. "What's the problem? What's going on?"

I wiped tears off my face, trying to keep my voice steady. "I'm fine, Nathan."

"Who was that guy? The one from that day? I don't like him."

I sniffed back tears.

"I have a bad feeling about him. I might've even seen him somewhere. He looks really familiar."

"Can I call you back later today?"

"Of course. Stay safe, Andriana."

I nodded before ending the call. I just couldn't sit here all day and wait for the worst to happen. There had to be something I could do to get Lila out of there. I pulled my hair in frustration.

This is sick, I thought.

"Hello."

I turned around to see the same guy from earlier with another bag. He didn't say anything this time. He just walked to the table and dropped the bag on it.

"What's in the bag?"

"Lunch."

"Get that thing out of here right now. You just dropped lunch here a few hours ago, and now you're back with another meal. What's your problem?" I didn't get it. It was like he was knowingly riling me up. Why the hell did I need to be eating this much when my friend was in danger?

"I'm acting based on command. I wouldn't be here giving you food if I wasn't asked to. I have more important things to do."

I took a deep breath and let it out slowly. "Get that thing out of here, or I'm going to fling it out after you."

He glared at me. "It's best you just accept the situation as it is; throwing tantrums and acting like this isn't going to bring a solution."

"Where's Alex? Is he back?"

"No." He turned to leave.

"Get that thing out of here right now! I'm not joking."

"What's going on here?" Alex's voice echoed through the hallway. I crossed my arms, waiting for him to come into the room.

"She has been refusing all the food I brought," the man said just as Alex walked in. He glanced at me with a little frown on his face before turning to the other man.

"You can leave, Joe."

Joe. So that was his name. I rolled my eyes, looking out the window.

"What's the problem, Andriana?"

I ignored him. Even a fool knows not to ask a silly question like that after witnessing what happened earlier.

"Mama?"

His voice sounded so soft that I almost turned to look at him. This wasn't what I needed right now. I needed a solution. I needed Lila out of there.

"Andriana?" He was so close, his voice sent shivers down my spine. I ignored him, but my heart was beating at an unbelievable rate. I could smell the scent of his cologne even before he touched me. And when he did, I felt my whole body shaking in surrender to him. I turned to him, my eyes glistening with tears.

"They're going to kill her. Look at what they've done to my poor girl. She's innocent in all of this."

He rubbed my cheeks softly before pulling me into his arms. I cried till I couldn't help myself anymore. He didn't say anything, and he just held on to me. It was almost like he needed the hug too.

"Do you trust me?" he asked suddenly, rubbing my back softly. I was quiet for a while before I nodded. After all, he had been the one protecting me from Blade's wrath.

"Yes, I do."

Silence.

"Your friend is safe."

I eased off him quickly, watching him suspiciously.

"What did you say?"

He shrugged. "She's safe. We rescued her earlier this afternoon."

"Alex? Are you being serious right now?" My lips gradually curved into a small smile.

He ignored me, walking to the table where the food had been sitting. "I don't joke around, Andriana. You can always take my word for what it is."

I squealed excitedly, running to catch up with him.

"Well?" I prodded, waiting for him to tell me everything that had happened.

"Well?" He asked, his lips curving into a knowing smile.

"C'mon, Alex, talk to me."

"Why haven't you eaten any of these?" He shook his head disapprovingly.

"Because my friend was in danger. I lost my appetite."

"You should eat. I'm not sure you've eaten anything this afternoon." He turned to me. "Have you?"

I shook my head. "No, food has been the last thing on my mind today."

"C'mon, eat something. I'll be going to meet the men now. There's an important issue I have to discuss with them before we leave."

I nodded, looking around with a frown. I couldn't wait to leave this horrendous place.

"I will, but where's Lila? You said you rescued her, and she's safe. Where is she now?"

"Receiving treatment."

"Can you take me there? Oh my God! I'm so happy. How was she when you met her, and how is she doing now? I really need to see her. I miss her so much."

He stopped walking and held my shoulders.

"Take a deep breath."

I rolled my eyes. "C'mon."

"Take a deep breath and then release. Do it about three times."

"I don't want to—"

"Do it. I mean it."

I did as he said, and he nodded once after I was done. "How do you feel now?"

I looked away from him, ducking my head shyly. "Let's just go and see her."

He smiled. "Give me a moment. I need to talk with my men. And you have to eat!"

I nodded, watching him as he walked down the hallway, a huge smile on my face. Lila was safe, and that was all that mattered. He turned back suddenly. "Why are you standing there?"

I watched him uncertainly. "You said you wanted to talk with your men."

"I didn't ask you to wait out here all alone. Come with me."

I didn't care about the meeting he had with his friends; all I wanted was to see Lila and to find her in good shape. Nothing else mattered to me, but I didn't say anything as I walked toward him.

———

Lila was lying down on the bed with her eyes closed when we walked in. Thankfully, she didn't look as bad as she did when Blade called earlier. She looked okay, except for the bruises on her neck and face. I glanced at Alex and was surprised to find him already watching me. I looked away immediately, my heart racing.

"She's on deep sedatives right now. She needs to rest. She won't be able to talk with you for now."

I nodded, checking her whole body for any hidden injury that the doctor hadn't seen. "She looks okay." I glanced at him.

"I made sure they took care of her. She looked a mess when she came in."

I held her hands softly. "Don't worry, you'll be fine, Lila."

I remained that way for several minutes until Alex cleared his throat. "It's getting late, mama. We should head home now."

I turned to him. There was something extremely captivating about him tonight. He was looking so good and so attractive. I glanced at his shirt. It must be that shade of blue; I've always liked that color. An image of one of Alex's men wearing that same color crossed my mind, and I made a face. Nope. It definitely was not the color. It was the man—this gorgeous man standing right in front of me was making me feel things I hadn't felt in years.

I picked up my bag and practically sashayed over to him. "Are you ready to go?"

He eased off the wall, and I stood in front of him, blocking his way. I didn't know what I was doing, but I knew I wanted him. I needed him so badly. He watched me, his gaze unreadable. I reached out my hand to his cheeks and caressed his beard softly, feeling my heart pound against my chest. This was the first time I was making the first move with a man.

I moved my face gradually toward his neck and kissed it gently, holding onto him tightly as if he might escape.

"Andriana—"

"Shh." I placed my hands on his lips before kissing him softly and nibbling gently on his lips.

"God, mama." He picked me up in one quick movement and pinned me against the stark white wall.

"Don't start what you can't finish," I said.

I pulled him close to me, completely oblivious to what was going on in the background. All I had in mind was Alex. I wanted nothing more than to feel him thrusting in and out of me. Nothing else mattered.

"Kiss me. Touch me. Just do something to me, Alex. I need you so bad." He drew my top down, and my breast came into view. I wasn't a fan of bras, and thankfully, I didn't put one on today. He stared at me with so much lust in his eyes that I knew he wanted me as much as I wanted him. He brushed his hand softly over my already hard nipples, and I moaned, holding his gaze.

"Alex," I said almost pleadingly, and he lowered his head to my breast, sucking it gently. I had never been so aroused. I moaned in pleasure as Alex worked wonders on my breast, my voice getting higher and higher. At this point, I didn't care who heard me. I was experiencing the best feeling in the world, and no one else mattered.

"Shh." Alex laughed softly, placing a finger on my lips. "You'll get us in trouble."

I glanced at Lila, who was sleeping peacefully on the bed a few meters away from us. I hoped that she would hear my moans and experience the most sensual dream of her life. I chuckled at the idea.

"Um, so she just needs a few—" Alex eased off me swiftly and adjusted my blouse just as the doctor walked into the room. She glanced from me to Alex, a disapproving scowl on her face, but didn't say anything. I was sure she saw us. My face reddened with embarrassment, but Alex had a serious expression on his face as he walked to the doctor.

"You were saying?" he asked.

She cleared her throat. "Excuse me. She's fine. She just needs some rest, and in a day or two, depending on her health, she should be discharged."

"Great." Alex nodded, his face blank. "I guess that's all."

She nodded, her earlier scowl appearing on her face. "But we'll need her to be alone now."

Such a killjoy. I glared at her. We weren't disturbing Lila in any way.

Alex nodded, reaching for my hand. "We'll leave now."

She nodded, making way for us to take the first step out before shutting the door softly.

Alex turned to me after she walked away, and we both burst into laughter. "She's such a killjoy," I muttered.

"There's a really nice hotel around here," Alex said, holding my gaze.

"If you don't get me there right now, I'm going to fuck you right here."

"Gosh." He laughed softly, and we practically raced to the car.

The ride to the hotel was extremely short, and I couldn't wait for Alex to conclude whatever he was saying with the receptionist. I needed us beneath the duvet as soon as possible. He turned to me, shaking the access card in his hand. "Done."

I didn't have the time to marvel at the beauty of the hotel as we walked to our room. I had other things on mind. Alex had barely shut the door when we both pounced on each other. He kissed me with so much fervor that I ran out of breath, but I didn't care.

"Take off your clothes," he said, easing himself out of his own clothes. I did as instructed, and in less than a minute, we were both standing naked in front of each other, our chests rising and falling. He captured my mouth in a kiss, moving his way down to my collarbone, neck, and shoulders.

Oh lord, what else was better than this?

When he reached my breast, I wanted to pull away from him, but the moment his tongue made contact with my nipples, I lost every bit of control I had. I writhed and whimpered, clinging to him as my body erupted with pleasure. But I planned to be in charge tonight, so I eased off of him, my gaze meeting his confused eyes.

"I'm going to ride you till every part of me is ingrained in that big mind of yours." Even my own words surprised me. But I knew I meant every bit of what I said.

He led me to the bed and laid down on it, waiting for me to take the lead as I had promised. I crawled slowly over to him and stroked his hard organ softly, before taking him fully in my mouth. He stifled a groan as I pulled and sucked. I wanted to suck him till he came, but my body couldn't wait. I needed him inside of me. I needed to feel every part of him within me.

I climbed his body and settled myself slowly onto him, moaning loudly as my pussy gripped his dick tightly. I couldn't wait any longer, so I got us both into a rhythm that would take us into bliss. I was pretty sure heaven itself didn't feel better than this.

CHAPTER EIGHTEEN: A CROSSROADS OF HEARTS AND DUTY

ALEX

NOTHING PREPARED ME FOR the way I felt looking at Andriana as she slept peacefully next to me. I had spent over half of my adult years putting this part of my life behind me. I never wanted anything to do with a lady, as that would cause a dent in the reputation I'd built for myself in the mafia. No one, absolutely no one in all my years of being there, had been able to use anyone as leverage against me. It was what made me one of the best.

She stirred softly beside me, and I impulsively caressed her brows, which were creased with worry. I knew in my mind that I did it deliberately, but I wasn't about to admit that.

"Alex," she said softly, touching the space on the bed to see if I was still there. "Oh, he's gone again." She muttered, her eyes still closed.

"I'm here," I whispered, moving closer to her and wrapping my arms around her body. "Come here."

She scooted closer to me, a little smile on her face as she went back to sleep. I couldn't sleep. I had gotten a text earlier that I needed to be back and active in the mafia. I wanted no part of this anymore, but I knew how impossible that was. Leaving the mafia was like filing for a death sentence. It was a do-or-die affair, and I'd known that since Marcel picked me up in the street several years ago.

I glanced at the wall clock a few meters away from the bed. It was 11 a.m. This was the longest I had stayed in bed.

"You didn't sleep a wink," Andriana muttered softly, her back facing me.

"And how do you know that?"

She was quiet for a while before shaking her head. "Never mind."

"How would you know that, mama?" I asked, trying to make her face me, but she wriggled out of my grip.

"Come here." I lifted her swiftly and turned her to me. "How are you?"

She smiled, looking away from me. "I'm good. How are you?"

"What do you think?" I asked.

She shrugged. "I don't know. You didn't sleep. You're going to feel really tired during the day." She looked at my face, caressing my hair softly.

"I slept." I laughed shortly. "It was the longest I've slept in a long time. You won't believe it."

She narrowed her eyes. "Are you serious?"

I nodded. "I feel charged with renewed energy."

She chuckled, getting off the bed. "Go away."

I remained on the bed, watching her as she went around the room, looking lost.

"What's the problem?" I asked her. She looked at me for a while, her eyebrows furrowed in confusion.

"Lila! I need to go see my friend right now!"

She didn't wait for me to say anything after that. She dashed into the bathroom, yelling out my name and telling me to get ready as soon as possible. My phone buzzed on the table close to the bed, and I raised it to see a text from an unknown number.

The message read, "The commission wouldn't take kindly to you getting soft, Alex. This has gone on for way too long. Get yourself together and get back to business."

The commission wouldn't take kindly to you getting soft. Those words echoed through my mind until we got to the hospital, where Andriana was making her way hurriedly toward her friend's room.

"The doctor said you should give them a few minutes," I said to her as she hurried to Lila's room.

She frowned. "He should've just been direct—five minutes, ten minutes. I'm bad at being patient."

I shook my head, pointing at a nearby seat. "Come, let's sit here. You'll have to wait patiently until they're done." I emphasized the *patiently*, and she chuckled, taking the seat close to me. My mind went back to the mafia and all of our activities, and I knew I had only a few more peaceful moments with Andriana. The last message was a strong reminder of that.

"Did you see the way that man looked at that lady dancing in the middle of the road?" She threw her head back, her laughter echoing in the hospital room. I forced a smile, my gaze shifting nervously to the doorway.

"Don't tell me you missed that!" She slapped my arms softly. "Did you?"

I had no idea what she was talking about, but her excitement was starting to rub off on me. "Where did this happen?"

She shook her head in distaste. "You didn't see it. There's no point explaining anything to you. You're not observant."

"Really?"

She shrugged. "Obviously."

I crossed my arms and faced her. "Then did you see that man stealing from that old woman's bag while she was waiting in line for her parcel?"

"Alex?"

I tried to stifle back laughter when she looked like she could commit murder.

"Did that happen?" she asked, frowning.

I nodded, rising to my feet when I saw the doctor walking over to us.

"And you couldn't do anything? You're such a bad guy." She made a face at me.

"Why are you making this about me? I didn't do anything."

She waved me off, turning to the doctor. "Can we go in now?" she asked hopefully, squeezing her hands nervously.

"Of course. She's doing great."

"Thank you, doctor!" She turned to me. "And you..." she said, but she just shook her head before turning to walk away from me.

I held her hands, feeling a great urge to explain myself to her. "I was driving, mama. You can't expect me to stop the car in the middle of the road and start running after some random guy."

"You're forgiven." She pecked my cheeks softly, a blush blooming on her face, before she turned around and walked inside the door. The world seemed to tilt on its axis after that. I, a man who stared down rival bosses without blinking, felt a heat crawl up my neck. My fingers, which were used to the weight of a loaded pistol, twitched with nervous energy.

I stood frozen after she left, the ghost of her peck lingering on my cheek. I sank into the hospital chair, the smooth leather suddenly uncomfortable. I laughed softly, finding myself in an unbelievable position. Love, it seemed, hit even the toughest mob boss harder than a brick wall.

———

I walked into the room several minutes later after receiving a phone call from Falcone, one of the mafia bosses. He was usually calm and cool, but his voice was urgent when he told me he needed to see me.

"Andriana?" They both turned to me as soon as they heard my voice.

"Hello." Lila waved at me, a strained smile on her face.

"How do you feel?" I asked.

She smiled. "I'm fine. Thank you for coming to my rescue."

I nodded, turning to Andriana. "We have to leave now."

She started to shake her head. "No, Alex. My friend needs me here."

I sighed. I needed to head over to Falcone, but I couldn't leave without making sure she was safe. "Andriana, listen to me. We have to leave now."

"No. What the hell, Alex?" She folded her arms stubbornly on her chest, her gaze hard.

I sighed. "I knew you were going to say this. Joe is on his way here, and he'll keep watch over you guys until I'm back."

"Joe? Can't it be anyone else? He's so annoying."

"What's wrong with him?" I asked her, a smile playing on my lips. I could see Joe making his way into the room from the side of my eyes.

"He's just so annoying!"

Lila chuckled softly, glancing from Andriana to me.

"Andriana has something to say to you, Joe." I turned toward him as he made his way in.

Lila burst into laughter, smacking her friend's arm playfully.

Andriana turned red before cocking her head arrogantly. She pointed at Joe. "I said that Joe here is annoying and doesn't listen to me." She met his gaze squarely, daring him to say something.

I patted his arm, turning to leave. "Keep her safe, and listen to her."

He nodded. "Roger that, boss."

I paused on my way out. "On second thought, don't listen to everything she says. She can be very stubborn. Especially if it has to do with them leaving this room."

He nodded. "Of course, boss."

"Alex!" Andriana called, pouting her lips in disappointment.

"He knows you so well," Lila said with a chuckle.

"You just shut up." Andriana threw her a glare.

"I'll be back soon." I nodded at her. "Stay right here, mama. Can you promise me that?"

Joe glanced at me with a surprised expression on his face. It was probably the first time he had seen me show genuine interest in someone.

"Andriana?" I persisted.

"On one condition," she said, walking slowly over to me.

I narrowed my eyes at her, warning her to behave herself. Either she was pretending not to understand what I was talking about, or she was blatantly ignoring my order. She crossed her arms over my neck, gazing softly into my eyes.

"What?" My voice came out in a hushed tone.

"You'll do whatever I ask of you when you're back," she whispered in my ear.

"In your dreams. See you later." I winked at her before turning around and shutting the door.

Falcone was waiting at a bar close to the hospital, so it didn't take long before I saw him. He pushed a steaming cup of coffee over to me when I settled into the chair across from him.

"Alex," Falcone began, his voice low and measured. "This ain't funny anymore. Your behavior to all of this is rather lackadaisical."

I snorted a humorless sound. "Lackadaisical? That's one way to put it."

"Six months you've been gone, Alex," Falcone continued, his voice laced with sympathy he wouldn't dare show on the streets. "What's going on? I'm hearing there's a girl, and then your company. What's really going on?"

"I had a good run," I conceded, a flicker of longing crossing my face as past activities crossed through my mind.

Falcone leaned forward, his voice dropping to a conspiratorial whisper. "Look, Alex, the group remembers your impact. Respects the hell out of it. But respect ain't gonna stop what's coming. They see you going around town, granting interviews for your company, poking around here and there with that lady—they ain't gonna like it."

I set my jaw, the spark of defiance returning. "I left that life, Fal. I paid my dues. Nobody can touch me."

Falcone shook his head, a sad smile twisting his lips. "Alex, you can't just walk away. This isn't some nine-to-five you quit. It's in your blood. They see you, and they see weakness. It'll be an accident, a stray bullet, or a bomb explosion. Heard from Simon lately? No? Exactly."

My hands tightened around the coffee cup, my knuckles turning white. I'd left that life behind me, and I had no intention of ever going back.

"We got you a way out, Alex," Falcone said, softening his tone. "One last job, clean and quick. Pull it off, and you disappear for good. They won't even know where to look."

I narrowed my eyes on him. Falcone must've forgotten who he was talking with for him to try to lure me with some silly words.

"Are you done? Can we both go our separate ways now?"

"Alex?" His jaw flexed with suppressed anger. I could see it, even as he tried to act unbothered.

"One last job. You're our last hope to make this work. And I'll do my best to make sure they leave that girl alone."

That was all I needed to hear to make my decision. I knew Falcone was probably lying, but it wouldn't hurt to take a chance.

I'd used these same tactics on newbies in the mafia, and I wondered why I was letting myself get into the same situation. It was hope. It was what most of the other guys had wished for. A chance at getting the life they dreamed of.

The silence stretched, heavy with the weight of a life sentence. My gaze flickered to the window, catching a glimpse of the bustling city outside—a world I thought I had escaped.

"One last job, huh?" I finally murmured, my voice rough with unspoken emotion.

Falcone nodded, a flicker of hope sparking in his eyes.

"So, what's this job about?"

CHAPTER NINETEEN: LOVE UNDER FIRE

ANDRIANA

ONE OF THE BEST things about staying with Alex around the clock was the fact that I'd gotten to know him reasonably well. So when he walked into the hospital several hours later, I knew something was wrong.

"Hi." I smiled at him, trying to figure out his mood. He nodded in my direction, whispering something to Joe, who was nodding severely.

"Why do you have that look on your face?" Lila asked, sitting up.

I shrugged. "There's something wrong. I know it."

She sighed. "I don't know, Andriana. I'm so worried about you. Sooner or later, I'll have to leave you, and you'll be left with these dangerous men. I'm just so sad, but what can I do?"

I pressed her hands reassuringly. "Don't be bothered, Lila. I'll be fine. Trust me. I've always taken care of myself."

She sighed. "Please try to stay safe for me. You know you're the only friend I have."

I nodded. "Lila, don't forget the plan. I'll call Nathan now because he's been blowing up my phone with calls."

She chuckled. "I didn't know he cared for me that much until now."

We both laughed softly.

"Brothers have their way of hiding how they feel from their sisters. I've seen it in many movies. They love them the most," I said, smiling. I had no experience with this, but after watching thousands of movies depicting brother-sister relationships, I could figure it out.

"So," I said, getting back to our earlier conversation. I took her hand. "You can't tell Nathan what happened. He's already getting a bit suspicious that maybe something like this happened, but you can't tell him. He'll want to get revenge for you, and that would be very dangerous for us all."

She nodded. "I know, Andriana. You've said this a million times."

"It's because I want you to always remember it. These mafia guys are not kind guys. They're so wicked that they'll kill an entire family without feeling a bit of guilt. Please try to keep everyone safe for me."

She nodded. "I'll tell them a thief got my bag in the airport. I tried chasing him, and they ganged up on me and beat me really bad."

I beamed at her. "That'll work. Just try to make sure there are no loopholes. Yes! You can also say someone finally rescued you and got your things back." I paused, shifting in my seat. "Just so they won't want any more investigations. That'll settle it all."

"I'll say just that." She smiled at me.

"I'll call Nathan now."

"Andriana!" Alex called, his voice sharp. I turned to look at him.

"Yes?" I asked cautiously, glancing at Joe.

"We have to leave right now."

"Can't I stay a few more minutes with her?"

He shook his head. "We have to leave now. Joe here will keep her safe until her family gets here."

I turned to her, and she nodded reassuringly at me. "I'll tell them Joe was the guy who saved me. You can go. We'll talk on the phone."

My eyes glistened with tears as I watched her, although she looked physically okay, I still thought I had a few more moments with her before we would say our goodbyes.

"Don't do that, Andriana, or else I'm going to kick you out!" She smiled.

"I thought we would spend all our time together this time around, but look what's happening."

She sighed. "We'll always have time to spend together, Andriana. Try to stay safe for now. That's all that matters."

I nodded, glancing at Alex, who was shifting his feet impatiently.

"I'll call you," I said, giving her a peck on the cheek.

She nodded. "Keep me updated, Andriana. love you."

I couldn't say anything after that. I just followed Alex quietly until we were inside the car.

"What's the problem?" I asked him, as he turned on the ignition.

"What do you mean?"

I shook my head. It was obvious he wasn't in a good mood, and he didn't feel like saying whatever was bothering him just yet.

We were both quiet for a long time, and just the noise from the road echoed through the night.

"There's an elderly couple, and Falcone claims to have killed their son when the couple was younger," he said, holding on tightly to the steering wheel, his gaze fixed on the road. I kept quiet, expecting him to say more, but when he didn't, I turned to him.

"Who is Falcone?" I asked.

"One of the mafia bosses."

"So why is he telling you this?"

He was silent again. Finally, he said, "Because this couple just moved into their million-dollar apartment. They just retired. They're holding a party to celebrate their success, and he wants me to kill them both."

I gasped, covering my mouth with my hands. "My lord! You're not going to do that, right?"

He glanced at me but didn't say anything.

"Say something. You don't do things like this, right?"

He laughed softly. "I'm not a saint, Andriana. You have the wrong impression of me. I've done way worse than that. This is small compared to what I've done."

Oh, lord, how did I get myself into all of this? I thought.

"So, what you're trying to tell me right now is that this is just a piece of cake, and that you're going to do it?"

"I should do it, and it'll be my last job before finally leaving all of this behind."

I scoffed. "And who told you that? Your last job is the last wicked thing you did, not the one you're about to do! If you do this, then you're not leaving anything behind, you're starting all over!"

He glanced at me with a flicker of confusion in his eyes. He looked like he had thought about this several times.

"Don't worry about me, Andriana."

I shook my head. "I will! You can't do this! You won't! Why do you even have to do this? There are a thousand other men they could use for this."

"I said *never mind*!" he shouted, his tone harsh.

I didn't care. If my words would make him rethink what he was about to do, then I would keep on talking. And if he was even thinking of killing that innocent couple, then he was a fucking monster. A heartless creature.

"What are you going to do? When are you supposed to do this?"

"Tonight."

"What do you want to do?" I pressed on, looking at him.

"I'll do whatever I like, Andriana. I'm not having this conversation with you anymore."

"Murderer," I muttered, hating him for even considering what those criminals told him to do.

"What did you say?" He turned to me, a frown on his face.

"I called you a murderer. Are you offended? Because that's what you are." I laughed shortly, feeling angrier with each passing second. "If you're considering killing those people, then even I'm not safe with you." I chuckled, feeling sorry for myself. "It's only a matter of time before they tell you to kill me, and you just point a bullet at me and *boom*!"

"Shut the fuck up, Andriana! Shut the fuck up!"

I crossed my arms stubbornly. "Drop me. I'm no longer safe with you."

He narrowed his eyes on me. "You're going nowhere. Sit your ass down, or you're not going to like what I'll do next."

"What's the worst a mafia criminal like you can do? Kill me?" I asked. I was way past caring at this point. I wanted nothing more to do with him and his mafia ties.

"You don't know what you're saying." A flicker of hurt crossed through his eyes, but it was gone as swiftly as it came.

"Please, Alex. I don't want to go anywhere with you again. Stop the car! I want to get out." I pulled on the door of the car, but it wasn't budging. "I don't want to stay with you anymore. I'm tired of all of this!"

I kept pulling the door, desperate to leave.

"Stop it, Andriana!" He brought the car to a halt. "I'm doing this for you! All of this! It's because of you. You won't last a day out there without me. Just—just stay calm!"

"Don't kill anyone for me, Alex. I would rather die than have you kill an innocent couple so I can live."

He started the car again, driving it at an even greater speed. "Alex!"

"It's obvious you have no idea how any of this works. I'll need you to keep quiet and do as I say from now on, or else you won't like the consequences."

I shifted in fear. "Where are you taking me?"

"Be quiet."

"Where are we going?" A sob escaped my lips.

He didn't even throw a glance at me.

After what felt like an eternity, he turned to me. "You'll have to stay here for tonight—no phone calls, no internet. Nothing! Just stay quiet till I'm back. If you do the opposite of what I say, then you're putting yourself in serious danger."

"Where's this place?" I looked around the dark neighborhood, fear enveloping me like a second skin. He brought the car to a stop and hurriedly got out to help me open my door. "Quick," he said, looking around carefully.

"Alex, what's going—"

"Come with me."

I watched him fearfully as he looked at the receptionist, a thousand emotions running through my mind. I looked at the exit, thinking of escaping, but the eerily silent neighborhood changed my mind. I would rather be cooped up in here than be out there all alone.

"Sarah, come with me," Alex said to me, watching me impatiently. The receptionist smiled at me when she caught my gaze.

"Your husband said you're sick, it's a little bit cold out here. It's best if you go up as soon as possible."

Mind your fucking business, bitch. I made a face at her.

Alex walked toward me and grabbed my hands gently, smiling at the receptionist.

"Have a good night," he said.

She nodded. "You too."

"Stay right here, Andriana!" Alex said as soon as he shut the door to the room. "I have to sort out a few things tonight, so don't go anywhere. I'll be back. You can go to bed if you don't see me in time." He rushed around the room, grabbing different items.

"You have a few things to sort out, or you have a few people to kill?"

He paused before turning to the door. "I'll go with the key. I checked around, and there's food and everything else you'll need in here before I'm back."

I shook my head as he walked out the door, feeling sick to my stomach. This was the life I was living now. How did I even get myself into this mess? An image of Jose crossed my mind, and I frowned, feeling renewed hate for him. "Thank God his restaurant got burned," I hissed. I felt bad immediately after I said that, so I burst into tears, hating myself and all that was happening right now.

"I should call Lila," I muttered, standing up to look for my phone. I didn't care about Alex and his threats. I would call whoever I wanted to call. I raised my jacket and checked both pockets. It wasn't there. I searched all around the room and frowned when an idea came to my mind. "Did Alex take my phone with him?" I yelled, feeling frustrated.

"That motherfucker!" I sank to the ground in anger. I wanted to yell out loud, but at the same time, I didn't want to draw attention to myself. I looked at the door. Maybe I should go out there. Yelling out in the dark, quiet street seemed a whole lot better. I was just about to rise to my feet when Alex's last words came to mind: *I'll go with the key.*

I sat back slowly. If there was anyone who was going to commit murder tonight, it would be me.

———

I was dozing off slowly where I sat when the door to the room was pushed open. I jumped to my feet, fear enveloping me. It was Alex, and he looked at me with pity when he saw me shivering in fear.

"Come here, mama," he muttered, opening his arms wide. I shook my head, taking several steps back.

"Stay away from me, Alex." I raised a warning finger at him.

He looked so tired that I wanted to get into his arms, but the thought of him killing that couple crossed my mind, and I took another step back.

"I didn't do it. Come here," he said, opening his arms wider, and I practically ran over to him, clinging to him. He held me tight, caressing my hair softly.

"You changed your mind," I said, smiling softly. "You did the right thing."

"We have to leave, mama." He pulled away from me, staring into my confused eyes. "Right now."

"To where? But I don't have my things with me."

He held my shoulders. "That's not necessary. We need to get out of here as soon as possible."

I nodded, noticing the urgency in his voice. "Okay."

He held my hand, leading me out the door. "We're getting out of here, mama. It's going to be a very long journey."

"Out of here? What do you mean?" I hesitated by the door, watching him uncertainly.

"We're leaving town."

"What? Do you want to leave all you've ever known just because of me? Do you want to leave it all behind? Who'll be running the company?"

He sighed, reaching for my hand. "There's someone in charge of that already. Let's go."

I shook my head. "It's not the same. Remember what Enzo did? You can't just leave like that. Stay back, and settle this with your people. Let me be the one to run away from all this."

He shook his head. "I can't leave you all alone, Andriana. I can't do that."

I held his hand, my eyes misty. I couldn't bear the thought of him leaving behind all he had worked for all these years so he could keep me safe. It would haunt me forever.

"Please, Alex, let me go. You can't leave everything behind... for me."

Shame flushed through his cheeks, a rare occurrence. "You ain't just everything, Andriana. You're the only thing that's ever felt right." He reached out, his hands hovering over me for a bit before his calloused fingers intertwined with mine.

His voice was low and gravelly as he continued. "From the moment I walked into that restaurant, it was like the whole damn world came into focus. You... you make me want things I never thought possible."

My eyes welled up. The gruff, intimidating Alex, feared by many, was laying bare his heart for me. I couldn't believe it. It was terrifying and exhilarating all at once.

"Alex," I whispered, my voice thick with emotion. "I never thought you could feel this way for me, or for anyone. It's almost unbelievable."

A sad smile played on his lips. "C'mon, let's get out of here."

He gently tugged me to the door. And as we hurried out of the hotel and to the car, a flicker of hope ignited in my chest. Maybe, just maybe, there was a future for us beyond the shadows of his world.

"But where will we go?" I asked him as he started the car, his face etched with worry. "Are they close?"

He didn't answer. The car sputtered, coughing on the wet road, and he swore under his breath. "This was all I could bribe from the mechanic on such short notice," he said, referring to the car. He pointed to the door. "Lock it. Stay down until I say."

A guttural roar ripped through the night as soon as I locked the car. Headlights cut through the dark, and a black heel barreled down the street. Alex didn't waste time as he threw the car into gear, tires spitting gravel as he lurched away from the hotel.

"Do you think it's the mafia, guys?" I shrieked, my voice barely audible over the screech of tires.

"I don't know," he snarled, his eyes fixed on the rearview mirror. The Jeep was gaining on us, its monstrous shadow growing larger with each passing second. I turned to Alex in fear, and his smile caught me off guard. How could he be smiling right now?

"Fasten your seatbelt, mama, and hold on tight!"

Oh, God, save me from death tonight and I'll never—

"Alex! Slow down!"

CHAPTER TWENTY: A NEW BATTLEFIELD

ALEX

T HE RUMBLE OF THE approaching muscle cars vibrated through the cracked asphalt, a tremor that mirrored the tremor in my hands. I gripped the steering wheel tighter, my knuckles white, my gaze fixed on the endless stretch of dusty highway ahead. Beside me, Andriana kept her eyes glued to the worn leather satchel in her lap, its contents far heavier than its size.

In the tense silence of the car, the only sound was the ragged rhythm of our breaths and the relentless growl of our pursuers.

"Slow down, Alex!" Andriana glanced at me for the umpteenth time, her face etched with worry. "You can't go this way. We're going to have an accident."

I glanced at her, trying to keep my attention fixed on the road. "It's okay. Just try to stay calm."

She nodded, shifting in fear as I turned sharply to the other side of the road. It seemed like Ferd and his guys were bent on getting her this time around, and I would do anything within my power to make sure that didn't happen.

"I don't think they're going to stop," she said, turning to me and rubbing her head softly. "We've been running for hours. They're not going to stop."

"Neither are we."

She was quiet for a while, but I could see her watching me in my peripheral vision.

"Thank you, Alex."

"It's okay."

She peered into the rearview mirror, her eyes opening wide in excitement. "They're slowing down! I think there's something wrong with their car."

I looked back, surprised to see the car had actually stopped a few meters behind. "Now, Andriana, I'm about to step on this accelerator, so hold tight."

She nodded. "Anything to get away from these bloodthirsty monsters."

I chuckled softly, the smile disappearing from my face as swiftly as it came when Andriana's high-pitched voice echoed through the car. "We gotta lose them, Alex. I can see a hotel over there!"

I didn't think going to the hotel at this moment was a good idea for us, but we were running really short on options. "I don't know. They'll definitely check in here."

"Alex?"

"Alright." I turned the car toward the little inn, and faced her when we pulled up to the front door. "The car is going to give us away."

She nodded, looking around frantically. "There!" she shouted, pointing to a gated house.

"What are you talking about, Andriana?" I glanced back worriedly. We didn't have much time before they would catch up to us.

"We could park the car in there," she said, starting to unfasten her seatbelt. "Wait here. Let me go in and talk to whoever is in there."

I turned off the ignition of the car, shaking my head slowly. "I'm not letting you go into some random stranger's house alone."

She frowned. "Alex, listen to me. My plan is going to work. Trust me," she said, looking back nervously. "They'll be here any moment, and we have to think of something really fast."

We were both getting out of the car now.

"Okay, so what's your plan?" I folded my hands once we got out of the car. She stretched her body lazily, whining in tiredness. "Oh my God, I can't believe I've been inside that car for over nine hours."

"Andriana?" I called impatiently, smoothing her hair. "What's your plan?"

She nodded. "I don't like to think of a plan in cases like this. It'll come once those gates are opened."

"You're doing no such thing." I frowned when I noticed she was already walking over to the gate. "Andriana!"

"Stay back, Mr. Mafia."

"Shh." I looked around worriedly, hoping none of the people passing by heard her. She chuckled. "Relax, and stay right there."

I couldn't do it for more than a few moments after she knocked on the gate, and I slowly made my way toward her.

"What the fuck are you doing here?" She frowned. "Go away, Alex. Someone's coming, and you'll jinx the plan."

"Think of another plan ASAP. They're not here yet."

"Oh my God, leave Alex! You being here will make this extremely difficult," she whispered.

"Who's there?" someone asked, approaching the gate.

Andriana narrowed her eyes on me. "Hello," she said.

I turned to her, shocked to find out she could use a voice as tiny as that.

The gate was pulled open, and an elderly man appeared by the gate, his face hard. "What do you want?" He glanced at me.

"I'm so sorry to disturb you, sir." She glanced at me, her face etched with worry. "But my brother here is really, really sick. He's been throwing up for more than a day now. He's so weak, he's limping now. He's all I have. I'm so tired and worried." A sob escaped her throat.

The man turned to me, searching my face uncertainly. "I don't know; he looks okay."

Andriana turned to me, cleaning tears off her face. "Ben, ask him for help. Or do you feel better now? Can you walk now? Do you have the strength?"

I shook my head, hating myself for what she was putting me through.

She turned to the man. "He can't even talk, and neither of us has had anything to eat for the past few days."

He shook his head, his eyes filled with compassion. I noticed the rosary on his chest and decided to try my luck. "I hope God has mercy on—on me. I'm so tired," I stuttered, looking down.

"Are you Christians?" His eyes lit up with joy when we both nodded.

"Why, come in! Come in!"

"Oh my goodness! Thank you very much, sir. May the good Lord bless you!" Andriana beamed with a smile.

He nodded. "There's no problem. It's what God expects from us."

"Can I park my car inside?" Andriana asked hopefully. This time around, we both turned back toward the road leading up to the main road.

"Of course, let me open this wider."

I didn't know if she could drive, so I tried catching her gaze, but she was hell-bent on doing things her way, and she didn't even look at me. Thankfully, it didn't take long before she drove the car into the house. We both sighed in relief when the man pulled the latch on the door.

"Come with me," he said to us as he walked inside the house. Andriana stretched out her hand to me. "Can you walk?"

I narrowed my eyes at her, and she smiled softly. "Here, let me give you a hand."

"No way. Don't be silly." I waved her off, and she glanced at the man walking ahead.

"Better not jinx this. Now give me your hand."

She held my hand, and I limped slowly as we walked in, earning a proud smile from her.

"We have visitors!" the man announced as soon as we got into the house. Andriana glanced at me. I looked toward the staircase, patting my pocket to ensure I still had my rifle with me in case of any foul play. Andriana noticed my movement and scooted closer to me.

"Visitors?" An elderly woman appeared on the other side of the room, a large smile on her face. "It's been so long since we've entertained anyone in this house. Hello there!" She walked over to Andriana, smiling softly at her.

"Come, let me show you your room. Who is the young man?"

"Her elder brother. He's sick and hungry. They need shelter and food."

"My goodness, come, come. Let me show you where you'll stay in the meantime."

"Thank you very much." Andriana smiled at her.

I nodded in her direction. "Thank you."

"Come," she said, starting to lead us to one of the doors in the living room. "I'm Martha, and that's my husband, Dan. Our son is upstairs. His name is David, but we all call him Dave." She laughed fondly.

"Here," she said, pulling the door open. "This is where you'll stay, girl."

Andriana turned to her. "What of Al—my brother?"

"There's another room he can stay in."

"Can't we stay together?" She peered in. "There are two beds in there. I'm so worried about him that I want to keep him in sight." She sniffed. "He's all I have."

Martha started to shake her head. "He's not well, and we have to treat him so he can get better." She glanced at me. "It looks like your sister wants you both to be together."

I smiled at her. "Can I just sit for a bit?"

She nodded. "I'm so sorry, of course. Let me get you something to eat and drink."

"Thank you."

Andriana faced me after she had left. "Now, what next?" she whispered.

"We stay here for a day or two, you know, to distract the mafia guys."

She nodded. "I'm so tired, I could sleep all day."

"You should. You've been so helpful."

She narrowed her eyes on me. "Why does that sound like you're making fun of me?"

"Huh?"

There was a loud bang on the gate just as Martha brought in a tray of food, and we both jumped to our feet. "Who in God's name is that?" she asked, looking around. "Dan just left the house, and we don't usually have people coming in here."

"The knock really startled me," Andriana explained to her when she kept looking at us like we were insane.

"Give me a minute, Dave!"

"Grab your bags," I said to Andriana as soon as Martha left the room. She stared longingly at the food on the table. "Andriana, get the backpack already. Let's find a way to leave."

She peered through the window. "No one has answered the door."

She grabbed a bag from a nearby table and emptied all of the contents of the tray inside it. "What do we do?"

"Let me check who's there," Martha said from outside the door. "Stay calm. I'm sure it's nothing serious."

I turned to Andriana immediately after she left. "Let's go."

"What if it's not them?" she asked hesitantly, waiting by the door.

"We can't take that chance. Come." I held her hand, leading her through the back door.

"How do you know we can go through this door?"

I shrugged. "Just my instinct."

The pounding on the gate grew louder and louder as we rushed out the door.

"Go out," I said to her, turning back toward the main entrance. "And wait for me here; don't come out for any reason."

She started to shake her head. "You must be joking. I'm not going anywhere without you, Alex."

"Go! I don't want them to find you here. I'll see what's going on. I don't want to put these people in danger."

"Alex, where will I go? I don't know this area." She looked around uneasily.

"What are you both talking about?" We both turned sharply to see a young boy of about twelve staring at us with amusement in his eyes.

"Uh," Andriana glanced at me. "Nothing."

"Are you trying to hide from someone? There's somewhere you can stay. I hide there when I want to be alone."

"Uh, I don't know." She looked from me to the boy.

"Go with him. We have limited time, and I can't hear anything from outside."

"Come!" The boy dashed up the stairs, turning back to see if she was coming with him.

"Hopefully I'm safe," Andriana muttered, running along with him.

The only reason I let this bullshit go on for this long was because of Andriana, and now that she wasn't with me I didn't care what happened to whoever was at that gate. They had to pay for the stress they had put us through.

"No!" I heard Martha's high-pitched scream and dashed to the door leading out. The mafia guys were all around the house. Martha and Dan were shaking fearfully by the corner. I recognized the three of them and as soon as they saw me, and they bowed in unison.

"What's the fuss about?"

"We need the girl. The boss's order," Anthony answered, watching me.

"You have only one boss, and you should listen to only him. I don't recall telling you to bring any girl."

"What's going on?" Martha asked, her voice quivering slightly.

"Keep quiet!" Anthony shouted, cocking his gun. "If that girl is not out in three minutes..." He pointed the gun at Martha. "She goes first."

"Please," she begged, looking down. "Please don't kill me."

"I said *quiet*!" He smashed her head with the back of his pistol, and she fell to the ground, groaning in pain.

"The girl, Alex." He turned to me.

"I will count to three, and if you remain present after the third count, rest assured, you will not be pleased with the ensuing events." He laughed shortly. "You can't kill your gang members because of a lady, Alex. Gang rule. You of all people should know that."

"You of all people should know not to disobey the boss, but here we are."

He narrowed his eyes on me. "You deliberately left the gang, Alex. No group can exist without a master. Everything that's going on now is all your fault."

"Leave."

He shook his head, nodding once at the others. I recognized that movement from my days in the mafia, and before the men took another step, I turned around, shooting straight at their legs. I had no intention of killing anyone, but if that's what I had to do to get everyone out of this situation, then so be it.

Anthony pointed his gun at me. "Drop your gun, right now!"

"Leave, Anthony. You already know I'm not in for all of this."

He shook his head. "No one disobeys the boss's order. Either you get out of the way, or I shoot. This is your last and final warning." His hands shook as he held on to the gun.

There was a reason Marcel found me worthy of being in charge of the gang before he died, and one of them was the fact that I never lost a fight. I fought with everything I had in me. And looking at Anthony right now, his hands shaking as he held on tightly to the gun, I knew how easy it was going to be for this to be over.

"Now!" Anthony said.

"If there's anyone dropping their guns, it won't be me," I replied.

"Let's go!" someone said to him. "We already know we can't do this. I'm losing a lot of blood!"

"Shut up," Anthony said.

I stared knowingly at him. "It's up to you to decide what you want now."

He groaned, rushing to the wounded men on the ground. He turned to me, his face blazing with anger. "We're not the only ones chasing after you. It's only a matter of time, Alex, and then it'll be like you were never here."

I nodded. "I'll be waiting."

"Coward! You're not even a true heir to the empire. Ferd is, and he is acting like a true master. You're nothing but a puppet."

His words meant nothing to me. The mafia had been my home for as long as I could remember. I would always be grateful for my family, but this was not the life I wanted, and there was nothing anyone could say to me to change that.

"They'll find her soon, and I would love to see what you'll do when you're overpowered."

I watched as he dragged the other men out of the gate, a smile on my face. "I'll be waiting."

Dan jumped to his feet after they left. "Who are you? Please leave! Look at the trouble you've caused us."

"Leave him, Dan," Martha stated as I helped her to her feet. "He saved my life."

"Bullshit. He brought this upon us. I want you to leave, right now!"

"Are you okay?" I asked Martha.

She nodded. "But you have to leave now. They promised to come back. We're in danger."

I nodded. "It's okay. We're leaving now." I had no intention of staying another day and putting Andriana in more danger.

"Are they gone?" Andriana's voice echoed through the air, and I turned back to see her running to us, the boy by her side.

"So you both knew about this? You deliberately decided to put us in danger?" Dan asked, glaring at her.

"Dan," Martha called softly, touching his hand softly. "It's okay."

"I'm so sorry. We didn't mean for any of this to happen. Were you hurt in any way?"

"Of course! What do you expect when you willingly invite the bad guys into our house?" He turned to his wife. "I wonder why she's acting all innocent now."

"Alex, what happened?" She opened her eyes in shock when she noticed the blood stains on the ground. "What the hell happened here? Where are they?"

"We need to talk," I said to her, turning around and walking inside the house.

"And where do you think you're going?" Dan asked, cornering me. "I've had enough of this. Please leave immediately."

"We're leaving. Please be patient." Andriana turned to him. "Look, I have my bags with me already."

"Why's everyone acting so weird?" Dave asked, looking from me to Andriana. "What's going on? And why are there blood stains on the floor?"

"Come here, baby." Martha threw one last glance at me before leading Dave toward the door. "Go inside. I'll be with you shortly."

He yanked his hands away from her. "I've told you to stop treating me like a child."

"What's the problem, Alex? Where are they, the rest of the men?"

"They left. We have to leave now."

She sighed, holding onto the bag in her hands. "I don't want to leave. I'm tired of running around. I thought this was our final destination."

"I thought so too, but now that we have to leave, please listen to me. It's not going to be easy, but I can guarantee your safety with me."

"Oh, Alex. What about your own safety? You're not even talking about yourself."

They knew who they wanted, and they weren't joking about it. One short encounter with them, and all of this would be over.

"Let's go."

I held her hand, they would be here any moment, and the earlier we left, the better.

CHAPTER TWENTY-ONE: STAND OR FALL

ANDRIANA

MARTHA AND HER HUSBAND would always be special to me. Even after they sent us out of their house, they were still some of the nicest people I'd met.

"Why are you smiling?" Alex glanced at me, walking down the narrow pathway leading to God knows where. This was the second day after leaving their house. There had been no place to sleep, no extra food to eat, and no water to drink. All of the extras I got from Martha were now finished.

"I thought of something."

Silence. I knew he wanted me to go on talking, but instead, I kept silent, following quietly behind him.

He glanced at me. "Are you talking or not?"

"Well, you didn't let me know if I could go ahead or not. I told you I couldn't tolerate your moods."

"Watch it! Don't step on that!" Alex pushed me suddenly, and I landed painfully on the ground.

"My back! Oh God!" I screamed, holding my legs.

"Did you step on it?" Alex asked, rushing over to me. "Let me see."

I slapped his hands away, frowning.

"Step on what?" I asked in irritation. He was so clueless.

"I'm so sorry. Come, let me help you up." He stretched his hands toward me, but I couldn't stand. My legs shook as I tried to stand.

"I can't. Let's just rest a while, Alex. I'm tired."

He nodded. "You should've told me before you got so weak," he said, scooting down and facing me. "How do you feel?"

"Weak, tired, and hungry."

He sighed, looking around. "I don't even know where this is or what sort of place it is. But I know we'll soon be out. Can you try to stand?" He stretched out his hands again.

"No." I dragged him down with me. "Here, sit. It's okay to rest."

"This is not the time for rest, mama. When that time comes, we'll both know. You're still in extreme danger."

I wanted to ask what happened with the mafia guys who came the other day, but a part of me still didn't want to know the entire story.

"So we're out of food, water, and everything!" he stated suddenly, looking down.

"I'm more concerned about the water," I answered.

"This must be a really small area. The fact that we haven't seen anyone else is a big concern."

I shrugged. "I'm actually happy I haven't seen anyone."

"Why? What exactly is your reason?" He folded his arms, leaning on a nearby tree.

"Because a lot of people are greedy and selfish, and it wouldn't take much before they exposed us to them."

He was quiet for a while. "Or people are extremely hungry and would do anything to provide a meal for them and their families."

"That's the wrong perspective. A greedy, selfish person is a greedy, selfish person. Nothing more, nothing less."

He smiled shortly, and I knew he was about to say something smart.

"What would you do if for the next three to five days, we don't see anyone—no food, water, or anything—and then some random strangers asks you if you've seen a random couple walking by?"

"Well, I have eyes. If I sense trouble or danger, I'm definitely keeping my eyes shut."

"Hmph."

"What?" I chuckled. "What's that about?"

"What I'm trying to say is that at such a time, whatever action that person takes doesn't make them a bad person. They just had to compromise for things to get better."

"I don't agree with you, but that's a topic for another day. What can we eat, Alex? I'm famished. My stomach hurts so bad."

He dipped his hands into his pocket and handed me a chocolate bar. "Manage with this for now while we think of a solution."

"Thank you!" I wasn't expecting anything from him, so I opened the bar happily, my mouth watering at the sight of it.

"I'd save some if I were you," he muttered, rising to his feet.

"Okay, relax, macho man. We just sat down. Where are you going again?"

"I told you we can't stay here longer than necessary, so can you try to get up?"

"No."

He shook his head, moving toward me. "You're real trouble." He lifted me up and flung me across his shoulder, walking briskly down the pathway.

"I feel so nasty and dirty. I wish I could have my bath," I whined, taking a bite of the chocolate and leaning my head softly against his back.

"Wishes do come true sometimes."

I nodded. "If only I was one of the lucky ones."

"Well, maybe you are."

He dropped me gently on the ground, and my eyes opened in surprise. "What?"

We were both facing a really clean pond. I looked at him in disbelief. "Oh my goodness! Finally! Thank God."

I didn't care that he was by my side. I yanked my top off and did the same with my trousers, ignoring the way his gaze traveled around my body.

"Stay near the edge here. We don't know how deep this is."

I nodded, walking happily to the water to clean up. This meant there was still a chance we were going to get out of here alive and well.

"You thought we were going to die here?" he asked with a smile. I ignored him, my gaze meeting his as he eased off his shorts and entered the water.

"Oh, this feels so relaxing," he muttered, washing his face with water.

"Oh yeah?" I touched his chest softly, and his eyes popped open.

"What are you doing?" His voice sounded hoarse, but he didn't move away from me. I kissed his chest slowly, earning a suppressed grunt from him.

"Andriana, we don't have the—fuck it, mama!"

Action speaks louder than words. I smiled to myself as he held a handful of my hair to help me get the full length of his dick. I had never been more aroused. I had no idea if it was because I was doing this in a not-so-private area or because of the stifled groans Alex was making, but either way, I realized I was more likely to come from the sheer carelessness of the whole thing than the man being touched.

"Mama." He tried pulling me away from him when he was about to come, but I wasn't budging. I wanted to feel all of him inside me, to taste him, to own him.

"I'm going to come, mama."

I nodded. "Go on. I'm all yours." Those words hadn't fully left my mouth when he erupted with a force I had never seen before. I was still battling with the euphoria of it all when he grabbed me by my waist and pulled me against himself, positioning his organ at my entrance.

"What are you waiting for? Fuck me already." I breathed, waiting to feel his full length inside me. My heart was pounding dangerously in my chest. Anyone could choose this moment to pass by and see us fucking each other.

"Alex?" I called impatiently, turning around to see what was taking so long.

He captured my breast in his mouth the moment I turned around, as if he had been waiting for that moment. I threw my head back in pleasure, a moan escaping my throat. I would give myself away to only one mafia guy—the one sucking on my breast like there was no tomorrow.

Suddenly, I heard the high-pitched voices of children approaching. We both froze before moving into action, running out of the water to get our clothes. Who were those goddamned kids? I looked around in irritation, wondering where we heard their voices from.

"Maybe it was just our imagination," I muttered, trying to hide my disappointment.

"I highly doubt that. I heard them clearly. Oh! There!" He pointed to the left of the bush. "There they are! Come with me." He stretched out his hand to me, but I shook my head. "I'm fine."

"We need to hurry. They'll lead us out of here. I'm starting to think we've actually been going around in circles all this time."

I shrugged, trying to catch up with him as he practically ran toward them.

"I think it's best we just wait till they've gone a little bit farther, then we start to trail them. What if they get startled?"

He laughed shortly. "Have you seen me around kids?"

"Then why don't you want one if you really love them so much." I regretted my statement the moment it came out of my mouth.

"And who says I don't?"

I looked away, embarrassment burning my face. "That was totally unnecessary. I'm sorry."

He glanced at me. "There's nothing to be sorry about."

By this time, we had started walking slowly behind the kids as they all walked out.

"You're just curious," he continued.

He didn't answer my question, but that was okay. I had overstepped my boundaries by asking that question in the first place.

"There!" he said. "I think that's where we've been making the mistake! Instead of turning right, we've been turning in the other direction."

I nodded my head in affirmation, the both of us increasing our pace to find out what was at the other end. By the time we stepped out of the bushes, my mouth was wide open as I looked around. We were standing atop a mountain with various small houses surrounding us.

"Wow," I muttered. "What do we do?"

He held my hand. "Come with me."

We walked around the houses, neither of us saying anything.

"What if we find somewhere among these houses to stay? Would you like it?"

I beamed at him, imagining how private it would be and how hot the sex would be. "Totally."

He narrowed his eyes at me. "I didn't realize you were so easygoing."

"Is that a compliment?"

He scoffed before walking briskly over to a man standing by the door. "Good day, sir."

The man looked up at him, his face uncertain. "Hello."

"Me and my wife need a place to stay. It's our honeymoon. We chose this place because of the ambiance."

His face transformed into a beautiful smile. "Wow, of course. There are a few more places around here. Hold on. Let me inform my wife."

We both glanced at each other after he walked away. "I hope there's space. I'm so tired. I need to sleep," I said.

He nodded. "I'll do everything within my power to make sure you have a good sleep tonight."

"Aw, Alex."

"Okay, let's go. Sorry for the delay." The man rushed out of the room, throwing an apologetic smile at us.

Just take us there, man, I thought.

He ended up showing us only one apartment, and it was far away from the rest of the other houses.

"Are you deliberately keeping us far away from the rest of the neighborhood?" Alex asked.

He laughed shortly. "This is what we have available, but it seems like you don't like it."

I watched as they talked about the apartment, eager to go inside and just relax. It had been almost a week of running around from these mafia guys, and we both deserved to rest. I wondered how Lila was doing, if she had gone back, or if she was even okay. I wanted to talk to her so bad, but we didn't even have our phones with us.

I was still waiting when I was reminded of Enzo. I shook my head, getting pissed.

That is none of your business, Andriana. You tried your best already, I tried to tell myself.

"Poor Enzo," I muttered to myself.

"What did you say?" Alex asked, standing right next to me.

"Nothing. Just thinking."

He wiggled the key in front of me, and we both chuckled.

"I can't wait to go in and sleep," I said.

He turned to me. "Reduce your expectations, mama. This is just a small village house."

I rolled my eyes. "Open the door, Alex. I wasn't expecting a mansion."

The moment the door clicked open, I dashed in, looking around to see if it was something we could manage, but then I heard loud explosions coming from outside.

"Alex." I turned to him, my heart pounding with fear. The mafia guys were here again. Was I ever going to have a single peaceful life to myself?

"Stay quiet. I don't think—"

Another explosion sounded through the air, and he faced me, looking around our small room.

"It's over. They're finally going to take me away."

He narrowed his eyes at me. "Wait here. I'll be right back."

I held his hand as he turned to leave. "Please don't go. I'm scared. Is this the final destination for the both of us?"

He sighed, holding my shoulder gently. "You'll be fine. I'm still promising you that. As long as I'm alive, then no harm from any of these guys is going to come your way."

I nodded, feeling a lot more confident. I was safe with him. He had made it clear time and time again. "Okay."

"So just wait right here. Trust me. Okay?"

I nodded, my heart resuming its frantic pace as he walked out the door.

The silence that followed was the most intense I'd ever heard. It was like all the activities, noises, and everything going on out there suddenly came to a halt the moment Alex stepped out.

I paced around the room for several minutes after that, still wondering why everything was suddenly quiet. Minutes turned into hours, and I became extremely restless. Something was wrong, I could feel it. I tried peering out the window several times, but it was no use. It just looked like a normal day outside.

Had he been shot? I looked at the door fearfully. Maybe they were waiting for me to go out? Of course, it would be fun for them to finally catch the rat that had been running around their trap for all these months.

I was so nervous that my body started to shake. I tried to stay still to calm my nerves, but nothing was working. It was at times like this that I wished I could talk to Lila. My eyes watered at the thought of her.

The door was pulled open before I could dwell fully on that, and Alex walked back into the apartment, his face hard. I remained where I was, unsure of what to do or say; I couldn't really tell his mood.

"Get some rest Andriana. It's been a really long week. You need to relax. Have your bath, eat, and sleep. I've discussed food with some people. They'll be here in a few minutes. So try to get some rest."

I nodded. He was talking to me, but he had his attention on other things, like the clothes he was currently folding into the bag. I wanted to ask him many questions, but from the way he set his face, I knew it wasn't the right time. Whatever they had discussed out there had been very different from the conversations they had been having before.

"You can't keep running forever. That's not the life I want for you." He said to me several hours later as I lay down on the bed to sleep.

"Uh?" I turned sharply toward him. "What are you talking about, Alex?"

"It's not reasonable. I need you safe and free, out there, living the life you've always wanted and not running around some goddamned places like this. No, it's not worth it."

I was quiet for a while, trying to decipher what he was talking about. It could mean so many things, so I needed to take my time to really understand what he was saying. "What exactly is your plan now?"

He turned to me, his facial expression still the same as it was the moment he walked in several hours back. "I'm setting you free."

CHAPTER TWENTY-TWO: HEARTBREAK AND REVELATIONS

ALEX

ANDRIANA REFUSED TO SAY anything further after my statement about our whole situation yesterday. I wanted to make her understand my reasons for saying it, but she was purposely ignoring me, so I just decided to leave her. It was the best decision I could make. I had to leave her life for her to ever have a chance at living a happy, normal life.

"Your breakfast is ready, Alex. Would you like to eat now?" She crossed her arms, looking everywhere but at me.

"Yes, please. I'll come get it now."

"Great." She nodded once and turned to leave when I grabbed her arms, turning her to me. "What's the problem, mama?"

She tried to wriggle her way out of my hands. "Leave me alone, Alex. I don't want to talk to you."

"Why?"

She narrowed her eyes on me. "Why? When you know the reason why, maybe then we can have this conversation, but for now, just let me be." She was saying one thing, but her hands were doing something else entirely. I noticed she was holding on to me now.

"Talk to me. Why are you pissed?"

She looked straight ahead, out of the window and into the silent street. "Never mind," she said. "In fact, stop asking me that question. Think about what you said, and then you'll know if I should feel a certain way or not. Now is not the time to ask me what the problem is. Think about all of this and what you said to me."

She eased off my body and walked away from me. "Maybe we should be apart," she muttered, sitting on the edge of the bed and looking out the window. I pretended not to have heard her, but her statement disturbed me all day.

When it was almost dark, she turned to me, a concerned expression on her face. "Why are we still here, even after the mafia guys caught us? Aren't we supposed to be on the run?"

I sighed. "I already told you, Andriana, I don't want that life for you anymore. I want you safe and well. You know, walking around the street freely without the fear of being followed or harassed. We can't have that if I keep running around with you and hiding you from them."

She watched me with the same expression on her face.

"I can't do that to you," I continued. "So that's it."

"For us to still be here, almost twenty-four hours after the mafia guys were here, something must've happened. Don't leave me in the dark here, Alex. What was your conclusion?"

It was best if she just faced our present situation now and did not worry about the conversation I had with the mafia guys. "You shouldn't worry about that."

"So what should I do? Stick around till you're ready to leave? If you're not telling me anything, what do you want me to do?"

"Just be patient, Andriana. I'm thinking of something."

She scoffed. "You're trying to enjoy your last days with me, and then after that, you make up your mind like the mafia boss you are and then disappear to keep me safe, right?"

We both glared at each other, her chest rising and falling as she watched me.

"That's so wrong."

She shook her head. "Are you leaving me or not? I need to know now so I can plan my life accordingly."

"This is not the time for this kind of question, Andriana."

"Am I safe from the mafia guys now? Can I walk around here freely? Is that why we're still here?"

"Andriana—"

"Just answer me, Alex, and stop beating around the bush. I'm asking you a simple question. I just expect a yes or no response. Am I free to go around?"

If I said no, then she would start questioning why we were still here. If I said yes, that was going to be another conversation entirely.

"Yes, you're free."

She nodded slowly. "Then I was right all along. You were waiting for the perfect time to discard me." She stood angrily. "I'll leave since that's what you want. I'm a free lady now, right? Thank you."

I stopped her when she got to the door, blocking her way out. "Where are you going?"

She was quiet for a while. "On a stroll. Alex, what the hell is wrong with you? Get out of the way, you've made your decision, stop making me feel stupid."

I made my decision, but that didn't mean it was an easy one to make. I had grown to like her so much, and leaving to keep her safe was a very touchy decision I knew I had to make, even though I didn't want to. "Come here." I pulled her toward me, but she didn't budge. "Mama,"

"Please, can you let me leave? I need to be alone. I need fresh air."

I had no idea what her plan was. She could be planning to leave, and it wasn't safe for her. We had come a long way. "Okay, let me grab my jacket. I'll be with you shortly."

"Alone." She met my gaze. "Stay away from me, Alex."

I held her hands, but she yanked them away from me. "Just leave me alone!" She sniffed, tears welling up in her eyes. "I just need to be alone."

"Okay," I said, opening the door for her. "Be careful."

She shot me a glare, cleaning tears off her face as she dashed out the door. It took every ounce of courage I had not to run after her and just bring her back in, but I had to let her do what she wanted.

"Good evening, uncle!" I heard someone say and turned around to see a young boy walking past me. Andriana was running down the street.

"Hey man, come here."

He glanced at me but kept on moving.

"Hey, you!"

The kid froze. "Please don't hurt me. I'm so sorry."

I knew word had spread after what happened yesterday, and I sighed. "No one's going to hurt you. You see that girl?" I pointed toward Andriana, who was walking at a faster pace now.

"Follow her," I told the boy. "Let me know where she stops when she finally stops walking."

He nodded. "And if she goes far?" he asked. "How do I quickly find a way to tell you?"

"That's very smart. You can send any of your friends to me."

He nodded. "Okay, she's almost out of sight. I'll go now."

I watched him leave, my mind filled with different thoughts. Nothing was making sense. Andriana wasn't safe going around with me, and I didn't want any harm to come her way. This was a really hard decision to make.

I was still in that same spot almost an hour later when I saw a young boy running toward me.

"Some men have her with them! My friend told me to tell you this!" he panted, trying to catch his breath.

I eased off the porch. "Okay, try to calm down. Take a deep breath."

He nodded. "They're currently at—" He paused. "Just down this road. That's where they are."

I nodded. "Thank you."

I dashed down the street, looking around to see if they had changed directions. I stopped a few meters away from them when I saw some men standing in front of her, talking with her. What could they be talking about?

They hadn't seen me, so I used the chance to get closer to them, trying to figure out what they were talking about.

"Leave! I've had enough of this. I have no interest whatsoever in what you're saying."

"We're asking you to leave politely. It's for the best. The boss can't settle with you. It's totally against our rules, and it's not wise for you to be running around your whole life."

"Don't demand anything from me. I've told you. Just leave."

"We've given you more than enough chances, Andriana, and the only reason you're still alive is because of the boss. It's only a few moments before you're eliminated."

"Remember all we told you. That'll be all for now."

She fell to the ground as they walked away from her, tears streaming down her cheeks. "This is so fucked up, man."

I came out of where I was and sat close to her, but she didn't even look up. I pulled her into my arms, hugging her as tightly as I could, and she cried like never before, holding on tightly to me as she wept.

"It's okay, mama, you're fine. Everything's fine."

She cleaned her eyes. "No, Alex. Everything is not fine, everything just got worse. We can't be together anymore, and new things are coming up every day."

"What are you talking about? What did those guys tell you?"

She shook her head. "Nothing, it's not something you should worry about." She met my gaze, daring me to ask anything else.

We remained that way for a long time. Neither of us spoke, and when I glanced at her and saw how stressed she looked, I knew it was my duty to make a decision.

"Here, you can have your phone." She looked up at me. "Thank you, there's something very important I need to do now."

"And what's that?"

She shook her head. "I need to confirm if it's true or not. I won't believe anything they say until I've confirmed this myself."

"What did they tell you, Andriana?"

She folded her arms. "Those were the guys from your gang. I'm sure you know. They're saying something I need to be sure of. He mentioned my father's and mother's names."

"He did?" I narrowed my eyes on her. It was possible to be extremely stressed and start acting weird. "Let's go back, Andriana. I think you need to rest."

She shook her head. "I'm good, there's nothing wrong with me."

I nodded slowly. "Okay."

"I wish my laptop was here. This will take longer to get with my phone, but I'll have to work with what I have. And, Alex..." She glared at me. "It's okay if you think I'm acting really weird right now, so just be patient with me. I need to figure this out as soon as possible."

My phone started to ring, and I excused myself to go to a quiet place. It was Enzo.

"Do you feel better now?" I asked him the moment I heard his voice. He was the last person I wanted to talk to right now. I still felt the same way I did the first day all of this was exposed.

"The doctor told me all that happened, and I'm very grateful."

"Of course, is there any other thing you would like to say?"

He was quiet for a while. "How's Andriana?"

"What do you want, Enzo? If you don't have anything to say, I'll end this call right now."

"I'm really so—"

I ended the call before he could say anything else. Only someone who was loyal to a fault would stick around with their bosses in our business. It was difficult, but it happened all the time. Enzo should've thought about all of that before he got himself involved with my rivals.

Andriana's little gasp caught my attention, and I turned to her. "Alex!"

"What's the problem?" I walked over, taking a seat beside her.

"You really need to relax your body and mind. I think we should go for a swim. You know, relax and blow off some steam."

"I think I need that really badly right now."

"Well, it's entirely possible."

She had a surprised expression on her face as she spoke. "Alex, my parents were mafia members. I can't believe this."

"Now how do you know that?" I crossed my arms, gazing at her.

"I did my research. Your gang members came here threatening and saying all sorts of things. Then they somehow expected me to understand how things were run in the mafia. I clearly told them I didn't, obviously, but they didn't believe me. So I had to check, and I just found out that my parents were active mafia members."

She went on, an amused expression on her face. "I also told my friend to do some findings for me, and that she should find out as much about them as she can."

"And what did she say?"

"Exactly the same thing I just said. She also said they were killed by a rival group because my father was almost made the don."

I scooted closer to her, trying to take in all that she was saying.

"If your father was almost made the don, mama, you should have a whole lot of properties and money now. There are some things that should've been given to you. How come you were left with nothing?"

She rolled her eyes. "Because I was a little kid in an unknown location. I couldn't talk. So I was taken to the state."

I held her hands. "How do you feel, Andriana? This is a lot for one person to find out all at once."

She chuckled. "Then you don't know me. Nothing is too much for Andriana Rodriguez to handle."

She was coming back to her usual self, and I was beyond ecstatic. I knew the last couple of days had been rough for us both, but this was the lady I needed now more than ever. She smiled at me.

"Why do you have that expression on your face?" she asked, jabbing my arms softly.

"Nothing, how about our swim?"

"I need it right now, urgently." She laughed softly. "That's the break I never knew I needed."

I looked at her, contemplating whether or not to let her know Enzo called, but I knew it would make her feel much better, which was what I needed now.

"Enzo called earlier."

She turned sharply toward me.

"Is everything okay?" she asked.

I nodded.

She frowned. "Then why did you sound that way?"

"How should I have sounded? Excited?"

She shrugged. "Learn to forgive, Alex. No one is perfect. Neither are you. We all make mistakes."

"That's not a mistake. It was a deliberate act, Andriana, or are you saying you can also betray me for a small amount of money?"

"What?" She shook her head. "Of course not! Unless it's a large amount of money, why should I betray you for a small sum of money?"

I narrowed my eyes at her, and she burst into laughter, trying to hold my hand as I got to my feet.

"No wonder you like each other," I said. "You're the same."

"No, I'm not." She chuckled. "I just don't want you to have any hate in your heart. It's difficult, but it's possible."

"Hmph. Until it happens to you."

"Is there anybody who hasn't been betrayed?" She glanced at me. "I've been betrayed before by my parents. They died and left me all alone as a baby. That was the first betrayal."

"That wasn't intentional. Don't be silly. That's not betrayal. Betrayal is something deliberate and intentional."

"They died together as lovers. That was deliberate."

I shook my head and she grinned. "Don't mind me. I've been reading too many romance books."

I told the mafia guys to give me a day to think of a way to let go of Andriana, but right now, staring into her face as she laughed, I knew I wasn't going to do that. I couldn't let her go.

A beep on my phone caught my attention, and I raised it to see who it was.

The message read, "Your time is over, Alex. Stop making this hard for us. The next time we're seeing that girl, we're shooting on sight. And this isn't going to be on us. We've given you more than enough time, more than we've given to anyone before, because of who you are to us."

CHAPTER TWENTY-THREE: A UNITED FRONT

ANDRIANA

A LEX CHANGED HIS MIND about us staying in the house that evening, which I found amusing because several hours before, he had promised us both safety and security in the same house. Now we were inside a cab heading somewhere we had no idea about.

"If I decide that we travel out of the country in the meantime, they'll track us and get us. So it's making all this a lot harder for me. We can't keep running around like some crazy couple. But at the same time, I can't act all macho because they won't hesitate to take you down."

I watched him as he spoke, different emotions running through my mind.

"It's a really tricky situation, and we have to plan very carefully and strategically," he continued.

I nodded, dialing Lila's number. He glanced at me.

"What are you doing, mama?"

I shrugged. "Trying to reach my friend."

He grabbed the phone from me. "You're not even listening to me. You can't use phones for now, and neither can I."

"But you gave it to me yesterday. I haven't been able to reach her in a long time. I don't even know how she's faring now with all that happened."

"You should've called her yesterday. It's too dangerous for now. By the way, she's doing great."

I narrowed my eyes at him. "And how do you know that?"

He shrugged. "I have my ways."

I nodded softly. "Okay."

"Don't worry. Sooner than expected, you'll be able to call anyone anytime you want, after all of this has been settled."

I nodded. "I'll need a laptop, Alex, with a different SIM and identity. Do you understand?" I lowered my voice so the driver wouldn't hear our conversation.

He leaned closer to me. "Why?"

"The same way they're tracking us is the same way we're going to track them!"

I grinned at him. "Two can play at that game, Alex."

He watched me, trying to hide the smile that was starting to form on his face.

I patted his shoulder gently. "It's okay, Mr. Mafia," I whispered into his ear. "You can smile. You have a genius with you."

He rolled his eyes. "A genius who has been sleeping this whole time."

I chuckled. "She's awake now."

"Remain in the car when we get to where we're going. I'll still be looking around, so just wait here for me."

I nodded. "Roger that, captain."

A few minutes later, he asked the driver to stop. "Is there a problem?" the driver asked, turning around to look at us.

"Just give me a few minutes. I'll need to get something in there." He pointed to a small building across the street.

"I'll wait for you," I said to him as he got out of the car.

He nodded his head. "And behave yourself while you wait."

"Just leave." I waved him off and turned around to see the cab driver watching me.

"Is he your older brother?"

I ignored his comment. "You should mind your business, man." I watched him.

"Your boss?"

I narrowed my eyes at him. "Please, I don't like small talk."

"Then what do you want me to say while we're both inside the car doing absolutely nothing? You should've gone in with your husband then. Or he's not?"

I decided to ignore him after that. It would help us both.

He started to complain after a few minutes when Alex still hadn't gotten back. "Where is he? I can't wait all day for the both of you. I have a lot of other things to do."

"Relax. He'll soon be here," I said to him, looking at old images of me and Lila on my phone. "Go in and let him know I'm in a rush, or I'll leave."

"What? I'm not going in." I turned to him, shaking my head disapprovingly.

He started the car, holding my gaze to let me know he was serious.

"What the hell are you doing? You can't leave yet!"

"Watch me," he muttered.

I looked around frantically. Alex had told me not to get out of the car for reasons known only to him, and this crazy driver was making it really hard for me.

"Alright, we'll tip you really well." I smiled at him, earning a glare in return.

"Keep it and use it to take care of your hair or something."

My hands automatically went to my hair, and I couldn't help the anger I felt as I turned toward him.

"You're a really shitty man. You have no idea how your words make others feel. You just talk without thinking."

"I don't care."

"You should."

"Get out of my car. I won't repeat this again."

"No! I won't."

He got out of the car and dashed over to my door, trying to pull it open. I pushed the central lock once he got out of the car and faced him. Now I could have some peace.

He banged on the door angrily, his face blazing with anger. "Open up! You silly bitch!"

I turned to the other side of the street to see if Alex was coming out and sighed in relief when I saw him rushing over to the car, a worried expression on his face. I didn't open it until he knocked on my window.

"What's going on, mama?" he asked, getting into the car. The driver pulled the door open angrily and turned to me, pointing his hand at me. "You silly bitch!"

Alex grabbed his hand and twisted it back. He winced in pain, trying to get away from Alex's firm grip.

"What made you think you could do that while I'm here?"

"And who the hell do you think you are?" he asked.

Alex pressed down on his hands again.

"Stop! Stop!" the man yelled.

I patted Alex's arms softly, my heart beating crazily in my chest, and he released him.

"Now, drive this motherfucker out of here!"

The driver turned around to start the car, his hands shaking as he tried to fix the key in the ignition.

"Go on," Alex said to him, facing me. It was times like these that I was reminded he was a mafia boss. "I have everything with me."

"You did everything I mentioned?" I asked.

"Yes, everything is ready."

"Give it to me then, and I'll start working ASAP."

He handed me the bag in which everything was placed, and I brought them out, my eyes opening in shock when I noticed he bought the latest model of the laptop I needed.

"How did you pay for this?"

The driver glanced at us through the rearview mirror. He probably thought we were thieves. "I paid for it."

"I thought you didn't want us to pay for or do anything with our credit cards."

He shrugged. "There was nothing I could do. They don't take cash."

"So that would mean we're currently being tracked. They'll track you to that place."

He nodded. "Go on with what you're doing, and don't bother yourself about that."

"Of course." I started to transfer all the apps I needed from my phone to my laptop. "I'll need their phone numbers and every one of their personal information," I said to him, and he nodded.

"I'll send it now."

"Great."

I contacted Camilla, letting her know I would need her assistance with a few things. It was easier and faster for her to get out some of the information because of where she worked.

"One of them is close to us." I peeped into the screen so I could get a clearer view. "Anthony. I think the moment he got information about your whereabouts, he started his search immediately."

"That fool," Alex muttered, shaking his head.

"We'll need to change drivers, Alex," I said, packing all our things inside the bag.

"Stop the fucking car!" Alex barked at the driver, throwing a glare at him.

The man brought the car to a halt without glancing back, and we both got out.

"Leave."

I turned to Alex and said, "We haven't paid him yet."

He shrugged. "He should've thought about that before he started acting like a lunatic." He turned to the man who was hesitating by the corner. "I said leave!"

I watched in amusement as the man drove away. This was one of the perks of being in the mafia.

"My friend booked us a hotel around here," I said to him, looking around to see if I could see the name.

"Your friend? Lila? She's too close to you to be helping with something like that. We'll get tracked."

"No, not Lila. I know about all of that, and I won't do anything that'll put us in harm's way."

He nodded. "Alright."

"There, that's it!" I pointed to a tall building right ahead of us, and I wondered how I missed it in the first place.

"You paid for this place?"

I laughed as we made our way in. "No way. She did. But I promised we would send her back every penny she spent once we're out of this."

He nodded, looking around with an impressed expression.

"She paid for our first day here, though."

"That's very kind of her."

"Hello," I smiled at the receptionist. I then showed her the receipts and transactions for all our payments.

She smiled at me. "Welcome back, ma'am. Here's your card."

"Welcome back?" Alex asked as we made our way to the elevator.

I nodded. "She told me she uses this place a lot. So the lady probably saw it on the computer. Let's get in before Anthony comes."

He shrugged. "Let's go."

The hotel rooms were as exquisite as she described them on the phone, and I sighed in contentment. We could remain here for the next couple of days, recuperating from our past weeks of being on the road and struggling for survival. I frowned when I remembered what the cab guy said about my hair earlier. I hadn't had much time to look in the mirror, and now I was too scared to even take a glance at myself.

"Why do you have that look on your face?"

"My hair."

"What's wrong with it?" His gaze scanned my face.

"Hm?"

"The cab guy said it didn't look good. It's been on my mind."

He laughed. "What did that unserious guy say?" He shook his head. "You should eat and rest, Andriana. You should actually relax; they have a pool here and a game room. Just relax."

I smiled at him. "Order us something to eat while I take my bath, please."

"Of course."

After we had both eaten and settled down, I heard a beep on the laptop. "Okay, so here's the thing." I glanced at Alex. "Drew sent a message to Anthony informing him that he's staying at The Tulip Hotel for the night. His room number is eighty-six."

"I need to reach out to someone," Alex responded.

I watched him. "You can chat with the person through this laptop. Let the person know what's up."

He nodded as I pushed the laptop over to him.

Sooner than expected, Alex's men were heading down to the hotel room. He smiled proudly at me. "They'll just abduct him and keep him away, for now, no punishment. They're just acting based on instructions."

I nodded. "That's fine."

He faced me. "Any other updates?"

"Uh, let me check. Yes!" I grinned. "They're almost there. There have been no further messages between Anthony and Drew, but there's a text that just arrived from Ferd to Anthony."

He leaned against the bed, picking up the remote. "What does it say?"

I read through it quickly, my heart pounding in my chest. This sounded like it was sent from the main boss.

"What does it say, Andriana?"

"Kill him the moment you set eyes on him. Enough of the games. End this once and for all." I said to him without looking at him.

"And what was the response?"

"No response yet."

He chuckled. "It's a really tricky one for Anthony."

"Why?" I faced him, eager to know everything I could about this gang since my parents were also active members of the group before their death.

"It's a crime to kill a mafia leader in our gang. Different gangs have different rules. If someone is found guilty of that, their entire family and friends will be wiped out immediately."

"So what's tricky about it?" I made a face at him. "Because of his family and friends?"

He shook his head. "Anthony is a lone ranger, and he has no ties with anyone. Only the gang members."

"That makes this very easy, Alex. What the hell?" I pushed the tray of food away from me, suddenly losing my appetite.

"It's tricky because I'm the boss Andriana, the one Marcel put in charge before his death."

"And who is Ferd?"

"Marcel's biological son. He's automatically supposed to be the one in charge. That's the law, but Marcel broke the law and announced me as don shortly before his death."

"Oh."

"The majority of the mafia gangs weren't in support of this and decided not to listen to my orders, so we had a division. Half of the group is listening to Ferd, and the other half is listening to me. That's where this whole thing started."

"Wow. So then you decided to leave because Ferd was getting in your way."

He shook his head. "I decided to leave because two masters can't coexist. We both wanted different things. Ferd wanted violence, and he didn't care who died in the way of getting what he wanted. I did. Every life matters to me, except that of a wicked person, one that has refused to change."

"Oh, I can now see why you said it's tricky. You are both leaders. It won't be an easy choice, and if he's found guilty, he'll be killed."

"Exactly."

"Wow." A beep from my laptop caught my attention again, and I leaned into the screen to get a clearer look. "Guess who's in the building, Alex?"

"Anthony?"

I nodded. "Yep."

He reached for our gun and grabbed his jacket.

"Where are you going?"

"To meet him halfway."

I chuckled. "He doesn't know we're here, Alex. He's probably here to see someone. We're using all of my friend's details and a random person's SIM."

"Oh." He paused halfway. "Any new update?"

"There's actually a message. He just sent a message to someone. A lady, I presume."

"Why?"

"I have a surprise for you. It's at your door. That's what the message says." I met his gaze, but the look he was giving me made me feel stupid.

"What?"

"He's literally delivering a package to someone, or he killed a person's loved one and is delivering the body to them. It could be any of those things. Love is the last thing on Anthony's mind. Don't be silly."

I peered into the screen. "Oh! Your men have gotten Drew. They're on their way to the warehouse."

"Great! We keep taking them down one by one until I think of a better way to handle this."

"And..." I drawled. A smile played on my lips. "Anthony's lover has replied. She said she's waiting for him in his favorite underwear. Ah!"

"That's a lie."

I turned the screen toward him. "Look at that."

His face transformed into a bright smile. "Check everything you can about her, Andriana, ASAP."

I nodded. "I'm working on that already. He just sent her another text. He said, 'Delete this immediately.'"

"Now that is a discovery."

"Why do you want me to look into the lady's profile? She's innocent in all of this. Just like me." I crossed my arms, thinking of what I was about to do.

"It's not to harm her. Just do as I say," he said, throwing an impatient look at me.

"Promise you won't put her in the way of danger?"

He nodded. "You have my word."

"Something is wrong, Alex," I said, gazing into the computer screen just as Camilla's chat came in.

"What's the problem?"

"They're all coming into this hotel. There's something fishy going on."

CHAPTER TWENTY-FOUR: THE PRICE OF LOVE

ALEX

"WE CAN'T DO THAT, Alex. We're impersonating Camilla. We can't put her in danger!"

I had had enough of all their drama. The earlier I took charge, the better it was for us all. Taking down two or three of the gang members would let them know I still had it in me.

"You can't, Alex," she continued. "You need to be patient right now." She reached for the gun in my hand and jumped back in fright when I pulled her out of the way.

"I've been patient enough, Andriana. It's over."

She sighed. "And this is what they want. You're falling right into their trap. And by the way, they don't even know we're here. I've said it a million times already."

She walked back to the table where she dropped the laptop. "Before you do something we'll both regret, let me check if there are any new updates."

I nodded. Now that I knew Anthony had someone he considered dear to him, it would make my plans a little bit easier to get through. "What's the room number of that lady?" I asked Andriana.

"What lady?" Andriana glanced at me, a confused expression on her face as she typed on the laptop.

"Anthony's girl," I answered impatiently, glancing at the door.

Although Andriana had said they had no idea we were in there, I was still on alert. She sometimes underestimated the prowess of the group.

She threw her hands in the air. "And why should I give you her room number?"

"Because I need it. That's why I'm asking for it."

We were both in a bad mood, and I wished she would just see that I was doing all of this for her. Now wasn't the time for disagreement between us.

"I don't know." She avoided my gaze.

"Mama..." I dropped the gun on the bed and started making my way over to her. She raised her hands when I was almost by her side. "Don't come any closer, Alex. What do you want?"

"I need her room number, Andriana. Please don't make me ask again." I wasn't used to being disobeyed. I grew up with every one of my demands being met without any questions being asked.

"You're only going to put her in danger. It's exactly the same thing that's happening to me. Can't you see it?"

I moved to the laptop and turned it toward me. There was no point in explaining further. I searched through the laptop for almost an hour before finally stumbling on a page where she saved all of the information about the lady. She was in room number eighty. All I needed was just to keep her hostage, and Anthony would do all I wanted.

"I can't believe you," Andriana said once she realized I had seen it. "You're just like the rest of them. Whether you kill one every two months or you kill every day, you're all the same."

Hearing all of this from her hurt a lot because all of this wouldn't be happening if I decided to let them have her. The genesis of this whole thing started with her. But even with all she said, I still couldn't imagine letting them have her. I almost chuckled at what the old me would've done. I guess people do change. I turned around when I noticed I wasn't hearing anything from her and saw her cleaning tears off her face.

"I told you I'm not giving out her information to anyone. Why are you making this so hard? With this, we can figure out a way to stop all of this."

"I'm just tired." She sniffed. "With all that's been happening, I don't think I can handle this anymore."

"What are you talking about?"

She shook her head. "I'm tired. The men got into a fight at the warehouse. Jose has been killed."

"What?"

She looked away from me. "Doesn't life mean anything to you all? You just end lives like it's nothing to you. My goodness!"

"You sound so ungrateful right now, Andriana. I'm doing all I can to get you out of this, and what do I get in return?" I shook my head. "Nice."

"I'm not ungrateful, Alex. I'm just fed up. I'm getting more involved with mafia activities, and I don't want that for myself. Why does it feel like I'm getting more involved than getting out of this?"

"Jose died?" I still couldn't believe it. What the hell was going on? If I didn't find a way to change things, they would all kill themselves before they realized what was happening. "Can you update me on what's going on with the mafia guys here?"

She turned around to the laptop screen. "Nothing for now—no incoming messages, no calls," She glanced at the wall clock. "They're probably asleep. We should sleep too. I have a feeling it's going to be a really long day tomorrow." She looked down.

"They're not sleeping; they're planning! Together. You said earlier that they're all together, right?"

She looked at me but didn't say anything. I didn't realize how tired she looked until right now. She had bags beneath her eyes, and her hair needed care. That damned driver.

"You should rest. I'll walk around. Try to see if I can find anything."

She shook her head. "Please don't go anywhere tonight. They don't know we're here. I can promise you that. Today is the first comfortable sleep I'll be having in almost a month. I don't want anyone to get in the way of that. Please."

I nodded. She deserved it. I watched as she changed into her night-gown and settled on the bed, turning the other way so we couldn't see each other.

I walked over to the table, preparing to keep watch of all their activities until morning. I knew it was only a matter of time before they were done with whatever meeting they were planning.

"I turned off the laptop, Alex. They're resting. You should rest too and replenish your strength. You'll feel better tomorrow, I promise you."

I sighed. "We both can't go to sleep while in the middle of danger, Andriana. Can I know the passcode?"

Silence.

"Please," I drawled, hoping she wouldn't make this difficult for me. When she still didn't respond, I turned to her side of the bed to see she was fast asleep. She looked more at peace as she slept, the worry lines that had been on her face for days now were absent. There was nothing I could do. I climbed into the bed, my gaze fixed on the door. I turned around to be sure I had my knives and guns by my side in case of any sudden disruption.

"It's okay. You can sleep," Andriana muttered, her eyes closed. "I can promise you that."

——

The morning light speared through the sliver beneath the heavy drapes, painting red and orange stripes across the rumpled king-size bed. Andriana stirred in her sleep, adjusting her body to a more comfortable position.

We couldn't stay here forever. We couldn't keep running forever, so I had to come up with a plan.

A sharp rapping on the door shattered the fragile silence, and Andriana bolted upright, looking around in fear. My hands instinctively reached for the silenced pistol beneath the pillow. Andriana's eyes flew open as I made my way to the door.

"Room service." A clipped voice spoke from the other side.

Room service didn't announce themselves. My gaze darted to the peephole, but it was useless against the darkness of the hallway.

"We didn't order anything!"

A beat of silence. Then the person said, "Housekeeping. Urgent maintenance request."

Andriana started to shake her head. "We didn't demand anything," she muttered.

It could just be the hotel workers, but I didn't want to take any chances. "Come back later. I'm busy."

Silence. "This isn't a choice, sir. Everything is being monitored from the head office, and they seem to think there is some electrical issue within."

"Just a moment," I said as I walked back to Andriana, who was watching everything without saying a word. "Can you..."

"Just let him come in. I'm not moving from here. I don't care who is by the door. If it's my last day, then so be it."

"Excuse me, I just got a call, and there's been a mix-up with the room number. I'm so sorry for any inconvenience caused!"

"Alright, thanks."

Andriana jumped to her feet after we were sure the man by the door had left. "I don't think I can do this anymore, Alex. I know you've been a great help to me, but at this point, I can no longer continue with this."

"What do you mean?"

"They won't stop." Her voice was quiet, laced with a weariness that cut deeper than any scream.

"But I'll keep protecting you. You're safe with me."

"Safe from what? Living a normal life? Going out without someone following me around?" Her voice rose, tinged with desperate frustration.

"How long is this going to go on, Alex? We can't keep hiding, running for fear of the unknown."

I reached for her, but she flinched away. "Just be patient, Andriana, and I'll figure out a solution soon."

She shook her head. "You and I both know there is no solution, Alex. The only way this can stop is if you go back to being the mafia boss and denouncing me." Her eyes welled up. "We both know I'm right."

The tears spilled over, tracing a glistening path down her cheeks. "I'm done, Alex," she continued. "I need to breathe. I don't care how long I stay alive after leaving here today, but what I do know is that I'll die with a good heart."

The silence that followed stretched for an eternity; she had every reason to feel the way she did but leaving wasn't the best option.

I grabbed my phone from the table. "I think you just need a little time to yourself, so I'll leave you for now. Try to relax."

"Alex, no. I'm leaving. I've made up my mind. I can't do this anymore. I need to be free, and you also deserve your freedom."

"It's not safe for you, Andriana."

But she had already put her dress on and was picking different items up from the table.

"Don't worry about me. I can take care of myself." She hoisted the bag where she kept all of her things over her shoulder and nodded once at me. "I can't thank you enough, Alex. But thank you for everything you've done for me. I appreciate you." She offered a watery smile and turned toward the door.

"Andriana?"

She wiped tears from her face as she stepped out of the apartment, the door clicking shut behind her. There was nothing else I could do, so instead, I picked up my phone and dialed Anthony's number.

"Leave the girl alone, and I'll be back in the group in less than an hour."

CHAPTER TWENTY-FIVE: PATHS DIVERGED

ANDRIANA

O NE MONTH LATER.

"Andriana, we'll need a report on Victor James, ASAP." My boss rushed past me, an impatient look on his face.

"Roger that, Phil." I pushed my chair forward to the laptop so I could get a better view of the computer screen.

"Seems really important," Anna muttered, making a face at me as I hurriedly typed the name on the keyboard.

I smiled at her. "They've been on a murder case all day."

"Probably one of these mafia guys." She shook her head, adjusting her collar. "I just wish something would be done about them before they eliminate the whole city." She frowned.

I sighed. I had decided not to think about anything relating to Alex and his gang members, but watching Anna talk about them brought back so many memories I didn't want.

"Is everything okay, Andriana?"

"Yes, and I've gotten it!" I smiled at her. "Victor James, thirty-six-year-old medical doctor, blah-blah-blah." I scrolled down as we both chuckled.

"I bet he's in the mafia," she repeated, peering into my screen to see what other hidden information there was.

"He's a computer hacker!" I said with a smile, clapping my hands happily. If he had been in the mafia, my day would've been ruined.

She narrowed her eyes at me. "Uh, is everything okay, Andriana?"

"Oh." I threw my hands in the air. "Don't mind me, just playing around."

She nodded slowly. "Better find your way to Phil before he comes back here."

I eased off my chair, winking at her on my way out of the room. This job was one of the best things that happened to me after I separated from Alex, as it took my mind off everything that had been going on.

Phil rushed out the door just as I was about to knock. "Oh, what's up? What's the update?"

I nodded. "Thirty-six-year-old medical doctor. Also involved in cybercrime."

He shook his head, glancing at his wristwatch. "There's more to this than what you're seeing, Ms. Rodriguez. The day is over. I'll advise you to do a thorough check on this tonight. I'll need a positive response tomorrow."

I groaned softly as he walked away from me. I had planned to binge-watch movies all night with Lila, but now I would be glued to the computer all night while she had the best time of her life.

My phone started to ring as I made my way back to the office. A smile took over my face when I saw Lila's name appear on the screen. She was on a two-week school break, and thankfully she decided to spend the time with me.

"What's up, baby?"

"I'm outside your office. If I don't see you in five minutes, I'm gone."

I chuckled, picking up my bag from the table. "Why are you outside my office?"

"Because I got bored, so I ordered some pizza for us. You know, to spice up our movie night."

Phil's words echoed through my head, and I groaned.

"What's the problem?"

I turned to Anna, who was also tidying up her table. "Bye, see you tomorrow."

She winked at me before nodding.

"What's the matter, Andriana?" Lila asked. "You have two minutes left."

"Nothing, just chilling."

"Sixty seconds, and I can't hear you running out of there."

I was heading to the main exit now and could see her through the transparent glass. She was wearing a blue woolen sweater, which looked extremely familiar, and a black flared skirt.

"That jacket..."

"Oh, please." She chuckled as soon as she saw me. "I'm taking it along with me."

I shook my head, grabbing the bottle of water she offered me and taking a large chug from it.

"It seems like you had a really busy day." She glanced at me as we walked down the street.

I shrugged. "Just the usual stuff."

We both fell silent as we walked. I preferred walking all the way home instead of taking a ride. It helped clear my mind.

"How's Nathan?" I asked.

She shrugged. "Good. He's having the time of his life."

"Oh, I'm so jealous." I groaned, making a face. "I could use a vacation right now too. I would be the happiest woman on Earth."

She chuckled. "Fair."

Lila glanced at me. "Have you heard from Alex?"

It was the first time in weeks she asked about him, and I wished she hadn't. I had been trying to take my mind off him ever since I walked out of the hotel room several weeks ago, but I just couldn't. Everything about him was plastered in my memory, never to be erased. I missed him so much, even after the short, bittersweet time we shared together. Sometimes, I regretted leaving, but a part of me knew that was the best decision for both of us.

I shook my head. "No, Lila. I haven't heard from him."

"He's such a douchebag, just like the rest of them. Not even a phone call to confirm your safety? Thank God you left him. Good riddance."

"C'mon, Lila." I faked a glare in her direction. "Don't talk about him like that."

"Don't talk about him like that." She repeated after me, irritation evident on her face. "He was pretending all along, Andriana. He's part of the mafia. He's only pretending to be better than the others, but they're all the same. You're just lucky he liked you, and you would have been dead a long time ago if he didn't."

My mind drifted back to my time with him, and although he seemed like a tough guy, he was never really mean to me. He treated me like a lady until the last minute.

"Alex isn't like the rest of them, Lila. I know it. I saw it."

She shrugged. "If you say so, okay. But explain why he hasn't called you yet." She crossed her arms, staring at me. "I'm waiting."

We both stopped to make way for a kid riding a bicycle to get across.

"The real question is, why is no one coming after me? Throughout the time I spent with him, it was one threat to the next. It was like they wanted me dead as soon as possible." I glanced at her. "That's the real deal, Lila. Everyday I go out, I pray it isn't my last day. But it's been more than a month now, and not even once since I left has anyone threatened me or even..." I sighed. "I don't know what to feel."

She narrowed her eyes at me.

"What?" I chuckled, slapping her arms playfully. "Why are you looking at me like that?"

"You should be glad they aren't coming after you. Not sad."

I chuckled again. "What? I'm not sad. I'm just... what's the word? Confused. I know how these men work. I'm just trying to figure out why they're not coming after me."

She shrugged. "Don't worry about that." She smiled at me. "Let's just be glad you're safe and out of that dreadful situation. The keys, please."

I searched my bags for the keys to the house, different thoughts running through my mind. Alex was such a fool for not reaching out to me. I missed him a lot. I missed every single thing about him.

"You know, someone texted me yesterday and was asking for your number."

I ignored her, picking up the letter in the mailbox on my way in.

She turned to me. "Aren't you going to ask who it is?"

"I don't know. I don't care, Lila. I have no interest whatsoever in who it was."

She laid the pizza box on the table and sighed, taking a seat on the chair. "You should mingle more, Andriana. I don't like this lifestyle of yours."

"Maybe when you get yourself a man, I'll consider having one too."

She burst into laughter, hitting me with one of the throw pillows on the ground. "You're such a fool!"

I laughed. "Let's start our movie date now. It's going to be a busy night for me."

"What?" A huge smile covered her face, and she scooted closer to me, rubbing her hands in excitement. "Who are you going on a date with? Where did you meet him? Who is he?"

I shook my head. "Official assignment, Lila. C'mon."

"Oops. My bad. I got carried away. Don't worry. I'll keep you awake till you're done." Lila patted my shoulder. "You have a message," she said, passing the phone to me.

I was busy opening the pizza box, so I couldn't get it. "Just read it. It's probably my boss."

"Okay, give me a second." She paused, scrolling through the phone.

"It's nobody." She chuckled. "Mistake."

A beep from my laptop caught my attention. Another mafia member had been arrested. I entered the search button, hoping it wasn't any of the guys I met through Alex.

Well...

CHAPTER
TWENTY-SIX

ALEX

"I SHOULDN'T BE HAVING this conversation or any other discussion with you." I dismissed the men in my room, stretching tiredly against the sofa.

"Look past my sins, Alex. I've apologized to you a million times. It's a miracle you even picked up my call today. I told you, I'm sorry. Very sorry." Enzo's voice seeped over the line, calm and relaxed. It reflected the man behind the voice. He had been hospitalized for over two months now.

"What do you want, Enzo? Why are you calling me?"

"To let you know how sorry I am, Alex. I wish I didn't make such a horrible decision."

"Okay, I need to go now, Enzo. I hope to hear from you soon."

"Is that sarcasm I hear from you?"

"Goodbye, Enzo."

"Wait! How's Andriana? I heard what happened between the two of you, but I'm hoping you can still find a hidden way to be in touch with each other."

"Are you trying to fish out information from me, Enzo?"

"My goodness! No. It's nothing like that. I'm just saying it would be unwise of you to let her go like that."

"That's none of your business. It was a wise decision, and I'm glad I was able to ensure her safety."

In truth, I knew I had fucked up less than five minutes after she walked out the door, but he didn't need to know that.

Silence. If there was anyone I would discuss my feelings with concerning Andriana, it was Enzo. But the fool betrayed me, and now there was no going back.

"Please tell her I miss her so much. It's crazy, but I do. Also, tell her I'm very sorry all this had to happen, and I don't—"

I ended the call, placing the phone gently on the table. I had been battling with the thought of going after her ever since she walked out that door several weeks ago, but I knew there were so many things I had to put in place before that could happen. I had to inform the entire gang of my separation from Andriana for her to remain safe. It was a well-planned decision that I knew I couldn't make alone. Anthony agreed to be on my side after realizing I had more than enough information about his relationship.

I was back in charge now. Everything was under control, but I couldn't stay a day longer without hearing from her. The first few days had been hell, as I wasn't prepared for the feeling of loneliness that hit me after she left. What would her reaction be when she found out I was searching for her? Happy? Worried? I didn't know, but I was hoping for the best. I didn't care what her reaction was, as long as I got to see her again.

I clapped once, signaling for one of my bodyguards. Leo peeped in. He was the exact person I hoped would come in.

"Come in." I motioned for him to come in, adjusting my seat. "I'll need you to do something for me."

He nodded. "I'm always available to help, sir."

"Hm, get me Jack. I'll need the both of you for this assignment."

He nodded, walking hurriedly over to the door.

"This is a very private matter. I don't want anyone else involved in this. So you know what to do."

He nodded. "Of course."

A few minutes later, he walked in with Jack. They both remained by the door, waiting for my order. Jack was my newest employee, so I knew how tricky this was.

"I'll be leaving the house for a day. If anyone asks to see me, let them know I don't want to see anyone."

They glanced at each other. "Yes, boss."

"This is a really difficult task. Can you do it?" I watched them both, hoping this would turn out well.

They both nodded.

"Some of the men from the mafia will be here this evening, as usual. Let them know I have a migraine and wish not to be disturbed."

"Yes, sir."

"Good. Now Jack will stay inside my room till I'm back. Can you do that?"

"I can."

"Just in case they try to open the door forcefully, you press the lock from inside. It'll give them the reassurance they need that I'm inside. I'm doing all of this because I'm going somewhere, and I don't want to be tracked down yet. I just need a full day." I glanced at my wristwatch. It was eleven in the morning.

"What if they forcefully come into the room?"

I shook my head. "That's highly unlikely, unless they've heard about my plans. This is just between us. If this goes wrong and they hear about it, I don't care if you have a five-year-old daughter waiting for you, I'm taking you down."

Jack scratched his fingers nervously.

"So, make sure you put in your best and try to be as careful as possible. Leo, you are to remain outside my door till I'm back. Jack remains inside."

"Yes, sir."

I stood up from my seat. "That'll be all. I'm leaving now. I'll leave through the secret exit just behind you." I pointed at Jack, who shifted automatically as I approached.

"Good luck, guys."

I exited the room and was immediately hit with a blast of frigid air. I pulled my cap down and continued down the street. I was wearing a white shirt so none of the guys would notice me. White was one color I never wore. As I walked down the street, I felt like an imposter.

It took about three hours while driving at maximum speed before I got to Andriana's apartment. The windows were open, so I knew she was in. I fidgeted by the door. What if she had moved on and was with someone else? Before I could stop myself from having these thoughts, the door was pulled open, and a little boy ran out the door, stopping abruptly when he saw me.

"Mom? There's someone at the door!"

Mom? I looked at the house again to be sure I was in the right place.

"Hello." A man appeared by the doorway, holding the boy's hand. "How can I help you?"

I knew that what I was about to say next didn't make any sense, but it was the only thing I could think of. "I was so sure I was coming up to see my friend when I made my way here."

He nodded. "Okay?"

"A lady, short and..."

"Oh?" He chuckled. "We're new here. That should be Andriana, the lady who moved out of here. Such a cool lady."

"Do you have any idea where she moved to? Can you tell me?"

He looked so uncomfortable that I realized my question could've startled him. "Do you know how I can get to her?"

"And who are you to her?" His gaze swept over my whole body in one quick glance. I tried to put on a smile. Maybe that would make me look a bit better.

"I don't know. I'm sorry." He shook his head, leading the boy back inside the house. I knew he had the information. I just wished he would have done it the easy way. I blocked the door with my shoe just before it was shut. "The number, Mr...."

He shook his head, trying to slam the door shut. I didn't know what kind of relationship Andriana had developed with this man in such a short timeframe, but he sure liked her a lot. I flashed the gun in my pocket, and he went still.

"I don't have her number, but the last time she was here, she called with a friend's number. I think they're really close."

"Good, can I have it?"

He called out the number to me, shutting the door as soon as he was done. I dialed the number on my way out.

"Hello?"

"Hello, can I speak with Andriana?"

Silence.

"Hello?"

"Who am I speaking with?"

Oh God.

"An old friend of hers. Can I talk with her, please? It's urgent." I was pacing around the street now. It had been over six hours since I left, and word of my absence must've spread by now, if things weren't going as planned. Staying outside Andriana's house wasn't a good idea. I walked to my car.

"Can I know your name? You don't sound familiar." Her voice was firm, almost like she didn't want to be having a conversation with me.

"Alex."

Another long silence.

"I'm not familiar with any Alex. I'm sorry, but didn't you hear what happened?"

"What?" I pressed the phone against my ear.

"She died. Please don't call to ask about her again. I'm having a hard time as it is."

It felt like someone dropped a bombshell on my head. My head started pounding the moment my brain registered what she said.

"What? Who is this? Lila?"

She hung up the call. I leaned on my car, holding my head to reduce the pain I was feeling.

She died. What happened?

I struggled to open the car door and placed my head on the steering wheel, a thousand emotions running through my mind. Died? I couldn't believe it. I didn't want to. It felt like my head would explode at any moment, so I drove to the nearest pharmacy to get a painkiller. I needed my mind in order before I thought of the next step to take.

"Hey! Watch it."

That voice, I would recognize it anywhere. Even in my sleep. "Andriana?"

Our gazes met, and she gasped, shifting back in shock.

"Alex," she said, placing her hands on her mouth. "What are you doing here?" Her face creased into a frown, and she started to walk away.

"Andriana, wait. I'm sorry." I held her hands, but she yanked them free, walking quickly away from me.

"Wait, let's talk."

"Talk about what?" she asked without stopping.

"It's not safe having this conversation on the road. Can we talk in the car?"

She laughed. "So we're still hiding? It's still not safe to talk like normal people?" She shook her head.

"Go away, Alex. We shouldn't have bumped into each other. I should've remained indoors."

"I didn't bump into you, Andriana. I came out in search of you. Please talk to me."

She turned to me, her gaze softening as she watched me.

"Where are you parked?"

I pointed toward my car, and she sighed.

"You'll have to take me home. I'm hungry, and I don't want my food to get cold," she said, raising the bag in her hands. "I came out to get extra food for later."

I nodded. "That's fine."

The ride to her house was silent. Neither of us said anything, just throwing random glances at each other. She was even prettier than I remembered. I hated to agree with Enzo, but it was truly unwise to have let her go.

"Come in."

Her house still had that soft, feminine smell. I looked around the room; this time around it was painted white with nothing extra. By the time I turned to her, she was already watching me. I took a step toward her, perceiving the familiar scent of her perfume. I had a lot to say to her, but the moment my hand made contact with her skin, nothing else mattered.

"Come here." I pulled her into my arms and enveloped her lips in a kiss. Everything made sense now. "I've missed you so much," I muttered, kissing her all over her body.

She moaned in response, holding on to me like she was sure I was about to leave. I didn't realize how much my body yearned for her until now. I pulled at her top with my mouth and groaned when her breast came out, firm and erect.

"Oh God, mama. I missed you so much." I placed my mouth on her breast, pulling and sucking like it was my only job on Earth.

Her moan sent an electric jolt through my entire body.

"Alex, please," she muttered, holding on to me.

"What do you want, mama?" I whispered into her ear, watching with a smile as she shivered.

"I want you inside of me. I've missed you so much. I miss this feeling. Fuck me, Alex. I can't wait anymore."

I couldn't wait anymore either. I picked her up and settled her gently into the sofa, raising her skirt up. I yanked at her underpants with my teeth, and placed soft kisses all over her thighs.

"Alex, please."

I plunged into her with all of my weight, stopping only briefly to see if she was okay.

"Don't stop, Alex, please."

That was all I needed to hear as I began to pound into her. God, I missed her so much. She shouted in pleasure as I pounded her pussy. She looked so beautiful moaning for me. I was going crazy. I didn't realize how much I had missed her until now.

"Oh, Alex. Please, I'm coming."

I stopped, placing soft kisses on her cheeks and capturing her breast with my lips. I knew I was being selfish, but I couldn't help it; I wanted her to come at the same time as I was. The moment I thrust into her again, I knew I wouldn't last long because the way I felt right now watching her as she moaned my name was pure bliss. It felt like heaven.

"Ugh, Alex. Fuck it, I'm going to come." Her voice shook as her entire body vibrated violently.

"Fuck, I love you," I whispered into her ear as my own orgasm hit me like an electric wave.

CHAPTER TWENTY-SEVEN

ANDRIANA

I WOKE UP THE next morning sore but smiling. Yesterday was one of the best days of my life. I remembered having sex in the living room, but here I was, neatly tucked in my bed. My smile grew larger when I remembered Alex's last word to me before we both fell asleep.

Love!

"Alex?" I called softly, getting out of bed. The house was too silent for anyone to be around, but knowing Alex, he was probably cooped up somewhere in the living room, watching TV or something. He wasn't in the living room when I got there, and I tried to stop the tears that were threatening to fall. Did he come to see me just to have sex with me and leave?

I noticed a piece of paper on the table and grabbed it hurriedly. It was a note from Alex: "I'll be back in a few hours' time, love. I had to go settle a few things. You know how it is."

I placed the paper on my chest and heaved a sigh of relief. "Yay!"

I heard a sharp knock on the door and jumped in fear before realizing I was supposed to run errands with Lila this morning. She was the only one who knocked. I looked around the room, searching for my underwear and dress that Alex yanked off last night. The room was in order, so I knew he tidied it before he left. So sweet. I tried to stop myself from grinning.

"Andriana! Open this door right now!"

I rushed to the door and pulled it open. "Where did you put your phone? I've been calling for hours."

"I'm so sorry. I was sleeping."

She narrowed her eyes on me. "Why do you look that way?"

"What way?" I shut the door as we made our way back into the room. Now that Alex was back in my life, I needed to be extra careful with my security.

"You're acting suspiciously."

"What?" I chuckled, taking a seat beside the TV.

She shrugged. "There's just something different about you this morning."

"Hmm. Tell me already."

I wasn't ready for the safety conversation I was going to have with her if I brought Alex up, so I just ignored her question. "It's the weekend, Lila. Of course I'm happy."

She was quiet for a while, just studying me. "Did you have sex?"

"Lila!"

She laughed. "That's what happened! You had sex last night. I don't want to ask how it was because it's obvious you had the time of your life, but who is it?"

"I'm not seeing anyone, Lila. Stop it."

She sighed. "There's something I need to tell you, Andriana."

I nodded. "Go on."

She looked down. "I did the wrong thing, and I'm very sorry, but I'm doing it for your safety."

"What happened, Lila?"

"Alex called me yesterday, asking for you. I told him I couldn't reach you."

I nodded. "That's fine. You did what you had to do."

She narrowed her eyes. "Uh? That's it? You're not mad? You're not going to ask for his contact information?"

I sighed. "C'mon, Lila. It's fine."

She pressed her hands nervously, avoiding eye contact with me. My phone vibrated in my hand, and I saw it was a text from Alex: "I'll be with you shortly, not telling you when. It's a surprise."

"I told him you died and that there's no way he could reach you."

That did it for me. She knew how much I missed him, and she told him I was dead. What if I hadn't bumped into him when I did?

"I'm sorry, Andriana."

"That was wrong, Lila. I know you meant well, but why would you say that?"

She sighed. "I'm sorry."

"It's fine." I nodded. "I'm not angry, just disappointed. I didn't expect this from you."

She nodded, standing. "I had every right not to give this man your contact, Andriana. I know you might be mad at me, but I don't feel bad for not giving it to him. He's trouble, and everywhere he goes, there's trouble. You should steer clear of him, although it looks like you both found your way back to each other." She peered out of the window. The moment I heard the engine buzzing, I knew he was back.

"I'll leave now," she said, shaking her head. "I hope you know what you're doing, Andriana."

"Lila."

She pulled the door open just as Alex appeared in the door. They both watched each other without saying a word.

"Excuse me," she said curtly, walking away from him.

Our gazes met as he walked in.

"Did I interrupt something?"

I sighed. "Not really."

"Hey, why do you have that look on your face? Come here." He opened his arms wide and enveloped me in a hug. "Don't worry, everything will be fine."

"Where did you go?"

"I had some business I had to settle."

"Has it been settled?"

He sighed, holding my hands. "I want to be with you, Andriana, openly, without the fear of something bad happening to you. I want you to be able to walk around town freely and come home to me when you're done. I want you to be happy."

I smiled. "And what about you, Mr. Mafia?"

He chuckled. "I hate it when you call me that."

"Do you?"

We both chuckled. "I'm happy when you're happy, Andriana," he muttered.

"Then let's figure out a way to help ourselves. There has to be a way. Nothing is impossible, right?"

He laughed. "Of course there are impossible things."

He sat up, patting my back softly. "I'm back to being the boss of the gang."

"Try to be more positive, Alex. As the boss, this should surely be easy for you."

He shook his head. "No, it makes it harder. I don't do things just because I'm the boss. I like to do what's right; that's why I'm a leader."

I smiled at him. "That's great."

"So I might be the leader, but I still need to do the right thing, and the right thing in our gang is not involving myself with someone who is not a part of the group."

An idea came into my head. "Alex!" I jumped excitedly.

"What?"

"My parents were gang members! Remember?"

He was quiet for a while before a smile started to form on his lips. "That's a brilliant idea!"

I nodded. "They won't allow you to be with someone without having an idea about the mafia culture. I've read everything I can since we separated, and my parents also had ties with the mafia. What else do they want?"

"Get dressed, mama!"

"What?"

"I'm calling up an impromptu meeting for all of the gang members, and you're coming with me."

I started to shake my head. "What if it doesn't go as planned? They'll kill me. They've been wanting to for months."

"Try to be more positive, Andriana."

I glanced at him. He was using my own words against me now.

"Fine, let's go."

———

My heart raced violently as I waited to be led inside the room where Alex and his other gang members were. He had been with them for the last two hours, and I wondered what was taking them so long.

I hope you know what you're doing, Lila's voice echoed in my head.

What the hell was I doing walking into the lion's den? I had a peaceful life for the past month. Why was I here, where I was visibly hated for being with the boss? It was a wrong move; one I had started to regret when we drove out of my apartment. I was right in their midst now, and one single mistake and I was out. And what if this Blade they'd been talking about was around? What if he killed me and also killed himself in revenge? I placed my hands on my head.

"Ma'am? Your presence is needed in there," one of Alex's bodyguards said to me, stretching out his hands. He didn't look familiar.

"You don't look like any of his bodyguards." I shifted uncomfortably.

He nodded. "I'm one of his newest employees."

"I don't want to go in now," I said, shaking my head. "Tell Alex I need more time."

He nodded but paused when he got to the door. "There's one thing I've noticed in my short time here, ma'am. If they notice your fear, they'll feed on it. The only way to have the upper hand on these guys is to show no fear. Be fearless."

He watched me, his gaze softening when he noticed how scared I was. I didn't realize how obvious it was.

"It's okay. I don't know your reason for being here. But I know you can do it. Walk in there and never let them put fear in you."

I nodded. "Whew! You can do this, Andriana. Let's go."

"That's the spirit." He led me to a large wooden door and stepped back. "They're in there. I wish you luck."

I took a deep breath before knocking once. "Come in," a gruff, angry voice sounded from within.

"You can do this," the bodyguard muttered, taking a step back as I walked into the room. I was greeted by almost forty angry eyes. Were they always angry, or were these just their normal faces?

"As I said earlier, I want her to be mine officially. We've been through so much together and have figured out so many things together. It's almost like she's a part of the family."

"It's the rule, boss. We're only following the rule."

Alex sighed. "I'm also following the rules."

My gaze met with that of the violent man from Jose's, the man who started all of this. Instead of being fazed by the violent look he was wearing, I glared back at him. That caught him by surprise. Good.

"The rule says you can't be with someone who doesn't have ties with the mafia."

Alex nodded once in my direction.

"I have ties with the mafia," I said.

They all turned to me, their faces void of any kind of expression.

"And I'm not just saying this because I want to be with him. It's the truth. I'm a Rodriguez. My parents were really important mafia members."

Alex smiled proudly at me, and I felt my head swelling with joy. I didn't disappoint him.

"How do you know this?"

I wanted to let them know I worked with the Secret Service, but I realized that would make them feel uncomfortable. Instead, I went for the easier alternative. "I studied cybersecurity in college, so it was easy to find out about my past."

Alex listened to them argue, his gaze fixed on me. We both watched each other, our dream of being together was finally becoming a reality.

I didn't need to hide anymore if I was with him. The thought of that made me giddy.

After a while, someone spoke. "So, she's right. Her parents were the same Henry and Samantha Rodriguez. She's a part of us." He paused. "Some of the gang members already knew about this."

He turned to Alex. "I'm sorry, boss. But your woman is free now. Rest assured of her safety, always."

"Are you all promising me the safety of my woman at all times?" Alex looked around before standing from his seat and walking over to me.

They all nodded in agreement.

"Then swear. Swear on your allegiance to the group."

They all did as instructed, and Alex stretched out his hands toward me. "Shall we?"

CHAPTER TWENTY-EIGHT

ALEX

"THIS WAS NOT THE group Marcel struggled so hard to maintain," I said to my few trusted men. They had stuck by my side even after Ferd decided to go against the mafia rules and cause a separation.

"Look at what's happening. Have you seen the news lately? It means there's something terribly wrong. The mafia group is supposed to be a secret group, but now that Ferd has decided to start his own group, I don't think it's wise to just watch them go on this way. It'll definitely fall back on us."

They nodded.

"So I'll need your opinions, guys. What is to be done? How do we stop this madness Ferd is going on with?"

"He has almost twenty of the group's men with him, which is huge. But it's not impossible. We just need a good plan," someone muttered.

"Don't worry. Take your time, guys. Think this through and get back to me when you have answers."

They nodded. "Roger that, boss."

I glanced at my wristwatch. It was almost six, and Andriana still wasn't back from work. I was about to call when the door was pushed open, and she appeared by the door, a sweet smile on her face.

"I missed you so much. I was beginning to think you changed your mind about coming over for the weekend."

She chuckled, placing soft, sloppy kisses all over my face. "I'm stressed, Alex, and I need a release."

I pulled away from her. "Is your boss stressing you? Do you need me to warn him?"

She chuckled, raising her blouse up and unhooking her bra. I watched in hunger as her breasts stood firm, begging for my touch. I glanced at the door, but she pulled me down to her chest instead.

"It's locked," she breathed as my lips made contact with her skin.

My sweet, sweet baby girl. She made life a whole lot better for me.

"I need this release, Alex." She muttered, unzipping her skirt. I watched as it fell to the ground, my gaze meeting hers in shock when I noticed she was stark naked.

"You went to work without underpants?"

She chuckled. "I removed them inside my car."

Hearing her say that brought a smile to my face. It made me recall how happy she had been when I gave her the keys to the car several days ago.

"You can't be doing that, mama. Anybody could see you."

She placed a finger on my lips. "Shh," she said, pulling my trousers and shorts down at the same time, gasping in disbelief as my cock sprang up. "I've been thinking about this all day," she muttered, settling on top of me.

Thankfully, the chair was made with original materials. She eased herself slowly into me, gasping slightly as she tried to accommodate my size.

"Oh lord," she breathed, riding me slowly. "We fit so perfectly. I don't think I can ever get enough of this." She threw her head back, moaning softly.

I sucked her breast as she rode me. Her movements became jerkier just when I started feeling ecstasy. I held her still. "Not yet, young lady."

She frowned. "Oh, Alex. Stop doing that." She started to gyrate her body slowly against me.

"Fuck, mama." I held on tightly to her as my whole body shook violently.

"I love you," she muttered, gazing into my eyes. It was the first time she'd said that, but I'd known for several weeks.

"Let's go home," she mumbled into my ear. "I want to lie in bed with you all night and feel your body against me."

I kissed her softly, helping her back into her dress. "Ferd has gotten worse, Andriana. We can't ignore this anymore."

She eased off me. "What's the problem?"

I explained how he got some of the gang members he took along with him into trouble, and she smiled.

"Now, why are you smiling, Andriana?"

She shrugged. "Can't you see that this is the best time to get your men back? At this point, they're probably regretting their decision, but too scared to come back to you. Just offer them your unwavering support and watch them come back in droves."

It was a simple but reasonable idea. "I'm about to be very busy, mama, so please be patient with me."

She nodded. "That's fine. I'll be waiting."

Thankfully, most of the others were still on the premises, so I called them to let them know my plans, and they all seemed thrilled by the idea.

"A second chance is all they need," someone muttered.

"So how do we go about this? I'll need your opinion, guys."

"They have another operation tonight," someone said.

I turned to him. "Any idea where this is taking place?"

He nodded. "I don't know who offended Ferd, but he's attacking the house later tonight."

That rang a bell. "An elderly couple?"

He nodded. "That's all I know."

"Ask for more information from the person telling you all the things you know."

He nodded.

"Tonight, we meet them halfway, unexpectedly. Not one word of this can get to them."

They all nodded.

"Great. Let's meet at my place. What time are they leaving?"

"Nine tonight. Ferd is on his way there with the gang members. I think the couple is hosting a party at their place tonight."

"That's sad. I wonder what the couple did to them."

I kissed Andriana's lips softly and said, "Go home, mama. It's not safe for you to remain here. I'll ask Leo to come with you."

"That's fine, but please stay safe."

I kissed her once again and rushed out of the room. "Leave now, mama. I don't want you stranded."

"Okay. Go! Your men are waiting!"

I signaled to Leo, letting him know he was going home with her. "She's going straight home. Call me if she says otherwise."

He nodded. "Of course, boss."

I turned to the rest of the group. "See you guys soon."

I had no idea what the outcome of this journey would be, but I knew it was going to be the start of the peaceful revolution I always wanted. This was the final chance for my men to redeem themselves, and I desperately hoped they took it. My phone began to ring as I walked into my office.

"Hey boss, change of time. They're heading out already!"

"Get the vehicles ready, guys. I'll be with you shortly.

Andriana ran toward me, a concerned expression on her face. "What's the matter, Alex?"

"Do you remember the night I told you an some elderly couple I was asked to kill?"

She nodded. "I do."

CHAPTER TWENTY-NINE

ANDRIANA

"THERE'S SOMEONE HERE TO see you," Leo announced, peering into the room.

"Me?" That came as a shock because I was miles away from home, and no one knew where I was.

He nodded. "She's waiting outside."

"Are you sure you haven't let the wrong person in?"

"The boss let her in."

"Her?" I jumped to my feet, rushing toward the door. Leo laughed softly behind me.

Lila was seated in a corner when I got there, and she jumped to her feet when she saw me.

"Andriana."

"I'm sorry," was all I could mutter as I walked over to her. "I'm really sorry."

She nodded. "It's fine. I just had to be sure you're okay. How've you been?"

"Come with me." I dragged her to my room, shutting the door as soon as we got in.

"First, I'm sorry I haven't reached out to you. It's been almost, what? Five days now? I'm such a horrible friend."

She chuckled. "Not really. I've also not been the best of friends."

"You've been a good friend to me, Lila. You acted that way because you cared for me. I was too blinded by my love for Alex to see that."

She smiled. "That's true. It seems like you both are getting really close now."

I nodded. "We're in a proper relationship now."

She looked around the house. "I didn't know he was this wealthy. So how do you plan to do this with the whole mafia thing going on? What's your plan? Because I don't think it's wise to keep hiding all your life."

"No, no. We've gotten past that. Okay, so to be able to be with Alex, I had to have ties with the mafia. Can you believe that?"

She leaned against my pillow. "Of course I can. It's a secret group. What did you expect?"

I rolled my eyes. "I should've told you this a while ago, but guess whose parents were mafia members?"

She started to shake her head in disbelief. "You don't mean it."

"I couldn't believe it when I first heard it either. I even did an extensive investigation on it. I called Camilla so many times she got sick of me."

She chuckled. "Are you serious? That's incredible."

I nodded. "So it was a bit easy. Not totally, but there was nothing they could do. I'm one of them."

She frowned. "You're not one of them, Andriana. What the hell are you saying?"

"Okay, I'm not one of them."

She shook her head. "You need to be careful with what you're saying. I don't think you know how dangerous this group is. Do you see how they kill people?"

"So this is what you don't know. Alex, just like me, lost his parents when he was a young boy. Marcel, the one in charge of the mafia group, raised him. This was where he grew up, and before Marcel died, he made him the leader of the group."

"I just don't want you involved in all of this. I wish things would've happened differently."

I touched her hands. "I'm good, Lila. Alex doesn't support the unnecessary killings that have been happening by the rival gangs, and just yesterday, he gave them the chance to return to the group. Those who wanted to did so. But I can assure you, everything is fine."

She nodded. "So does this mean no unjust killings and punishment in Alex's group?"

I nodded.

"Are you just saying this because you don't want me to be worried about you?"

"Come with me." I held her hand, leading her to the door.

"Where are we going?"

"To the mafia's hideout. Things are being run differently now. You know, I think Alex has had enough of the killings over the years and just wants the welfare of those under his control."

She paused when we got to where my car was parked. "Are you kidding me? Now I'm mad at you. Is this your car?"

I nodded. "I'm sorry, Lila. It all happened so fast. You know I would still tell you. Everything was just happening so fast."

"Admit it. You were wrong. I wouldn't keep something like this away from you. Is this a Benz?" She looked at me in awe.

"You were mad at me. I didn't know how to relate any of this to you without seeing you."

She shook her head as she got in the car. "Stop making me look like a monster."

"If it's going to be safe for you, then I don't have a problem with it. I just want you to be happy, Andriana. I know how you suffered alone all these years, and I don't want that to repeat itself in any way.

"I'll tell you if there's trouble, Lila, but I can assure you that things are run differently now."

She narrowed her eyes on me. "Just shut up."

We were both laughing when I pulled into the driveway. Some of the men were gathered outside, and they made their way over when they noticed my car.

"Is it safe for me? I don't want to die now." She faked a cry.

"Shut up!"

She laughed. "Okay, jokes aside, look at these faces. Am I safe here? I can't forget what that evil man did to me that day."

"You have every reason to feel the way you do, Lila. I'm sorry I didn't consider your feelings in all of this."

She waved me off. "Everything will be fine, only if I don't see that bastard. Is he here?"

I shook my head. "He's on probation. Alex isn't sure whether to let him stay or not. He's a danger to the group."

"Alex is considering letting him stay? Why? He's a monster."

"He claims to want nothing to do with Ferd and his men."

"Maybe he failed to fulfill his part of the plan or something. What-ever the case, he's just looking for shelter for now. After whatever he's going through has been sorted out, you'll realize he was only pretending."

She had a point, and I was going to tell Alex what she said.

"By the way, how did you find me?" I asked as we walked inside.

She shrugged. "I called Alex. I wanted to apologize for lying to him, but he didn't let me. When I asked for your address, he sent someone to pick me up instead."

I smiled, feeling my love for him skyrocket. "And he didn't mention a word of this to me."

She laughed. "There he is!"

None of them noticed us from where we stood. They were discussing how to release those who had been unjustly detained by Ferd and his men.

"There's a girl that's been detained since Marcel was alive. I's been almost five years now."

"My goodness!" Alex exclaimed. "What's her crime?"

"She refused to sleep with him."

"Go and get her right away!"

Lila glanced at me. "I knew I hated this group for a reason. This just shows exactly why." She shook her head in disbelief. "Let's get out of here."

I waved at Alex just as we turned to leave, and he excused himself. He pulled me into his arms as soon as he got to us.

"Hey, Lila."

Lila smiled at him. "Hello."

"Where are you taking my wife?"

We both laughed. *Wife* was a really strong term to describe our relationship.

"Wife?" Lila repeated, glancing at me.

"Yes," he nodded, going on one knee. "I've never been more sure about spending my life with someone. My life has been so much better since you walked into it. I love you, Andriana, and I want to spend the rest of my life loving you." He pulled out a small box from his pocket, his gaze fixed on mine.

I gasped in shock when he pulled the lid open and I saw the dia-mond-encrusted ring he got me.

"Will you marry me, Andriana Rodriguez?"

EPILOGUE

ALEX

Two years later.

"I can't believe I now own a bakery!" Andriana announced with a big smile on her face.

I placed my hands on hers, caressing her hands softly.

"Not just any bakery, but the largest bakery in the country. That's not an easy feat! I'm proud of you, Andriana." Lila added, mirroring the smile on her friend's face.

We had just concluded the grand opening of Andriana's bakery and were now celebrating at home with a bottle of champagne.

"All thanks to my wonderful husband." She chuckled, her voice laced with a comfortable rasp. "I couldn't have done this without him."

I pulled her closer. "That's not true. You could do this and more, even without me there."

We stared into each other's eyes. Two years had passed since I got married to her, but it still felt like yesterday. My love for her grew stronger and stronger with each passing day.

"Hmph." Lila cleared her throat, standing. "I guess it's time to leave."

"What? No, no. You can't leave now." Andriana pouted, walking carefully toward her.

Enzo stood up too, smiling briefly at me. After taking back my place as the mafia boss and dismantling the rival gang, Andriana begged me to consider taking back Enzo.

It was a tough decision for me, as his betrayal cut deep. But with Andriana's constant reassurance, I was able to look past his mistakes and accept him back into the group. We weren't as close as we used to be, but Andriana still invited Enzo to most of our celebrations and hangouts. She always said she knew we would get along someday soon, but I didn't see that happening.

"You too?" Andriana whined, glancing at me.

"It's been a long day, mama. You need to rest, and they also need their sleep." I smiled at her.

"I thought you both were going to stay till tomorrow." She pouted.

Lila chuckled. "Wake up, Andriana. I have work to do."

"It's Saturday night. There's no work tomorrow."

Lila's face broke into a devious grin.

"Don't," Andriana warned, stretching a finger toward her.

They talked in codes like that most of the time. I tried understanding their weird way of communicating when we got married, but got tired of trying when it was obvious I was never going to.

"Bye, baby, I'll see you soon. You know that."

Andriana waved her off, sitting on my lap. "I'm hungry. What's for dinner?"

"But you just ate!" Lila chuckled, pointing to the empty plate on Andriana's table.

"She's hungry." I faked a glare at Lila before rubbing Andriana's gently rounded belly. "She's eating for two, so of course she'll get hungry easily."

Lila chuckled, walking out the door with Enzo following quietly behind.

"Bye, Enzo!" Andriana called out, waving at him.

He nodded, winking at her as he stepped out.

"You didn't even smile at him." She pouted, slapping my hand softly.

"I'm saving my smile for you."

She chuckled, rubbing her belly gently. "I can't believe I'm with a child. Whenever it crosses my mind, my heart just swells with joy."

My stomach swooped with the oddest sensation. And as Andriana wrapped her arms around my neck and placed her head on my chest, I finally identified the odd sensation gripping me. It was the joyful feeling of starting my own little family.

She ducked her head shyly. "I love you, Alex."

My eyes met hers and our gazes were filled with love that transcended time.

"I love you too, mama," I whispered, my hands finding hers. I squeezed gently, the simple gesture speaking volumes.

The coming child promised not just a new chapter in our story, but a vibrant continuation of the legacy we were building together, a legacy of the enduring strength of our love.

If you enjoyed *Stuck with the Mafia Boss* then you will love *Bound by the Mafia Boss*.

(Click Here to get Stuck with the Mafia Boss)

A tech graduate waitressing until her career takes off, unexpectedly lands a job with a mysterious billionaire, Alex, who is twice her age and the grumpy CEO of San Diego's largest construction firm. Despite their rocky start and his mafia ties, their mutual attraction becomes undeniable, Will she risk everything she is starting in her life for love?

Curious about what happens next? (Click Here to get Stuck with the Mafia Boss)

SNEAK PEEK

Stuck with the Mafia Boss

((CLICK HERE TO GET Stuck with the Mafia Boss)
BLURB and CHAPTER ONE:

He's twice my age, a billionaire, and shrouded in secrecy.

I'm a tech graduate, waitressing until I get my career off the ground.

Which happens much faster than expected when a mysterious billionaire offers me a job.

Almost twice my age, Alex is the CEO of the largest construction firm in San Diego.

This seems like a great opportunity, yet working with Alex is anything but smooth sailing.

He's grumpy and guarded. Everything's a secret.

And he makes it clear he doesn't appreciate my sassiness.

While we don't like each other, the attraction between us is electric.

It grows and grows until neither of us can hold back.

We kiss, and before long I realize I'm falling for Alex.

But then I'm exposed to the grim realities of his life.

Alex has ties to the mafia and staying with him could put me in the direct path of danger.

Yet the way he puts it on me I may be willing to take that risk.

(Click Here to get Stuck with the Mafia Boss)

CHAPTER ONE:

AURORA

I'm breathless and shaking as I slam the door to the cab shut. I'm barely able to tell the driver the address, and the look of concern that he gives me, tells me I look as bad as I feel. The day had started like all the rest; I had just picked up my Cinnamon Dolce Latte with a double shot of espresso and was on my way to see my dad at his office.

I turned the corner away from the coffee shop and was met with a group of men. I didn't think anything of it at first—It's New York City, there are a lot of people around. I started to walk around them, but they moved with me, and when I finally looked at them and started paying attention, I saw that they were holding rope and duct tape. I knew at that moment that I was in trouble. All my life, I had been taught what to look out for and taught how to defend myself. With my father's line of work, it was drilled into me that I needed to protect myself.

I have never been more grateful for that training than I am right now. I had thrown my coffee at them and turned to run. Everything that happened after that is a blur of kicks and punches. I didn't try and see who I was hitting, I just blindly lashed out and fought to escape. Jumping into the first cab I saw once I was far enough away from the men.

"Miss? We're here."

The driver's voice startles me from my panic, and I look out the window to see that we are at my dad's best friend and right-hand man Ronan's home. I'm confused why we are here and when I turn to the driver he says, "This is the address you gave me, is this not where you want to be?"

I gave him Ronan's address?

I don't remember what I said to him when I got into the cab, just that when he asked where I wanted to go, I struggled to answer.

"No, this is it. Sorry. Here."

I hand him some bills, hoping that it's enough for the ride and climb out of the back. Shockwaves are still running through my body as I stand at the end of the driveway, outside the gate. I try taking a couple of deep breaths to calm down, but it's not helping. On shaky legs, I make my way over to the speaker box and hit the call button.

"Can I help you?"

The voice of one of the many bodyguards my father employs comes through the box.

"Um, it's Aurora, I need to see Ronan."

There is a pause before the buzz of the gate opening.

"Come on in."

The tone of his voice had changed when he heard it was me. I never leave the city, and I've never shown up here without Dad. As the gates open, I start the walk up to the house, which is right outside of the city. Ronan is the only one of my father's men that doesn't live in the city. He bought a symmetrical two-story brick house that stood on a few acres of land, as far away from people as possible.

He's already waiting for me at the front door. He stands tall and imposing. He's dressed in a tailored suit, with his chocolate brown hair slicked back and his dark gray eyes trained on me. He's 6'2 and fit, his body filling out his suit and his muscles on display for everyone to see. He started working for my dad about ten years ago and they are thick as thieves now. I kind of feel like their job forces people to be close.

"What's happened? Where is your driver and why are your clothes ripped?"

I look down at myself; I hadn't realized that my shirt sleeve was ripped during the attack.

"Um, I was attacked."

I don't think he was expecting me to say that. His eyes widen and he is down the steps and in front of me before I can blink.

"What do you mean you were attacked? Where? What happened?"

My adrenaline must be wearing off because all I can do is stare at him as my whole body starts to shake violently. My legs give out and Ronan is forced to catch me. Before I can apologize for just collapsing on him, he swoops me up into his arms and carries me into the house. After setting me on the couch, he disappears for a moment.

Get it together, Aurora.

No matter how much I clench my muscles, I can't get the shaking to stop. Ronan is in front of me again, kneeling on the floor. He holds a glass of water to my lips and tells me to sip. As soon as the liquid touches my tongue, I start to sputter.

"That's not water."

Ronan chuckles as I cough from the burn of the vodka.

"No, it's not, but it will help with the shock."

When he lifts the glass to my lips again, I shove his arm away.

"Geez, Ronan. If I didn't know better, I would say you're trying to get me drunk."

The words leave my lips, and I freeze.

That sounded flirty, Aurora. Are you flirting with Ronan?

My eyes meet his, and I'm relieved to see humor reflected back at me. Ronan is known among my father's men, and everyone else in this world, as someone who is to be feared. He doesn't put up with anyone and will not hesitate to do whatever it takes to keep my father and his position safe. And I do mean *anything*.

He has always intimidated me, but there was also something there that seemed almost...soft. My father is Augustus St. James, one of the most feared and respected Mafia Bosses in New York City. I grew up in this world. I knew the ins and outs, and I knew better than to get close to anyone who worked for or with Dad, yet something about Ronan Thatcher fascinated me. I made sure to follow Dad's rules, and I stayed as far away from Ronan as I possibly could.

He was involved in every aspect of our life. He came to all the big events and came over for random dinners at the house at least once a week. I was fifteen when he started working for Dad and from the moment I met him, I was starstruck. He was my first serious crush and over the years that crush has lost its intensity, but I still catch myself thinking about him.

This is the first time he and I have ever been alone, and so close to each other. I can see the dark ring around his grey eyes and the salt and pepper that is starting to take over the hair at his temples. This man has never once looked in my direction, so having his complete undivided attention on me now is jarring.

"I have to call your father and tell him what happened, but I need you to tell me first. Are you up to that?"

He gently reaches up and brushes a strand of my hair out of my face with one finger. Trailing the tip across my forehead and down behind my ear. It's the lightest of touches and my body still breaks out in goosebumps. To distract myself, I start to tell him about what happened. The men, the rope and duct tape, how I fought and ran. I watch him as I tell the story and the more I talk, the more his fist clenches and his eyes darken.

"It was a kidnapping attempt. We will need to find out who it was."

He stands and pulls his phone out of his pocket. My eyes follow him as he paces the living room. I can see the barely controlled anger radiating off him as he barks orders into the phone. I'm not paying attention to what he is going on about until I hear him say, "And pick up a venti Cinnamon Dolce Latte with a double shot of espresso on your way to pick him up."

Did he just order my favorite drink?

He hangs up the phone, looks at me, then takes a deep breath and brings the phone back up to his ear. I know he's calling Dad now. The thought drains me, and I curl up into a fetal position on my side. I forget about the fact that he knew my drink order and snuggle deep into his surprisingly comfortable couch.

~~~~~~

I must have fallen asleep because the next thing I know I hear Ronan's soft voice and feel his warm hand on my shoulder, gently shaking me.

"Aurora. Come on, wake up."

I open my eyes and see his face above mine. I can't stop the smile from spreading across my lips, and he gives me a surprised one back. We stare at each other for a moment, and I forget in my sleep fog that I *shouldn't* be looking at him this way. We are pulled out of our bubble by the sound of my father's voice coming closer to us.

"I want you to find out who was behind this. Now. I don't care if you have to stay up for days; figure it out!"

Dad's angry voice jolts me from my fog, and I sit up, blushing at the fact that I was just smiling and staring at Ronan. Dad walks into the room just as I sit up and Ronan is standing a good distance away from me.

"You are not to go anywhere on your own anymore, understood?"

My father's green eyes lock with my matching ones and I know if I say anything other than "yes, sir," I'm going to get an ear full. I may be a grown woman, but no one argues with Dad.

"Yes, sir."

"You were smart coming straight to Ronan's place. It's away from the city and no one outside of the family knows it's his."

I tense and look at Ronan. That's not why I chose here, and I hope he thinks the same as Dad. No one needs to know that my instinct was to come here, not because of the seclusion, but because of Ronan.

I have always felt safe when I'm near him and after almost being kidnapped, all I wanted was to be near him.

"Aurora, honey, we all need to debrief about what has happened. Are you okay being in here by yourself?"

I nod. I know I don't really have any other choice. Dad and Ronan both turn to walk out of the room, and dad's driver walks into the room, holding a large coffee. He brings it to me with a smile, and as I take it, I see Dad look at him confused.

Ronan clears his throat, "She mentioned that it's what she threw at the men. She was in shock, so I figured the sugar would help."

It's a simple explanation, but as they both leave, I can't help but wonder if I had. I think about what I said to him, and I'm almost fairly certain that I did mention throwing my coffee at them, but not what the drink was, definitely not in such detail.

Does he know my coffee order?

I study him as he follows Dad out of the room and right before they turn the corner, he looks back and his eyes lock with mine. It seems like he's trying to tell me something, but I can't figure out what it is.

The quiet that follows their absence unnerves me, and I quickly grab the remote and turn on the TV. I pull my knees to my chest and curl up into a ball in the corner of the couch, flipping through the channels while I wait for them to finish with their meeting. I know they have all the security in there and are trying to figure out what happened, why it did, and who was behind it.

Why would they want to take me?

Dad's life has always been dangerous, and I was always taught to be cautious, but I figured that it was just that, being cautious. Never in all my life did I think someone would try and take me. I fiddle with the torn sleeve of my shirt and replay everything that happened. Thinking about what could have happened if I didn't get away makes my stomach turn, and I jump from the couch and search for Dad. I want to go home.

I find them in Ronan's dining room and as soon as they see me, they stop talking.

"Dad, I'm fine now. Can't I just have someone take me home so I can get some rest?"

Dad and Ronan look at each other before Dad turns to me.

"No, I don't want you anywhere near your apartment. You are going to stay here. In fact, I want you here for the foreseeable future. This is the safest place for you."

"What?" Both Ronan and I speak at the same time.

He wants me to stay here?

(Click Here to get Stuck with the Mafia Boss)

Printed in Great Britain
by Amazon